To Pett

Hope you enjoy... ...

Tony Berry

The
Sea General
by
Tony Berry

Published by Amazon and Silver Books NN36JF (23)
ISBN 9798703738979

Previous books by Tony Berry
Featuring John Ketch

The King's letter
Cromwell's Gold
Mutiny at Burford
The Golden Coins of Lombardy
An Unwise Marriage

Author's Note (1)

In February 1649 there were fears that a large part of the English navy was ready to defect across the North Sea to Prince Rupert. Parliament was concerned that their existing admirals possessed Royalist sympathies. They therefore appointed three of their successful land commanders to Head the navy. Three men Richard Deane, Robert Blake, and Edward Popham were appointed as Generals at Sea. The longest serving and most successful of these, was to be Robert Blake.

Chapter Headings

Chapter One   An unexpected introduction

August 1653.

John Ketch was sitting in his favourite chair in his garden looking across the Nene valley, enjoying the warmth of a hot Northamptonshire afternoon. He was in a reflective mood, conscious of his good fortune and the pleasures of his life. He was free of money worries, enjoyed good health and a loving wife. His son and heir was thriving and he had the good opinion of his neighbours.

He sat enjoying his satisfaction for some time. However, he was not so vain as not to recall the warnings of scripture "Vanity, Vanity all is Vanity". He smiled to himself.

"I *must not forget that such a happy state can be lost in a moment and that life is full of risk. Also, my situation in life is not all of my own making James Hedlow* is the man who has ensured my prosperity.".

James Hedlow had been Northampton's Clerk to the Council and had worked with Ketch on many of his successful missions solving crimes and mysteries. His recent death had been a blow to both Ketch and his wife Anne, who had been the old clerk's housekeeper. His inward thoughts about his life did not end there. Ketch was a secret agent who worked for Oliver Cromwell's Spy Master John Thurloe. In this alone there was enough to blight his life. He and Anne had often discussed when he would retire from his present employment. He had a growing family, a responsibility he could not ignore.

"I know Anne desires it. She leaves the matter in my hands, but she does expect it one day."

He looked down at his hands. There were marks and scars that memory told him had been obtained dangerously.

"And I am due to return to London in a few days. My time of inaction is over."

He mused on in the warm sunlight. He could not deny that the thought of fresh challenges set by his masters still filled him with excitement. He smiled.

"It was ever thus. I always opt for London. No doubt the time will come when I choose to remain here in Northampton. But not today"

He stretched in his chair and sensed his manservant, William, beside him.

"Madam has taken delivery of a basket of fresh plums and is trying them with some cheese and honey. She inquires as to whether or not you would wish to join her."

Ketch forced himself upright and out of his chair. He found Williams speech too flowery and a bit servile, but could not find a gentle way to raise the matter. He would discuss it with Anne.

"Thank you, William. Have you tried the plums with cheese and honey?"

"Only the plums sir. I am not fond of honey."

Ketch led the way back into the house looking forward to some fresh fruit. At that moment he heard the sound of splintering wood and the shrill cries of a horse in pain. It was close bye at the front of his property.

Derngate House looked out upon an open expanse of grass. To the left some thirty yards away was the Derngate, the main entrance into Northampton from the South East. To the right the same distance away was Beckett's Well, once used by the Archbishop when escaping from the castle. The road from the South East ran across from the well to the Derngate. Ketch burst out of his front door, followed by William. From the kitchen, Anne called out a warning.

"Be careful John."

Across the grass, just before the Derngate, there had been an accident. It was a sorry sight. A large coach pulled by two horses had collided with a light cart pulled by one horse. The coach looked undamaged and its coachman was already stood down, quietly calming his horses. The light cart was badly damaged. It had a splintered wheel and a broken shaft and had fallen on to its side. Its two occupants had been tumbled out on to the ground, where they lay groaning. The loud noise was from the horse trapped to the ground by the broken shaft and a tangle of reins and harness. It was desperately trying to free itself.

"William try and aid that horse," directed Ketch.

He made his way to the two figures on the ground. As he moved to give assistance a thick set, sternly dressed man, with a slight limp, joined him from the coach also offering aid. The casualties were a middle-aged couple, a man and a woman. Whilst Ketch tried to revive the man, the newcomer was seeking to care for the woman. Slowly, Ketch was able to raise the man to his knees and then to his feet. He seemed undamaged but Ketch knew there would be bruises later. He still asked his question, however.

"Are you hurt, arms, legs, head anything damaged inside.?"

The man joined Ketch in feeling his limbs and found he had a cut head. There was no great flow of blood but a dressing would be required. He straightened up.

"My wife! I must see to her!

He stumbled across to where his wife lay. She had managed to sit up and the sternly dressed man was offering words of comfort.

"Thank you, sir," said the husband.

"I must help her now,"

The man so addressed turned to Ketch.

"Is he alright? I think the lady has no physical hurts but is still very shocked."

They both looked about them to see what else was required. William and another man were soothing the fallen horse, whilst trying to free its constraints. The coach driver had not moved and was continuing to sooth his own horses. Ketch saw that there were two other men who had been standing by the coach, but were now walking over the grass to join Ketch and the newcomer, who turned to Ketch.

"Good, it appears that my gentlemen are unhurt. Let me introduce myself. I am General at Sea Robert Blake and I greatly appreciate your prompt assistance in this matter."

Ketch returned his slight bow.

"I am John Ketch, Captain John Ketch. This is my home and it is at your disposal. I must at the moment provide some aid to the fallen couple."

The Sea General and Ketch moved across to the man and woman, who carefully were examining each other for wounds. When each were satisfied, the man continued to hold the woman gently in his arms. Ketch made the offer of further help and pointed towards his house.

"This is my home, come and rest from your ordeal. Your good lady looks in need of somewhere to sit quietly.

"You are most generous sir, and I gratefully accept your kind offer. My name is Sir John Barnard and this is my wife Elizabeth."

Ketch began leading the new arrivals towards Derngate House. At that moment his wife Anne emerged from the house and quickly took over the care of the middle-aged couple. This allowed Ketch to return to matters with Robert Blake. The Sea General lightly caught Ketch by the arm.

"I see my servant and your man have quietened that horse and from here at least it appears unhurt. A touch of good fortune, and indeed your man and my servant also appear to be unhurt. However. my two companions are not totally unscathed as I had originally thought. I see what looks like a twisted ankle and a cut head."

"Unfortunate", replied Ketch.

"You must all come and rest. Some strong drink and bandages will help."

Whilst making his invitation, Ketch made a quick appraisal of the Sea General.

"After all this is no ordinary acquaintance. This is England's hero, a man of substance and influence, almost as much as Cromwell himself.".

Robert Blake was some fifty years old, of medium height, but generally ill-proportioned. His arms looked strong as did his chest and shoulders, but they did not go well together. It was the same with his legs and torso, both individually fine but they also did not complement each other. His face was round with large, brown eyes and he had the weather- beaten complexion of a sailor. He seemed to suffer from an intermittent limp. His clothing was well cut, but mostly black. There was, however, a strength in his manner that indicated a self-confidence to command. He turned to Ketch.

"You are most kind sir! Let me introduce you to my companions, but first you said your name was Captain Ketch."

Ketch replied with a modest tone.

"Yes! I am a military officer based in Whitehall Palace and I serve Secretary John Thurloe. My home, however, is here in Northampton."

The Sea General chuckled.

"One of Thurloe's men. I had better watch my step."

He waved the two men towards him,

"Captain Ketch may I introduce you to my travelling companions, my secretary Charles Beaumont and Captain Treddager, one of my aides. Gentlemen this is Captain Ketch who has kindly offered his home, for us to rest and deal with our injuries."

The two men bowed together said.

"At your service Captain."

The Sea General turned his attention to another two men who were holding back.

"My coachman and my servant have restored order amongst all our horses and will ensure they are properly settled. They are both always hungry so when they have completed their task, perhaps they may be offered some victuals and weak ale."

Unseen, William had appeared at Ketch's side.

"The lady and gentleman are being tended by the mistress. I can take the coachman and servant around the back to the kitchens, where something can be found"

"Good! See that is done," ordered Ketch.

With a wave of his hand, Ketch led his guests into his house where they could re-join Sir John and Lady Barnard. The Sea general showed a look of concern.

"Thank you for this Ketch. I must first have a word with them. My coach is a heavy slow thing but can cause damage when off course."

On entering the house Ketch spoke to Charles Beaumont and Captain Treddager.

"There is a decanter of brandy in my dining room, may I suggest you make use of it whilst waiting for my wife to examine your hurts. She will be with you when she has finished with the other casualties."

Ketch guided the Sea General into the parlour. There they found Anne sitting on the parlour's small couch alongside Elizabeth Barnard, holding a cold compress to the woman's brow. Her husband, John, had placed himself in a chair at a small table. His hand was tapping nervously. Robert Blake immediately approached the Baronet and his wife.

"Sir! My name is Robert Blake. I am most sorry that you have had such a tumble and such grievous damage to your cart. The broken wheel is quite useless and I doubt it can be repaired."

He paused to choose his words carefully.

"I am quite clear that I am in the wrong of this matter."

He paused and looked more carefully at their injuries.

"I see you have a cut to your head and your lady is in shock."

John Barnard rose to his feet. He was determined to respond in kind to such courteous words.

"It was our fault entirely. I was unfamiliar with the horse and he got away from me. I was pulling hard to bring him back when your coach appeared before us. The next I knew I was on the ground alongside my wife."

"Have you far to go," inquired the Sea General,

"may I offer you my coach for the rest of your journey."

"Very Kind sir! That is not necessary. We are less than an arrows flight from our destination. We are travelling to Abington Manor. It is our property but currently empty. Our home is in Coventry. Matters of business have required our presence here in Northampton. A gentle walk will see us to the manor."

The Sea General nodded in the face of his declined offer. Ketch stood watching this discussion. He wondered how long it would be before the parties began to see the differences between them.

"Despite these initial courtesies there may be some tensions in a moment."

Ketch's concern was a product of differences in dress. The clothing of the Barnards was the very opposite to that of Sea General Blake and his companions. Sir John Barnard wore a fine, dark green, coat which covered a white shirt, a finely embroidered, maroon waistcoat, knee length trousers, silk stockings and fine leather shoes. Elizabeth Barnard also enjoyed an embroidered blouse, a light blue scarf, a full-length blue dress and fur lined short boots.

"*These are not the clothes of Puritans,*" thought Ketch.

"*And Coventry is known as a town that retains royalist sympathies.*"

It became clear to Ketch that this was also dawning on to the mind of the Sea General. He was known as not only a successful commander but also a devout man of God. There was also a change in the Barnards. Their eyes betrayed a growing consciousness of their situation and the memory of past hurts that could not be forgotten. The easy manner of Sir John Barnard took flight. There was a stiffness about him and a colder tone in his voice.

"Captain Ketch, I believe it is time for us to depart. We have greatly benefited from your kindness, but now we must take our leave."

He reached across and firmly helped his wife from the couch and turned to the General.
"Shall we say no more of this matter. I will arrange all affecting our cart and I believe it is nothing but cuts and bruises amongst your company."

General Blake just grunted and nodded his approval. He turned to Ketch.

"I shall remove myself to your dining room to assure myself of Beaumont and Treddager and try your brandy. You have your other guests to speed on their way."

He gave a slight bow to all and left the room. Anne and Ketch rose to their feet. There was some sympathy in Ketch's voice as he addressed Sir John.

"Are you sure sir, that even a short walk can be managed by your wife. We have a very mild-mannered mule and a stable boy who knows her well. They could easily carry your wife and make her journey more comfortable."

Sir John and his wife exchanged glances. It seemed to Ketch that Elizabeth Barnard was very much in favour of accepting the offer. Sir John, however, stood in thought for a moment.

"Agreed!" He said.

"I believe that both the Good Lord and his mother rode upon mules frequently in their lives. I happily accept your kind offer."

Ketch led husband and wife to the stables, gave careful instructions to his stable boy, ensured that Elizabeth Barnard was comfortably seated and waved them on their way. Back in the house he found Anne.

"The old divide of King and Parliament threatened us there. The Barnards moving on came at the right moment."

Anne placed a reassuring hand on his chest.

"All is well husband. Now let us see to our other guests."

They agreed that Anne would take bandages, ointment together with food and drink into the coach party and Ketch would check on the kitchen When Ketch opened the door to the kitchen, he found the coachman and the General's servant sitting around the kitchen table together with William and

11

their cook, Mrs Langley. All were eating bread and preserves and drinking cider. Everyone quickly rose to their feet.

"Sit finish your food" he instructed.

For a few moments he discussed with the coach man the run up to the accident and how long they had been on the road. But as time moved on, he thought it wise to give them an early warning.

"Well as I say, finish your food, but be ready to resume your journey. I expect the General will want to move on."

He paused for a moment.

"Have you far to go?" He inquired.

The coachman quickly swallowed his cider.

"No master. The Sea General sleeps tonight in Northampton at the house of Sir Arthur Hasselrig."

Ketch laughed.

"Then your accident was very unlucky, both parties at the very end of their journey. I shall mention it to the Sea General."

He turned to the door to leave when Mrs Langley spoke up.

"Begging your pardon master but what is a Sea General? I have never heard of such a person. Is it not the case that Generals are to be found on land commanding armies?"

Mrs Langley was a forty-year-old widow, with sons and daughters, who now had families of their own. She had gladly accepted the position of "live in cook" at Derngate House. Besides being a fine cook, she could also read and write and had a general interest in the world.

"You are correct Mrs Langley. It is an unusual title."

Before Ketch could say anything else, the Coachman cleared his throat.

"May I explain master! I know all about this."

Ketch nodded his approval and the coachman sat up straight in his chair.

"Some years back, just as the tyrant Charles Stuart was being beheaded, Parliament had great fears that the admirals in the navy were all at heart royalists, ready to betray the fleet to Prince Rupert. So, they had to find some loyal soldiers to take their place and to head the navy."

The coachman paused to take another sip of his cider, checked that he still had Mrs Langley's attention and continued.

"Of course, they had to choose good men and they found three of them and they called them Generals at Sea and Robert Blake, my General, was one of them. These three men control all the ships in the navy and all the admirals follow their orders. And you must know that General at Sea Robert Blake is the best of them all. He chased Prince Rupert's fleet to the West Indies and destroyed it, recovered the Scilly Isles and the Channel Isles from royalists and three times beat the Dutch....."

"Yes! Yes!" Interrupted Ketch.

"Very good we are convinced that Sea General Blake is the Cromwell of the sea and Mrs Langley has had her question answered. Thankyou coachman but you must now get ready to move."

As he left the kitchen bound for the parlour, he reflected for a moment on the coachman's words.

"Yes, Sea General Blake is a very important man, we must see him safely on his way."

In the parlour Anne was sitting at his mahogany dining table, with a glass in her hand chatting to the Sea General and his companions. Charles Beaumont was sporting a bandage and Captain Treddager was somewhat flushed with drink. A bottle of brandy, an empty decanter and a bottle of port stood on the table. Anne spoke up.
"The gentleman managed to find the brandy and I offered a little port to go with the biscuits and small cakes from the pantry."

Inwardly Ketch felt very proud of his wife. There was a scar to her face that she had received following the Battle of Naseby. For years after she shunned all company and yet now, she was enjoying a conversation with some of the greatest in the land. He accepted that much of her new found confidence was related to their friend, the old clerk James Hedlow, but his love and care over the years had also played its part. As he took his seat, she rose from hers.

"I will leave you to discuss matters with your guests."

There was a smile on her face as she left the room. She was being the good wife.

The Sea General also came to his feet.

"Our host has found us enjoying the company of his wife. She has bandaged Beaumont and cared for us all so well."

Ketch leaned forward at the table.

"Please gentlemen take your repose for as long as you wish."

Beaumont and Treddager both looked at the Sea General. They clearly were both happy with the current situation. The Sea General coughed.

"Yes! Yes! We must move on. Captain ketch has had a disturbed afternoon."

He looked at Ketch.

"Like the Barnards we have almost completed our journey. We seek the house of Sir Arthur Hasselrig. He owns a property in this town and has opened it to provide us with accommodation for the night."

"You are virtually there General," exclaimed Ketch.

"Enter by the town's Derngate. Your coach is facing it. Then follow the road on a straight course through the centre of the town. You carry on past the church of All Saints and as you approach the far side of the town you will find it on your left. I promise you it is quite straight forward. Sir Arthur is a Leicestershire man and we rarely see him here. He must care greatly for your safety and comfort. "

The Sea General laughed.

"Oh! We have been brother Members of Parliament for many years, it will be a delight to see him and I know he keeps an excellent table."

He motioned to Beaumont and Treddager.

"We must get on. Ketch we can sort out matters for the rest of our journey but can you ensure that the cart and horse of the Barnards are dealt with. If there are difficulties, take it up with Beaumont."

Ketch gave a slight bow.

"It will not be a problem General and there will be no need to bother Mr Beaumont.

The Sea General was now clearly anxious to get away. "Chase my servant and coachman out of your kitchen Ketch. You have clearly made them too comfortable"

When they had all stepped outside, he glanced across the grass towards his coach, where in fact both the coachman and his servant were in their allotted positions. He gave a wry laugh at the sight. Then he shook Ketch by the hand.

"Thank your wife for all her aid"

With a final wave he moved across towards his coach preceded by Beaumont and Treddager. Suddenly he stopped and turned to face Ketch.

"I shall be dining with Sir Arthur this evening, perhaps you would like to join us. It will be a small affair, just ourselves and Arthur. I believe he has also invited the Mayor, who you probably know. If it is in order. I shall send a note, with times etc. This is the least I can do."

Ketch stroked his nose.

"Dining with Robert Blake and Sir Arthur Hasselrig could never be topped."

He gave his answer.

"I would be delighted.

The Sea General and his party moved into their coach. The coachman cracked his whip and they were speedily away through the Derngate. Someone waved from the coach window.

Chapter Two   The Dinner

Anne Ketch had suffered much in her early life. Unloved by her parents, abused by her neighbours, at the age of fourteen she was forced out of her home. For three years she survived in a way, that in later years, she wished to forget. Unwillingly she had found herself present at the battle of Naseby just outside Northampton. On the cold battlefield, after victory and defeat, she had been assaulted and the victim of a knife attack that had left her with a scar on her face. This had been the low point of her life. Wandering around Northamptonshire, she was constantly a victim of rebuffs from women and leering advances from men. Eventually in Northampton she had been taken up by the elderly clerk to the Council. He had seen something in her bearing that denoted resilience and humanity. She had first begun as an indoor maid and then became his Housekeeper. James Hedlow and his manservant, Robert, treated her with such simple honesty and goodwill, that the bad memories and continuing fears began to fade. Then events had led Trooper Ketch into her life and a succession of visits led to friendship, love and marriage. With such people in her life, she had not only gained strength in physique but also in spirit. Her confidence grew such, that now she would not suffer to be put down and no longer avoided the public gaze. She was as relaxed in the market place as in her own home. The scar on her face had not gone, but she felt no need to hide it. It became her badge of survival and defiance, and has not prevented her from being regarded as a beauty.

She was excited that great men had invited her husband to dinner and when he announced that he would not be wearing military dress, she cleaned and brushed his other clothes in a whirlwind of activity. When he was ready to go and collect William to accompany him, he was suffered to accept the most detailed of inspections along with a wealth of helpful advice on his behaviour. This included neutral topics of conversation and the need for caution in the matter of food and drink. Finally, he was given a clean, white handkerchief and pleasant-smelling herbs were placed in his pockets.

As she watched her husband and William depart, she remained in a state of great happiness. Whilst life had made her sensible, she could not deny a warm glow filled her at the thought of the news she would have for friends and neighbours. She would be the source of all information about the accident, the General at Sea and the dinner taking place at Hasselrig House. She was a happy and contented woman.

Ketch and William arrived at Hasselrig House at the same time as the Mayor and his servant. Ketch and Councilman Lugg were shown upstairs, whilst the servants were whisked away into the kitchens. The Mayor and Ketch were old friends, having experienced in the past, political and personal danger together.
As they mounted the stairs, they were able to express cordial greetings and share a few remarks on the size of the house and the nature of the evening ahead. They entered the dining room

to find Sir Arthur Hasselrig, Sea General Blake, Charles Beaumont and Ralph Treddager standing around an empty fireplace in amiable conversation. Sir Arthur turned to meet them. He was a tall, dark man, good looking with a thin moustache. Dressed in sombre clothes there was the look of a pirate captain about him. He smiled as he approached them.

"Mr Mayor, you are very welcome and this I presume is Captain Ketch who has been of such help to our Sea General."

There were bows and introductions all around and Ketch received a wave from Robert Blake. Then Sir Arthur led them all to the table.

"Come let us all sit down at once. Our food is ready, no special places as after all we have a round table."

His guests all found a place. Ketch himself was sat between Beaumont and Treddager and opposite Sir Arthur. From there he had a very good view of both his host and the Sea General. Considerable quantities of food began to arrive. A procession of servants laid out a cold collation of chicken and vegetables, a saddle of lamb, three large beef pies, and a dozen small venison tarts. There were three large platters filled with sliced duck and pigeon, bowls of onions and carrots together with jugs of meat juices fortified with red wine. Three large jugs of beer and ceramic mugs completed the meal, except on a side dresser were laid out bowls of cream and chopped fruits with cakes, puddings and sugared nuts. When the servants had left, Sir Arthur gently waved his knife.

"Sit gentlemen and for the moment let us forbid talking. That can come later, let us enjoy our food."

Everyone helped themselves and passed dishes and plates around between them.

"I find servants are quite useless with a round table. We can so easily have just what we want if we help ourselves."

Sir Arthurs voice was loud enough to convey his sentiments far beyond the room and Ketch wondered how they would be received and then he remembered that this property was rarely used by Sir Arthur. These would all be local, temporary staff. All the guests took full advantage of Sir Arthur's hospitality and there were quiet murmurs of appreciation. But in the silences Ketch ran over in his mind what he knew about Sir Arthur Hasselrig.

"Member of Parliament, famous as one of the five members who, together with Pym, Hampden, Hollis and Strode, so criticised and defied the King that he came in person to the House of Commons with two hundred soldiers to arrest them. Fortunately, they had been warned and escaped by boat to the City of London., and that really started the Civil War. For the rest he is known as a sworn republican and has a reputation for being hot- tempered and rash."

One by one the diners had eaten their fill and with the return of the servants came wine, brandy and port.

Sir Arthur looked about him.

"It is such a pleasure to entertain you all. I enjoy being with men who clearly enjoy their food."

There were further murmurs of appreciation all around the table. He turned to Sea General Blake.

21

"Robert Blake and I are old friends, the rest of you gentlemen are unknown to me, that is of course except Councilman Lugg, the Mayor of Northampton. We have from time-to-time crossed swords over the merits of our respective towns, but we remain friends."

Mayor Lugg nodded and replied.

"Just so Sir Arthur."

Sir Arthur returned his focus to Robert Blake.

"I understand Robert had an accident when less than a mile away and that Captain Ketch came to your rescue. No one seriously hurt I hope."

"No one Arthur", replied Blake.

"A small cart collided with my rather heavy coach, the cart's wheel was splintered and a middle-aged couple were spilt upon the ground. Captain Ketch
gathered us all up and treated our cuts and bruises in his home. His wife provided us with food and drink and then we were sent on our way. It was tidily done."

Sir Arthur had a question.

"The couple spilt upon the ground, who were they?"

It was Ketch who provided the answer.

"A Sir John Barnard and his wife Elizabeth. Their property is close to mine."

"Old Royalists," interrupted Beaumont.

"And very colourfully dressed. When they got a good look at us, they were quick to be on their way. They are not of our congregation."

The Mayor felt he could add to the conversation.

"An interesting lady is Elizabeth Barnard, she is the last living descendent of a poet and playwright called William Shakespeare, at least she and her cousin. A tragedy really, he was much admired in the old Queen's time and still has followers, indeed he is quite revered by many men of letters in the South of our County."

He paused for a moment.

"Indeed, there is a gentleman called Dryden, something of a poet himself who is always singing Shakespeare's praises and, in a heartbeat, will give you a reading from his poems and plays."

Some years earlier, Ketch had pulled young Dryden out of the River Thames, but considered it not politic to mention it with such a potentially dangerous topic of conversation.

Captain Treddager snorted with annoyance. "The theatres have been closed for over ten years, so perhaps lack of Grandsons is not such a misfortune."

Sea General Blake also grunted his disapproval.

"People should stick to their bible. Theatres and mummers, jugglers and the like, take the lower orders from their study of scripture. They are not helpful."

"How right you are Robert," echoed Sir Arthur.

"I once, years ago tried his poetry. Found it difficult to get anything out of it."

It was to the Mayor's credit that he was not nonplussed by such opposition, he had stood up to high-ranking military men before.

"Well, I like him anyhow and so do others," he muttered.

There was a brief moment of silence before Sir Arthur passed the brandy decanter towards Ketch, who remembering his wife's advice, demurred the offer.

"You are a military man Captain Ketch, in the time of our troubles, did you get involved in any fighting, what regiment were you in?"

Sir Arthurs question was asked in a careful neutral tone. This, however, was familiar ground for Ketch. On this topic he felt much more at home. He addressed the table.

"When hostilities broke out, I was barely 21 years old, but I signed up for Lord Manchester's regiment, but throughout the conflict I was moved about. A time with Colonel Butlers regiment and then I found myself on the right flank at Naseby."

He looked Sir Arthur in the eye.

"Our County Sir Arthur. It was a hard day. Charles Stuart's men in the centre stuck out until the end. There was much loss of life."

Ketch left it at that. Something at the back of his mind warned him that the names Thurloe and Cromwell may not now be happy subjects for Robert Blake and Sir Arthur. They were both known as fierce republicans. However, Robert Blake was very happy to continue with military reminiscing.

"This man here, Ketch, Sir Arthur was a doubty fighter, a very difficult man to kill. He fought in many actions but famously at Roundway Down. Stranded and surrounded, the enemies' musket shot just bounced off his armour."

He turned to his subject.

"That is correct Arthur?"

There was a nod in return.

"So as musket balls could not bring him down, they set about him with their swords, but he just beat them off. In the end his men re-joined him and he survived intact to give both King and Cromwell trouble."

Sir Arthur chuckled.

"Steady on Robert. I am loyal to our cause. I fought King Charles but I argue with Cromwell.

He turned to the company. He would not be backward in similarly lauding his senior guest.

"This Sea General here with us this evening was a hero on land noted for his defence of both Lyme and Taunton, but at sea he is a giant, Prince Rupert destroyed at sea, Scilly Isles and Channel Isles liberated, Dutch navy defeated three times, the Bey of Tunis bombarded and Christian slaves freed and I have no doubt there will be more to come."

Sir Arthur was clearly going to continue with Robert Blakes achievements when the Mayor cut across him.

"General, how was it that as a land commander you were able to become a successful sea commander. Surely it demands different skills."

Robert Blake looked carefully at the Mayor.

"Councilman Lugg you have raised a very delicate issue. It is three years since I moved on to the sea and I have learned that simply sailing a ship in the right direction takes considerable skill and deep knowledge. Even today my understanding of sails, rigging, masts, cordage, gunnery and interpreting the wind is incomplete. That is why I keep Captain Treddager by my side. He will admit he is too old for combat but in his head is all that is known of sailing, navigation and how to take a ship into battle."

Captain Treddager acknowledged the General's words with a lift of his glass. The General continued.

"I run the fleet; my sea Captains run the ships. Action at sea is so complicated and full of uncertainty. Keeping fifty, sixty, a hundred ships together operating as one is a nightmare. Signals are missed, the wind changes, collisions happen. Basic naval strategy says that if you can take the windward the enemy's fleet is lost. Frankly, there have been times when I had the windward only to find that the wind changes and it is I who am in mortal danger,"

He laughed.

"We do a lot of praying at sea especially about the wind."

His manner became more serious.

"What I do Mr Mayor, is make men want to fight, to believe that it is God's work we are doing. Make them convinced they will win because they have been given better officers and better guns, English seamen when they believe this are wonderful to be with. Every commander will tell you this. Treat them right and they will fight."

He took a sip of his brandy.

If I have any trouble, it is with the Captains rather than the men."

A serious moment fell upon the table.

"We shall have war with the Spanish! General?"

Asked the Mayor more as a statement than a question.

"Yes" was Blake's reply in a clear firm tone.

"It is the Governments' will."

To everyone's surprise, Sir Arthur uttered an oath.

"Government Robert! What Government! We have no Government. Cromwell has closed down Government. The House of Commons has been reorganised as an unelected chamber, full of so- called Godly men all chosen by Cromwell and Thurloe. In fact, what we have is personal rule by Cromwell rather than by elected representatives of the people."

He looked across to Robert Blake.

"I absolve you Robert from all this. You are always at sea fighting our enemies abroad. We have beaten our enemies on land, now is the time for civilian government."

He abruptly stopped speaking and took a strong pull from his glass of brandy and surveyed his guests. Ketch felt very uncertain. He had spent his last ten years working for Oliver Cromwell and his right- hand man, John Thurloe. These were uncomfortable words to hear from such men as Sir Arthur Hasselrig. Sir Arthur had more to say.

"I apologise gentlemen, especially to you Mr Mayor and you Captain Ketch. I know that there are many military men and civilians who have the highest opinion of the Lord Protector. Such an evening we have enjoyed should not be upset by political matters. Please drink up Mr Beaumont, I know nothing of you. How did you become involved with the Sea General?"

Charles Beaumont took the opportunity to give the company a detailed account of his school and university days. It was so full of incident and humour that the whole tone of the evening was changed and much laughter was heard around the table. The Sea General looked on approvingly at the social skills of his Secretary. The evening ended with Ketch and the Mayor profusely thanking Sir Arthur for a most wonderful dinner and a most stimulating evening. Everyone laughed at the word "stimulating." They collected their servants; both were standing at the threshold holding aloft torches. With final "Goodnights" they stepped out into the dark night and made their way back to the town centre. They walked in companiable silence for some time but as they approached All Saints Church, Councilman Lugg spoke quietly, his words just intended for Ketch.

"I leave you here John for my house is just beyond the market square. What an evening. I feel that the company of great men requires me to be constantly alert. I am exhausted. I have been battered by their words"

"I share that feeling", replied Ketch.

"I am most ready for my bed and sleep."

Chapter Three   For the Empire

January 1656

Philip IV by Grace of God, King of Spain, the Sicilies, Jerusalem, the Indies, Arch Duke of Austria, Duke of Burgundy and Milan etc.....

The ruler of an Empire on which the sun never sets, was sitting in his favourite room, in his favourite Palace peeling an orange. His Palace, the Escorial was a huge block of stone, built by his Grandfather Philip II. Located thirty miles North of Madrid, it was the seat of royal and ecclesiastical power for the whole of Spain. As a building it served not only as a Royal Palace, but as a mausoleum, a library, a treasury, museum, monastery and hospital. From here Philip IV administered his whole, wide Empire. As he skilfully quartered his orange, his mind pondered the state of the Empire.

"It is always left to me. I get no real help. My Chief Minister tries his best, but he never sees the whole picture. He worries about France, the Dutch, the Sultan of Turkey and of course the English. But once a problem is solved, he goes on to something else, endlessly busy but with no central strategy.".

He paused to order his thoughts.

"I fear we are in decline. The Grandees of Spain are of little use. Oh Yes! They will become Princes of the Church, and are happy to be appointed as Governors and Viceroys in Italy, Mexico or Peru. There they can happily make their fortunes but, I get no help in

managing the Government or the Army and Navy. It is left to me to carry the weight of decisions, to devise an overall strategy, policies that will secure the Empire for the future."

He threw his orange away and carefully wiped his hands.

"The sea is the heart of the matter. Spain is a world Empire. We must control the seas, all the seas. When Dutch, Portuguese and English ships dip their colours to our galleons, then I can rest"

He decided to share his thoughts with his Chief Minister, Luis Mendoza de Haro, he was to share in his King's enlightenment. He rang the small bell on his desk and ordered a page to "send for De Haro".

Whilst waiting he turned to look at himself in his large wall mirror. He was not tall and was disappointed to see that the nature of his face reinforced his reputation as morose. He scowled back at himself. He had discarded his wig and this had revealed the thinning hair of his fifty years. In contrast, he was pleased to see that his clothes were of the finest materials and fitted him perfectly. He turned this way and that and smiled as he still retained some grace about him. He peered closely and noticed he was squinting. His eyes were a problem. He had lost his pleasure for reading.

"Well, thought"

"This mirror fails to show that I am diligent and hardworking on the Empire's behalf and that my close friends and family think I am good company."

His further thoughts were lost in the arrival of his Chief Minister. Philip was uncertain whether or not Luis was a friend but their relationship required him to treat him as both friend and confidant. He took hold of him by the shoulder and guided him to a couch below a set of large windows and there they sat together side by side. It amused Philip, that Luis was obviously unhappy with such physical contact with his King. Luis was of a similar age as the King, but dark and wiry, a man of thin lips and all wrists and elbows. His family had long been servants of the crown and the King felt comfortable with him. Luis had no intellectual pretensions, relying on absolute loyalty as the basis of his position. He waited for the King to speak.

"Luis, I have been thinking on the state of the Empire and the war with the English."

Luis was very uncertain at what was to come, the King had a conspiratorial air about him.

"But Sire! You agreed that we must stop their continuing piracy and plundering of our country's ships, especially the treasure ships from the New World. There is so much at stake."

The King was already impatient with his Chief Minister.

"I am not suggesting an end to the war, just that we are not doing very well and with us still at war with France, something new must be tried. We have to gain mastery of the sea. That is the key. Every method including the unusual must be considered."

Luis was about to speak, but a lift of the king's finger forestalled him.

"Listen to my words Luis. We are fighting wars with both France and England. Now who is the greatest threat to Spain and our Empire?"

Luis was astute enough to know that the King was going to provide the answer.

"The answer Luis is the English. France is essentially an annoyance to Spain. They have a female Regent and a boy King and their interests are solely in Europe. The English are a sea-going nation. English expansion is aimed at the world and our overseas possessions. We are not winning this battle Luis. We need command of the sea, Luis. All success will come from that"

Luis remained silent; he knew that there was more to come. The King continued.

"So, if the sea war against the English is our priority! What can we do?

Luis again was silent but this time because he had no answer.

"Could we invade England Luis?

Compelled to answer Luis replied.

"I think not your majesty. Even your Grandfather failed in that."

"Quite correct Luis. We shall think no more of that. Then the question is how can we match and defeat the English at sea?"

The King was now coming to the very heart of his thinking.

"To defeat the English we need Admirals, skilful Captains, trained seaman, well-built ships and an enthusiasm for battle. Are we lacking in any of this Luis? No! Do not try to answer my question. We are lacking in them all."

The King's Chief Minister was feeling some distress. This conversation was taking an unhappy turn, but he did not see any wisdom in contradicting the King. The King was pleased with himself. Explaining matters to Luis had clarified his own mind.

"We must of course seek to improve our navy and strike where we see English weakness, but we need something more immediate. At the moment the English rely very heavily on one commander. He is their champion and hero. He is called Robert Blake. All their successes come from this man. Without him the balance of sea power can move towards Spain. We must ensure that he will never command an English Fleet again."

Chief Minister De Haro had not anticipated the seriousness of the King in this matter.

"Your Majesty, we should kill him? Assassination your Majesty.!

The King lowered his face close to that of his Chief Minister.

"In the war with the Dutch Provinces my esteemed ancestor Philip II offered 250,000 golden coins for the death of William the Silent and it worked. William was killed by a Dutchman, one of his own people.

Luis's mind began to consider the King's proposal.

"Your Majesty such a policy of public assassination would not be well received by the Courts of Europe. The suggestion of disreputable conduct would impact badly on Spanish Honour. It would be discussed amongst the common folk of Europe. It would be a sign of desperation, of weakness. There may be retaliation and remember Philip II lost many of the Dutch Provinces."

Luis was pleading with his King. He found a desperate last argument.

"Besides he is always away at sea, for months at a time."

"Ah!" Interrupted the King.

"They are not at sea all the time. In winter, poor weather and lack of supplies forces them to return to port."

The King rose to his feet, but pressed Luis to remain sitting on the couch. He gazed out of the windows.

"Luis I am not suggesting a public bribe to murder him. No! No! What would be of interest is an arranged accident, a fall, food poisoning, a runaway horse. Life is full of chance and such things could occur with no stain on Spanish honour. If such an accident could be arranged, think of the gains for Spain.

Luis could see that the King would not be deflected from this. He tried to gain control of the project.

"A powerful plan your Majesty, we of course must in no way be seen to be involved. It will require discretion and skilled men. We cannot involve Italians, Siciliennes or Turks I think your Majesty such a venture would be better managed from

Spanish Flanders. The right men for such a task are more likely to be found there, English speaking and knowledgeable about England. Also, there are plenty there used to brutality."

"Excellent," exclaimed the King.

"We will not be involved and what a coup it will be. Think Luis of the ships, commerce and treasure we will save. My son, Don Juan, rules in Spanish Flanders. Let him be brought into this matter. There must be no letters, no evidence that we here in Spain are involved. You must send a trusted man, properly briefed, to explain to Don Juan, what is expected."

The Chief Minister rose and bowed to the King. He would do what was demanded, but had little faith in its success. He was delighted that it was now the responsibility of the King's illegitimate son to get on with it. The King clapped his hands, he had managed a good morning's work. He was looking forward to his lunch.

Don Juan of Austria, Governor of Southern Flanders closed the door on the messenger from Madrid and walked back to sit at his desk. He needed time to think. It had been no ordinary message or messenger. It had been delivered by a Captain in the Royal Guard and a man known to him. As such he knew it as coming directly from his father. This he could not ignore, quite the reverse, it had to be done.

Don Juan had served all over the Empire and the use of accident as an intelligence option was not unknown to him. Indeed, in Naples it was a normal matter of policy and often

35

there was no bothering with an accident. His instructions had been quite clear. No records of any sort, verbal reports only, success only to be judged on results, a matter vital for the Spanish war effort.

He pursed his lips and looked at the ceiling.

"This is no back alley stabbing or beating. An accident requires skill and imagination. This is to take place in England. Finding the right people will be difficult. We have people in England but they will not do. They just count ships for Madrid. The English Spy Master Thurloe, almost certainly know all about them anyway. Surely, we can find sufficient English- speaking agents. They will need that pale, unhealthy look of the English and have some skill in spotting opportunity, but a small team must be able to accomplish this."

He looked at the casket on his desk. He looked at the heaped gold coins.

"At least I do not have to pay for this myself, although it does show that the King is serious."

He rang a silver bell and to the summoned page he gave the instruction.

"Find me Henrick de Ritter."

The man requested was the Chief of Spies for Spanish Flanders. On his arrival Don Juan waved him to a chair. Henrick de Ritter was forty years old and looked the typical Netherlander. He was of medium height, broad of stature, clear face, black hair and dressed in rich but conservatively cut clothes. He had all the marks of a prosperous merchant from Antwerp. He was relaxed in the Governor's presence. They worked well together and he knew he was a trusted man. Only two days ago he had warned the Governor, that his personal hairdresser was probably one of Thurloe's spies. Whilst angry at the deception, Don Juan was amused that De Ritter's advice was to keep him in post and use him to feed the English false information.

"I have a difficult and serious task for you De Ritter. It is a matter of great importance."

It took some time for the Governor to outline the nature of the instructions from Spain. He finished with some carefully chosen words.

"This will require careful trade craft, fortunately we have been provided with ample funds. I might add this comes from the King himself."

De Ritter pulled a face.

"The man is at sea most of the time. I know the English fleet winters in port, but early Spring is almost upon us, we have but four or five weeks to succeed in this. There is another problem that unfortunately I must raise with you. There are five of us in my department. Only myself and my deputy speak English well enough. The others are fluent in Dutch, French and German. Even if my Deputy is involved, we will need two new recruits and this will not be easy. This proposal has a very high possibility that any agent involved will lose their life No one easily contemplates suicide, yet the outcome must look an accident. Frankly Governor, I think you are asking a lot of new recruits. "

"Go and speak to our Generals there must surely be amongst the army at least three men trustworthy, English speaking with the necessary loyalty to Spain."

Don Juan did not like difficulties. He wanted action.

"Well, that should be possible. You must just get on with it. Keep me informed of progress."

De Ritter stayed in his chair. He needed clarification in one other area. He got a sharp look from the Governor, but he was given a nod to proceed.

"I have but one good contact in England who is in London. Madrid has agents in England, largely in the Southern ports. Are they to be involved in this?"

Don Juan spoke carefully and clearly emphasising every word.

This is your affair. Madrid is not involved. You have full responsibility from this moment.

Thank you, sir. Replied De Ritter.

"I shall get on with this at once."

He felt it politic to instantly rise from his chair, bow and make his exit.

De Ritter immediately scoured the local regiments seeking suitable candidates. He had decided that given the importance of this, they should be seen by the Governor himself. Within three days he had what seemed to him a reasonable selection. They were sent into the Governor one by one. The first was a lieutenant in the artillery, thirty years old, tall, muscular and a fine horseman. He had battle experience, good English and came highly recommended by his commander. The second was a twenty- four years old Captain of infantry, thin but wiry, good English and from an old Spanish family. Finally, an aide to his General, in fact his nephew. This candidate had excellent English, very keen, well-liked, a clever mimic and a good swordsman.

Each man had some thirty minutes with the Governor and De Ritter had high hopes for them. On entering the Governor's room, he was waved to a chair and settled down for the Governor's comments.

"No! No! No! They will not do Henrick. Yes! They are all loyal Spaniards, talented and trustworthy, but they are too clean, too well nourished and too well set. They are confident, take them out of uniform and put them in rags and they would still shine through and stand out."

De Ritter felt deflated and decided an apology was necessary.

"I am sorry Governor. I am clearly looking for the wrong type of man.

The Governor sucked his teeth.

"In desperation, the third candidate, the General's nephew, will do but that still leaves us needing two others. Forget soldiers, sailors. Where can we find English- speaking agents who are normal, who do not attract notice.?"
De Ritter was unfortunately thinking over a candidate who had all the qualities of normality, but was far too valuable to him. He felt, however, he had no choice.

"There is my Deputy, Michel Gauvin, bookish, a thinker, no swordsman, but he can shoot. He is very clever, has an exceptionally fine hand and speaks English. He always looks under nourished and is uncomfortable in the company of women."

"Excellent," cried the Governor,

"Just the sort of man we want. It sounds that he would blend in unnoticed anywhere. He must lead. Now with the General's nephew we have two. Who else can you bring to mind? Someone more villainous, used to back alleys and living with low lives"

The Governor's comments kicked De Ritter's mind to a name he normally would not have considered, but the Governor had spoken of low lives.

"There is a woman in the Ghent jail, who is English, a seductress and a trickster. Beautiful and accomplished in the arts and music. She is a dangerous and slippery criminal, that the Burgomaster mentioned to me. She seduces elderly widowers, preferably rich merchants, offers to help them in their business. Then at the right time she will gather together as much of his wealth as she can and then disappear. A former actress she has skills in disguise that make her hard to track down. But we have her now in Ghent Jail where she will remain for a very long time. Her daughter, who she loves very much, we have in a local convent. But, is this really the type of agent we require?" Her name is Mary Sharp."

The Governor clapped his hands.

"I think we have our agents, D Ritter. Raphael de Rousse, the General's nephew, will do this for Spain. Michel

Gauvin will do it out of loyalty to you and Mary Sharp will do this for freedom and her daughter."

He motioned to the casket on the desk.

"Make this happen Henrick. Let them know precisely what is required and then let them loose."

De Ritter rose, bowed and left the room. The Governor stood and looked out of his window into a bare garden. He rather wished he was in Spain.

Henrick de Ritter chose the security of the Governor's chapel as the place to fully explain to the three agents the nature as to what was expected of them and how it was to be achieved. He had ensured that they would not be disturbed by dismissing the local priest. He looked about him. The winter sun threw only weak shafts of light into the gloom of the chapel. Candles, without much success, tried to illuminate the frescos, gold hangings and the alter. He shrugged; it would have to do. He placed three chairs by the steps to the alter. He was confident that his words would only be heard by those for whom they were intended. As the agents arrived in the chapel, he led them to their places. They quickly settled and he took one final look around before he began.

"You Raphael have surprisingly volunteered for a very dangerous mission. You do not know what it is. You say this is out of loyalty to Spain, but I suspect it is to impress your uncle and get away from the boredom of soldiering. But I must tell you that now you have no choice in the matter, you will undertake this mission."

The two men and a woman sat in their chairs in a row before a standing De Ritter. Raphael looked up at De Ritter and beamed him a confident smile with just a hint of insolence.

"I am your man De Ritter, ready for whatever challenge you have for us. You may rest assured that together with these comrades I will get the job done."

Raphael de Rousse was twenty-eight years old, of average build. He enjoyed a blemish free face and curly-black hair. He wore dull clothes, but was permanently cheerful. He sat relaxed and at ease in his chair. There was a hint of arrogance in his obvious confidence.

De Ritter was not pleased by the familiarity or the lightness of his speech.

"I really cannot understand why the Governor thought this young man was suitable. Perhaps he sees himself in his younger days, carefree but lucky. He will be less carefree when he finds out what is expected."

He turned to Michel Gauvin

"Michel, you have been my Deputy for three years. Your work here in Flanders has been exceptional but the Governor has particularly required you to lead this mission and in this I have no choice. As you must go, it is a comfort to me that you and your experience will be available to your other team members.

Michel removed a delicate pair of glasses, wiped them carefully with his handkerchief and looked around him.

"Yours and the Governors are kind words but I would have more certainty in this, if I knew what exactly we are being asked to do."

De Ritter nodded agreement to Michel and looked hard at Raphael and Mary.

"Michel is your leader, listen to him and you may live to achieve your goal and return safely, ignore him or disobey him at your peril."

There were nods of acceptance from Raphael and Mary but no great enthusiasm. Mary Sharp sat up straight in her chair, she knew she was next.

"You madame are a thief, a fraudster and a liar. You are violent and dangerous. I state these facts for the benefit of these two gentlemen. They must be informed of the potential risk you represent. But in this imperfect world and the difficulties they may encounter, some of your skills may be of use."

Mary smiled. She had been brought straight from prison. She was quite used to hearing her character described in this way. She was tall for a woman and there was a strength in her body that prison had not yet conquered. Her long, black hair was greasy and unkempt. She had an unmarked face with brown eyes, full lips, and when its dirt was removed it could be considered beautiful. She was still in her prison shift, a thin grey garment, from throat to ankles, kept in place by a rope belt.

De Ritter was ready to put his proposition to her.

"You have been brought from prison, where at the moment you are destined to remain for twenty years Your young child has been taken from you and handed over to nuns. For the rest of her life, she can look forward to serving God."

There was silence in the chapel. Michel and Raphael were fully focussed on De Ritter's words. The chief of Spies cleared his throat. There would be no turning back from this.

"You can only hope to change your fate if you agree to take part fully in what has been planned for you three to do on behalf of Spain. You will share, if successful, in a large quantity of gold with Michel and Raphael, but in addition you will receive back your daughter and your crimes will be forgotten. You have the chance of a new life. I only add none of this will be available if you fail, in fact your troubles will increase. I need a decision now. From here you can return to jail, or you can earn what I have just offered by joining with these men in the mission. Like you, they have no idea what is involved."

The chapel regained its silence, light from the candles flickered over four faces. Mary held them in suspense, but for herself, she knew, of course, there was of no choice.

"I accept. I will do whatever unpleasantness that is required."
The tension in the chapel lifted. For a brief moment there was a moment of comradeship. She would be part of the group. They would share their future.
De Ritter grunted his approval.

"Now listen to exactly what is expected of you. "

His audience leaned forward anxious to catch every word.

"You are being sent to England, to London, to murder Sea General Robert Blake. He is the senior commander of the English fleet, which has been collecting on the South Coast of England. There may well be up to one hundred ships. This fleet is a dagger poised at the heart of Spain. He is a superb seaman as dangerous as Francis Drake. We have little fear of England's other Admirals, a very poor lot, but he must be destroyed. "

He waited to give them time to absorb the full measure of what was being expected and the reason for it. All three faces were devoid of expression.

"There is no honour in this, but the naval advantage will be immense."

De Ritter was watching very closely for any sign of disaffection or dissent.

"Now it is important that if possible, this should be, or look, an accident. Spain would then be seen as totally uninvolved. If I read in a dispatch, of an unfortunate accident leading to the demise of Robert Blake, that would be fine, but the central requirement is, that he must die."

Having outlined the heart of the matter, he began providing further details.

"You will each be given a substantial sum of money, together with travel papers. You will enter England legally from French Calais to Dover. You will travel to London and find a tavern called the Turk's Head in Billingsgate, by the London docks. You will approach the landlord, a brutish woman called Sally Stanley. She runs a gang of thieves, but receives a lot of money to be our agent in London. She deals directly with me; however, I do not recommend total trust in her. She will be expecting you, but it would be better if she does not know your purpose. You involve her only if absolutely necessary. It is you who must find Robert Blake. It should not be too hard. He has an extensive entourage: secretaries, clerks who will all work to his command and there will be a constant flow of seaman, captains, messengers and contractors visiting him on business."

De Ritter was beginning to feel weary and he had not yet finished his briefing.

"Now this part of your instructions is especially important. Once you have located him you must act as individuals. To work as a team is comforting, but an initial failure by one, invariably leads to all being lost. We want three separate attempts at least. You will have your own knives but I shall provide Michel with both a vial of poison and a fine wheellock pistol. If an accident becomes impossible these may be used."

He felt he was finished but he knew more was required of him.

"What are your questions?

He was another hour dealing with the careful, clever, sometimes foolish questions thrown at him. Eventually a silence of exhaustion fell on the chapel.

"You have some two to three weeks before Blake joins the fleet. That is the time that Madrid's spies on the coast have given us. I would like to hear of his death before then We shall speak again before you go. I have arranged rooms for you here in the Palace. You are not to leave the building. "

He cast a look at Mary.

"I will lock you in if necessary. In two days, you will be taken to Calais."

At last, he was finished. He rose and led all three out of the gloom of the chapel. He had to report to the Governor.

Chapter Four   Friends and Foes (1)

Ketch took a last look at the Abbey. He always enjoyed being in the presence of the Palace of Westminster, Whitehall Palace and Westminster Abbey. He felt the three great buildings symbolised the power of England. To him it seemed they would stand for ever providing protection for their people. Having filled his mind with these thoughts, he took a deep breath and strode purposefully past the two guards and through the archway into Whitehall Palace. He made his way to the staircase that led up to the headquarters of Cromwell's secret service. He expected to report to his friend and mentor, Major Richard Blake, but on mounting the stairway he was surprised to see the Major descending towards him.

"Hello Richard, I am on my way to see you. I have had a note from Benson that spoke of urgent matters.

"Indeed John, but even Benson, our chief clerk, cannot foresee all the events that crowd in on us. We are in the usual state of too much to do and not enough of us to do it. At this moment, I am on my way to Wales, to remind a particular General that he would be unwise to support the potentially treasonable activities that seem to be thriving around him."

Ketch frowned.

"That sounds very serious, are we talking about rebellion?"

"Pray God no! But Thurloe has the belief that I in some way frighten senior military figures into good behaviour. I seem to be regularly performing this task for him."

The Major looked about him.

"I must move quickly."

He grasped Ketch on the shoulder and made his way down the stairs, but halfway down he turned around.

"Our master, Thurloe, is in my office waiting for you. You have a problem, not as urgent as mine, but even more serious.......Good Luck."

With a wave he carried on down the stairs leaving Ketch in some uncertainty and concern as to what Secretary Thurloe wanted of him. Benson was waiting for him inside the main and only door into their headquarters. The dozen or so clerks were working feverishly at their desks, but as a body they raised their heads to acknowledge his arrival. Both he and Major Blake had survived almost ten years in the service of Secretary Thurloe and their work was frequently perilous. In fact, it was a great reassurance to the organisation that they were still unharmed. They had become talismans to the clerks, bringers of success.

"The Secretary requires you to go straight in Captain. He is waiting for you.

Ketch acknowledged Benson's instruction, strode across the room and knocked on the door. He had no idea as to what would be awaiting him. He knew the words from Secretary Thurloe would determine how his next days would be spent, Secretary Thurloe had occupied a number of different posts within the Republic, but being Chief of Spies had become a fairly small part of his duties. The whole range of Government now came within his compass. As Secretary to the Council of State, he was charged with ensuring that the decisions it made were implemented. Controlling the agenda, making recommendations, reporting on progress were what placed him at the centre of national affairs. Whilst Cromwell was truly master of England, Ireland and Scotland, it was John Thurloe who exercised much of that mastery. Senior Generals, Members of the House of Commons were frequently infuriated at his intervention into what they considered were matters for them alone. Nevertheless, his will would prevail. Nearing his fiftieth year there was nothing in his physical appearance to suggest his importance. His grey eyes indicated an intelligence and his close- cropped hair flagged a radical view of life, but it was when engaged in conversation that his energy, confidence and knowledge became evident. Then his true metal shone through. Ketch faced him sitting behind Major Blake's desk.

"Come! Come in Ketch and sit down. I have sent the Major to Wales so you must take up the next serious matter we face."

Ketch settled in a chair opposite the Secretary. Thurloe and leaned towards him. He spoke just above a whisper as if concerned someone was listening at the door.

"John, this is a really important matter. It must be handled with great care and discretion but also great determination. Get this wrong, frankly there will be consequences for you and indeed me as well as the country."

Ketch had never been briefed in such a manner before. In fact, often his missions had been introduced with a hint of humour or irony. He gave the Secretary his full attention.

"You have heard of Robert Blake our senior commander at sea. He enjoys the title of General at Sea. He is a man who has served the Government well. He, as a land Commander, won praises for the defence of Lyme and Taunton and holding the West Country for Parliament. When Parliament found there were no admirals without royalist sympathies, he agreed to take to the sea. There, amazingly he thrived, securing marvellous victories. I do not know how, for he had no experience of the sea, and had to learn all from the beginning. Yet, it was his victories that brought the Dutch to seek peace with us."

There he paused to ensure that ketch was following. He was about to continue when Ketch forestalled him.

"Mr Secretary, some years ago I met the Sea General when he was travelling through Northamptonshire. He was involved in an accident right outside my home. My wife and I treated his, and his companion's initial injuries. As a result, I had the pleasure, that same evening of dinner with him and Sir Arthur Hasselrig."

Thurloe could not hide that he was impressed.

"That was high flying Ketch. I hope you emerged unscathed?"

Ketch smiled and waited until Thurloe moved on to what was so urgent.

"Good! The Sea General knows you, that will ease matters."

Thurloe sat still, seemingly to take a moment to review what he was about to say.

"Following the Lord Protector's strategy, we are at war with Spain and Sea General Blake has been seeking to bring the Spanish fleet to battle. To date this has not been achieved, rather he has been serving our best interests, ranging around the Mediterranean. At this moment, the fleet is in winter quarters readying for sea. Blake is here in London, managing the thousand and one things a naval commander must do. He is preparing a fleet to take on the Spanish. Do you know anything about naval warfare Ketch?"

Ketch was silent. He knew nothing. Thurloe took silence to mean nothing.

"A fleet of almost one hundred ships is being prepared on the South coast. It means new ships and dozens being re-fitted. It is horribly involved and extremely expensive."

He began ticking points off his fingers.

"You would not believe the amount of wood and iron required for the body of a ship and setting its masts and spars. In addition, to fully prepare a fleet, miles of rope are needed for rigging and cordage, plus acres of sailcloth, cannons, gunpowder, saws, axes, firearms cutlases. Thousands of seamen need clothing, food and drink for at least six months. Maps, medical supplies, glass, lamp oil I could go on. There is then the question of men. The navy is always complaining that it hasn't enough. So, the Government ignored our traditions of liberty and have introduced "The Press." where able body men from the poor and idle are forcibly signed up for sea. This navy has come at a high cost."

Thurloe came to a sudden stop.

"I digress a little. The point I am trying to make is that whilst the Navy Committee pays for this and the Dockyard Commissioners implement it, the Commander in Chief has to ensure that it all happens and he becomes permanently harassed by his Captains that they in one matter or another have been forgotten or ignored. The point of this Ketch is that Robert Blake is in London, in this building dealing with all these matters. For this he Sea has a large entourage of secretaries and clerks, but come what may he must be in Portsmouth early in March. This means that there will be a large convoy of carts, carriages and waggons managed by some twenty people together with the Sea General's personal staff. Such a large transportation is necessary as the fleet will be away for at least six months, possibly more. The Commander in Chief must live and entertain, thus there will be in these waggons, quantities of food and drink, furniture and personal effects. I would expect at least two carts to carry the wine and spirits, alone, and others for the cheeses, coffee and small livestock. Of course, on the way down to Portsmouth there will be well-wishers and former sailors to see him on his way as well as the usual men and women seeking to make money any way they can."

He looked at Ketch and laughed.

"No obvious role here for you then Ketch. But there are serious concerns to consider,"

His face hardened.

"We have had whispers from our people in Dover of three persons who have arrived from the Spanish Netherlands tasked with the murder of Robert Blake. Such an act is, of course, a blot on Spanish honour, but they seriously want Blake dead. They see him and the fleet as a mortal threat."

Ketch could now see what was coming, he had had similar tasks before, protecting Generals, MP's great Lords and Ladies. He found them difficult, often actually unpleasant. Many times there had been complaints about loss of privacy, a lack of cooperation and at times total disobedience.

"Thurloe, knows my views on this, but I can see that in this case, my personal objections are to be overruled, something must be done,"

Thurloe, raised his arms in mock concern.

"I know your dislike of this sort of work and Cromwell when he heard of this wanted a troop of cavalry to provide an escort, but Blake would have nothing of it. He was prepared to place his trust in his seamen who are always with him. He is the one man in England who can outface the Lord Protector."

He focussed his grey eyes on Ketch.

"So, we have no choice, the two or three seamen who surround him are tough and hard men, but if we are facing Spanish assassins a wider understanding of what is possible in necessary. You have to be involved! For heaven's sake! I am involved. The Lord Protector is holding us responsible for Robert Blake's safety and that will be your task Ketch. You must get him safely to Portsmouth."

Thurloe poured them both a glass of water from the carafe on the desk and pushed a glass across towards him. Ketch accepted it gratefully. He could see they were not yet finished. Thurloe continued.

"There has as yet been no decision made as to when the move to Portsmouth will begin, but in effect your mission starts now. You will have sergeants Tull and Holditch to help you in this, but this requires some immediate action. You are at an advantage in that Robert Blake knows you. As such I am sure he will accept you as extra security, but somehow we have to get those two sergeants int his entourage."

Thurloe fell silent. It was now time for Ketch to speak.
"Do we know any more about the three Spanish agents. Any descriptions, any location.

Thurloe's reply was unusually apologetic.

"Unfortunately, the answer in both cases is no. I am sorry Ketch they seem to have gone to ground. You must take it that from this moment Robert Blake is in danger. You must quickly bring Tull and Holditch into this and get to work."

Thurloe' tone was one of concern and frustration.

"I am sorry Ketch, but I must get back to Hampton Palace, Benson will be here if you should need anything."

He rose from his chair, collected his papers and without any further word left the room. Ketch sat for a while in deep thought, after a moment he also moved. He had to find Benson.

The Turk's Head was a large, rambling building found amongst the wharves and warehouses of the Thames waterfront. Its clients were normally hard-faced men from the sea. It was popular with low life criminals and others desiring privacy or secrecy. As ever with such an establishment, the most permanent residents were a group of whores managed by the sister of the proprietor, who was herself a woman of considerable brutish presence. The establishment was under the control of Sally Stanley, but to everyone she was known as "Draught Sally." Closer to forty than thirty, Draught Sally was a large, muscular woman, wide in the shoulder and strong in the arm. There was always an unhealthy greasy, pallor about her and her ill-fitting, foul clothing was rarely washed. Her face had once been pretty, but now was puffy with small eyes and warts on one cheek, from which strands of hair straggled. She was master of the place, largely through the support of her sister and three sons, each of which was as ugly as the others. It was said that her former husband, the previous landlord, when given a sight by the midwife of his last son, groaned and fell down dead. Surrounded by her sons, none challenged her. The name "Draught Sally" came from her early days, when she earned a living, frequenting drinking establishments and encouraging drinking contests. Her regular call was "Who'll take a draught with Sally?" Subsequently a drinking contest would take place, with Sally usually triumphant. Even on the rare occasions when she was beaten, such was the merriment, that she rarely left without coins in her pocket.

This moment before the large, public room began to fill, she was taking food and drink to her special guests, who had been very happy to have the privacy of her cellar. Carrying a large tray of mugs and bottles she was preceded by one of her sons and followed by another. They carried platters of bread, cheese, ham and boiled eggs with bowls of oysters, mussels and other shellfish. Waiting for them in the cellar, sat around a large table were Michel Gauvin, Raphael de Rousse and Mary Sharpe, the three Spanish agents.
"Hello my luvlies. Food and drink and there is more if needed."

She and her sons distributed the victuals around the table. Some effort had been made to brighten up the cellar. There were three fairly clean mattresses plus blankets and for the moment the gloom had been beaten back by a multitude of candles. Sally smiled at them.

"All comfy then?"

She did not entirely care for this spying part of her business, but Mr De Ritter paid very good money for the reports he received and there were extra payments for any additional services provided. She turned to follow her boys out of the cellar, but could not resist ruffling Raphael's hair.

"What a pretty boy."

She did it again, laughed and left to re-join her sons. Raphael boiled inside but could only smile weekly. Everyone gave a sigh of relief at her leaving.

"She frightens me," admitted Raphael.

"If she had been a man, I would have struck her down, but how do you deal with such a monster.?"

Michel gave an answer.

"You don't. You behave exactly as you did; you smile and accept the insult.
Everyone watching knows how it is."

"It would be interesting," interrupted Mary.

"If you played up to her in turn. Give her a big smile and blow her a kiss. You may become a real favourite."

"Stop it Mary," warned Michel.

You'll get Raphael into serious trouble if you upset this woman. Anyway, we have much more important matters to discuss."

Michel's words brought the reaction he hoped. The two comrades became attentive.

"Our first task is to find the location of Robert Blake. De Ritter had no information so we must find him ourselves. I suggest at first light we divide up and make individual searches. Alas! It is a big city. Mary have you easy knowledge of London?"

Mary was happy to give a positive reply.

"Indeed Michel. Yes, I do. I think there is little point searching South of the river It is full of stews and the poor, unless you are looking for whores, gentlemen stay well away.

You will not find him there. The most likely places will be close to either the City in the East or The Palace of Westminster in the West."

"In that case," ordered Michel.

"Let Mary concentrate in the East and the City and I will take the West. Raphael you try between those two areas. Remember we have to be discreet. Try not to ask for Robert Blake by name rather try "Where are the offices of the navy"? That is a more normal approach as a request for guidance rather than a person."

Mary nodded.

"That is wise Michel, but one other matter must always be with us. London is not a friendly city to the innocent. It is full of thieves, fraudsters, and tricksters, all ready to gull the unwary and part you from your money. You are most at risk when you stop and ask directions. It marks you out as a new arrival a ready victim. "

Michel took this warning seriously; Raphael was more confident that he could deal with such low lives. For that day the three agents scoured the streets of London.

"Nothing!" The words were almost spat out by Raphael.

"I am exhausted and achieved nothing"

Mary and Michel, likewise had failed to find any trace of Robert Blake. They were back in the cellar in a tableau that reflected the previous night, sitting around the table, eating and drinking and making plans. Michel, in particular was looking morose, but he knew what to do next.

"We must ask Sally. It is dangerous. We are giving an insight into our purpose, but it cannot be helped. If we are successful or not, she will know who we are and her tongue may loosen, but I see no other choice."

He waited a moment and then took silence as consent. To their surprise asking Sally was extremely easy.

"Oh! He will be where all the Generals and Commanders make their home and place of work, He is in Whitehall Palace. You will find him in there. Mind you it is a big place, biggest in Europe, or so they say. He'll be there with all his clerks and secretaries and hangers on, with comfortable living quarters alongside. Having said that, it is full of rooms of all sorts, offices, bedrooms, kitchens, stables, ballrooms, the banqueting suite. He could be anywhere in there."

Sally was very pleased with herself, putting these foreigners to right.

"Thank you Sally," said Michel.

"But of course, not a word to anyone."

"Mr De Ritter pays well for silence Mr Gauvin."

Michel was very pleased with their success.

"Now we can move on, get closer to Robert Blake and get out of this damned cellar. At this point we can move more in step with De Ritter's plans. We can each devise our own separate plan of attack."

He addressed his companions.

"I think it is time for us to consider our separation."

"Agreed! It was Raphael with unexpected enthusiasm.

"I suggest that we spend the rest of this evening thinking about our own plans and where we are going to stay. Then tomorrow, take a look at Whitehall Palace and find our own accommodation. Then another council of war"

All three moved to a separate part of the cellar to consider the next day and the days to come. These were silent hours until one by one they extinguished their candles and took their rest.

Each in their own way, spent the following day in and around Whitehall Palace. Their approaches to those going in and out of the Palace were tentative. A questioning look, or a raised eyebrow was enough to make them break off questioning and retreat away. For the rest of the day, they either looked for their lodgings or developed further whatever plans they were devising. Michel caught sight of Raphael who smiled back from a distance, but of Mary he saw nothing. It was not until late afternoon that Mary re-surfaced and shared the last few yards to the Turks Head with Raphael. They found Michel in the cellar waiting for them. Mary was bubbling with excitement. They had barely discarded their coats and cloaks before Mary was sat at the table ready with her news. The two men joined he quickly.

"First thing this morning I spoke to Sally. I asked about the madams, who ran the brothels around Whitehall Palace. Where there are military men, there are always plenty of whores."

She paused, making certain that they were following and understanding how clever she had been.

"Sally was most helpful in giving me names, two of the madams being business acquaintances of her sister. So, today I visited these ladies and laid out a little gold, for information on clients from Whitehall Palace, especially those with a naval background"

She paused again enjoying her control of events.

"Get on with it," snapped Raphael.

With a hard stare at Raphael, Mary continued.

"One madam told me of a Mr Charles Beaumont, some sort of secretary to Robert Blake himself. It turns out that Mr Beaumont has a real fancy for one of her girls called Sally. She is a pretty young girl and he is quite a regular. So, I speak to Sally, who is a sensible as well as pretty about Mr Beaumont. He, is apparently quite free in talking about his famous employer and how soon they are to join the fleet."

"This is excellent," cried Michel.

"Excellent indeed, you must share all this with us.

"Of course," she retorted but there is more.

Mary's face was suffused in smiles.

"He needs more clerks Michel. He is desperate for men of letters who have some knowledge of numbers. You must take advantage of this."

Both Michel and Raphael came to their feet.

"Well done Mary", exclaimed Raphael.

"Very clever indeed. Such a source of information had not crossed my mind. This I must remember."

"I also," added Michel.

"Tomorrow morning, I will present myself to Mr Beaumont and astonish him
with my sweet writing and clear numbers. Mary you have moved our mission along, but I have not yet found lodgings, Raphael and Mary, have you managed to find something.?"

Mary nodded to indicate that she had made arrangements. Raphael explained that he was without anywhere. Michel was ready to move on and lay out their immediate future.

"We will spend tonight and tomorrow night here and then we must move on and take our plans to a new level, are we agreed?"

Both Mary and Raphael agreed. Raphael indicating strongly, his pleasure at getting away from that "damned woman."

Chapter Five   Friends and Foes (II)

It took Benson two days to find and bring Tull and Holditch away from their current duties to meet Ketch in Whitehall Palace. He did, however, speedily find them a private and secure room for their meeting.

"I leave you to your meeting gentlemen, may I assure you that I am always at your service."

The three men sat in silence as the sound of Benson's footsteps, first receded and then disappeared entirely. They burst into helpless laughter.

"I see Benson is as pompous as ever," remarked Holditch.

"He really has become something of a Major Domo."

Tull could not forbear from adding.

"He has also grown fat and slow."

"Yes! Yes!" Agreed Ketch

"But he is also very hard working, efficient and loyal. I know what qualities I prefer.

Only slightly chastened, Tull and Holditch knew they were here for something more important than Chief Clerk Benson's character.

Ketch had requested comfortable chairs and a table with plates of fresh bread, cheese and fruit together with mugs and two jugs of ale. He wanted his colleagues in a good mood. All three were old comrades, who met on the outbreak of the

Civil War by joining Lord Manchester's regiment at the same time. They had marched and fought alongside each other throughout the campaign. They stood up as one when facing danger and such unconditional support left them largely unmolested by even the hardest men in the regiment.

Tull was in his mid- forties, tall and dark. He was a married man, who had lived in Bridgewater until a fire destroyed his family. He had found some solace in religion, in soldiering and in friendship with his two colleagues. Somewhat taciturn, he had kept his West Country burr and was always quiet in manner. However, he would, from time to time, make a remark, that would send his audience into gales of laughter, or bring out a word that would completely clarify a situation or describe a person's character. There were also those that knew that although quiet Tull could be dangerous and best not upset.

His fellow sergeant Holditch was very different. An extrovert, he was well liked by both men and women. Always on the move, he was continually working on some scheme or other. There was a plumpness about him that the foolish took for weakness, but Holditch was quite capable of making a serious contribution to any confrontation. By nature, he was kind and merry, he seemed constantly surrounded by people enjoying themselves. It was no surprise that he was remembered by even bare acquaintances. But, above all else, at heart Holditch was a market trader, always on the search for buying and selling opportunities and inevitably he was usually the chief beneficiary of his commercial activities. It was said he could enter a market with a feather and come out with a chicken.

These were the two men who now faced Ketch. He had lost touch with them for a while having been recruited into the secret world of spying, but their unlooked-for help during the short-lived mutiny had propelled them into the same service alongside him. All three were highly valued by Thurloe. It was Holditch who spoke first.

"Well, Ketch, Benson tells me that you are in difficulties. You have a serious problem of national importance that requires assistance from trained men, qualified, first class agents and thus it is necessary that Tull and Holditch are involved."

His tone was light, faintly pompous and Ketch was forced to smile.

"Yes! Holditch you are absolutely correct. I cannot hope to solve anything without your valuable contribution."

Holditch carried on a little further.

"Well, it must be important, Tull here has been dragged halfway across London to be here, and I, who had been charged by Thurloe, to become extremely friendly with an ambassador's daughter, have had to withdraw from the field in confusion."

Tull grunted in support of Holditch's remarks. He could feign annoyance as well as anyone.

"Yes! Yes! Gentlemen, everything will go smoothly now that you have arrived, but I would value the opportunity to provide you with the details of this matter."

"Well, come on", railed Holditch.

"What is the delay?"

Ketch looked at them both.

"Take account of this."

He outlined to them his original meeting with Robert Blake in Northampton, the importance of the Sea General to the navy and the plans for a Grand Fleet to sail against the Spanish of which Blake would be the Commander in Chief. Tull and Holditch listened silently, but could not as yet detect how it affected them. However, it focussed their attention, when Ketch explained the presence and purpose of the Spanish agents. When he had finished the questions came thick and fast. He dealt with them as best he could, finishing with the news that the Sea General and his entourage would soon be travelling to Portsmouth and they would be going with it. He tried to make his comments meaningful.

"Our job is complete when we have Sea General Robert Blake safely in Portsmouth on the quarter deck of his flag ship the Naseby. Thurloe made it quite clear that there could be consequences for him if that did not happen, almost certainly consequences for me and definitely consequences for you."

He smiled. There was a long silence. Ketch moved on, he wanted to talk about individual roles.

"As Blake has refused the offer of troopers, we must take their place. My role as extra security close to the Sea General, Thurloe has cleared with the Sea General. So, I will be by his side all the time, but both of you somehow have to become part of the entourage, especially for the moving to Portsmouth."

It was Tull that was the first to speak.

"Ketch, I know nothing about boats and sailing. I cannot see me deceiving any seaman as to who I am."

Ketch stroked his nose; he had devised a particular role for Tull. He just had to introduce it carefully. He leaned forward engagingly.

"Tull we know you as a man of God with deep religious convictions and a very wide knowledge of the bible. Many times, when we were soldiering, I heard men tell of how you had helped them with their day to day and spiritual problems, that you should have become a preacher."

Tull was looking anxious. There was something unlooked for coming his way. Ketch had his total attention.

"I have discussed this with Thurloe and he agrees that it would not be impossible for you to play the role of a preacher, wishing to be a sea chaplain and an example to other religious men."

Ketch did not give Tull time to reply. He wanted the full idea to be presented.

"Sea chaplains are not unknown Tull. Agreed they are few in number, but it is a role you could easily perform."

Tull, simply could not respond. He felt his brain freeze. Holditch looked on with eyes wide open.

"This is blasphemy Ketch or at least religious deceit."

Ketch was determined to counter that.

"No! You will remember our chaplains in the regiments, how they inspired us. Did they not lead us, singing psalms and hymns on the way to Naseby? Were we not inspired by them? Do you not remember Hugh Peters in the front of the battle with us? He was but a self-made preacher. No! You have the knowledge, and people respect you."

Tull half nodded but still looked uncertain, but Ketch felt that he could make this happen.

"Now listen carefully Tull. This is not some wild scheme developed without some thought. For one, Robert Blake is known as a deeply religious man and he uses his religious strength to encourage his men to fight. Second, when as a land commander and defending Lyme against siege, he met Hugh Peters, who was acting as a sea chaplain to the relieving ships and Peters preached before him at the victory service in Lyme church."

Tull was beginning to understand that this was becoming a serious proposal. He saw some of his early reasons for refusal disappearing.

"Finally, Tull. Hugh Peters is on the Council of State and Thurloe, as its Secretary, is sure he can obtain a letter of commendation from him pressing the Sea General to take you to Portsmouth with him. The idea being you would be the first of many sea chaplains for the navy. That should finally convince you that there is a way for you also to be close to the Sea General as part of his entourage. There is no fake religion in this; our navy should also have sea chaplains. Placing you alongside Sea General Blake would genuinely create a momentum for the practice across the fleet."

Tull could see that in this he would now have no choice, but he made one last appeal.

"I accept everything you say Ketch and yes, I will do this, but I am not going to sea. "

"Agreed, when we reach Portsmouth, safely with the Sea General, you can go back to being Sergeant Tull."

Ketch turned his attention to Holditch, who sat up straight, wondering what was coming his way. He spoke first.

"What scheme have you got for me, Ketch? I cannot think what it might be.

Ketch laughed at the hint of uncertainty and concern in Holditch's voice.

"Nothing, Holditch. I can hopefully get Tull into Whitehall Palace, but I can think of no scheme to include you. Of course, we must, in some way, bring you into this matter as we move South. I shall have to leave it to your wit and skill to get yourself involved. In some way you must become useful as a driver or a groom, labourer or extra servant. I am told it will be a large convoy with many waggons, carts and carriages. I am sure there will be opportunities."

He leaned back in his chair to address them both.

"Remember the purpose of all this is to save a life and deliver a Commander to his fleet. Thurloe and Cromwell himself expect us to succeed"

"Well! That's that", said Holditch.

"Tull and I will require a considerable supper this evening for bringing us into your latest scheme. Something more than cheese and fruit."

Ketch felt a surge of relief, all three would do everything possible to protect the Sea General. There was now a chance they would succeed.

Having used half the morning walking from the Turk's Head to Whitehall Palace, Raphael decided that he must get on and find lodgings. It was a new experience for him. His life had moved between the comparative luxury of his Ghent family home and the barracks of Spanish armies. He was unused to negotiating about rent with people he did not know. He approached a number of establishments in the Whitehall area, but veered in his negotiations between excessive confidence and supplication. However, his growing familiarity with the process, eventually led him to secure an acceptable room on reasonable terms. His landlord, a cloth merchant's clerk, was not pleased when Raphael was unable to say, how long he would need the room, and demanded a week's money in advance. Raphael bristled but to no avail. As he left, he reflected on this new experience.

"Securing lodgings is no different than buying things in the market, except you get rooms and an unwanted companion in your landlord."

He enjoyed an inward thought that made him laugh.

"It is something of which my brothers would know nothing. They probably do not know the word lodgings."

71

He promised that he would bring his belongings the next day. As there were plenty of hours left in the day, he decided that he would take a look at Whitehall Palace, he might pick up some valuable information. Several attempts at different entrances received both polite and impolite inquires as to who he was and what did he want. On all occasions he beat a retreat. It was clear that it was no place for strangers.

"The Palace may be huge but everyone is either known or has a good reason to be here."

It was mid-afternoon when he discovered the entrance opposite the Abbey. This was larger and busier than the others he had tried. There were two guards, but some people were entering unchallenged and he decided to follow a group of four well-dressed men, who were making for the entrance, whilst talking and laughing. To his relief he followed through the large archway unquestioned. Within seconds he found himself in a spacious courtyard. Around him people were disappearing through open doors and stairwells. He would choose one at random.

"Look confident Raphael, you must appear to know where you are going Do not hesitate."

He chose one of the stairwells and followed the stairs up to the next floor. He was delighted with his progress.

"Now Raphael make it count. What can you usefully discover? Perhaps you might find yourself with the Sea General himself."

He continued to explore, by climbing up to the higher levels. His good fortune, however, deserted him at this point.

Two men appeared at the top of the stairs at the next floor above him.

"Who are you? Come here, explain yourself"

They began hurrying down the stairs towards him. Raphael panicked. His fear, however, served to quicken his reactions. He turned immediately into the nearest passageway and ran as fast as he could, turned into another corridor and then another. He could hear his pursuers behind him and realised his own footsteps betrayed him. He paused at an open door and quickly judged it as a place to hide. He found a room full of cupboards, cabinets, boxes and all types of furniture. He rejected it and turned back into the corridor. He could hear the footsteps coming closer. In desperation he chose a large freestanding cupboard in the corridor itself as his final refuge. He leapt inside amongst coats, cloaks, scarves and hats. He quickly shut the door and stood as silently as possible with his heart pounding and his hand firmly on his sword. His pursuers entered the corridor and headed straight for the open door.

A voice called out.

"This is where he will be. Have you your sword ready?"

"I do, lets flush him out"

There followed a series of bangs and crashes as doors were flung open, furniture toppled, boxes kicked to one side. In a split second, Raphael had to make a decision, to stay where he was or make a dash for it. The continuing noise from the room signalled that it remained the search area. With a

73

pounding heart, as quietly as possible, he slipped out into the corridor, past the open door, and on the lightest of feet, he swiftly retraced his steps. At the end of the next corridor, he paused for a second and could still just hear, the continuing noise of the search for him. He descended down to a lower level and moved at a reasonable pace trying to find a way out. After some minutes he rested.

"That will not do Raphael. You will not be so lucky again. Running is no good. You must find a reason to be here."

He resolved he would be a messenger who had delivered a note to Robert Blake and had lost his way amongst all the corridors and stairs. He knew that using the Sea General's name was a risk but it added a touch of believability and who would dare approach the General to verify it? In fact it turned out that people were always losing their way in the Palace. Twice when politely challenged, his tale was accepted and the directions he received finally got him to an exit into Whitehall itself. He gave a sigh of relief. He decided it was probably best not to mention this to his fellow agents. He had gained no valuable information and almost certainly he would be scolded for rash behaviour and putting their mission at risk. He decided to return to the Turk's Head. On arrival, he found his colleagues in the cellar. He was the last to return. They sat around the table together sharing their experiences of the day. The best news came from Michel. He was obviously eager to share it

"I have secured the position of clerk. I was seen by a gentleman called Charles Beaumont. As soon as he saw the clarity of my script he called in his only other clerk, a man called Turner, and straight away they agreed that I was the man for the job. Then I was introduced to Robert Blake himself. It was good to get so close to him."

There followed a lengthy discussion on the nature of Robert Blake and the various other people who worked alongside him. Michel was very careful to share every shred of information about what he had seen.

"Well done Michel." Enthused Mary.

"That was all valuable information, especially about the seaman and this Captain Treddager. At last, it is beginning to feel real to me."

"We can leave all this to you now Michel," suggested Raphael with a grin.

"Mary and I can take a holiday. You are so close to Robert Blake that you will have no trouble completing our task."

"No, no," answered Michel.

"This is a good start, but remember De Ritter requires all three of us to be centred on Blake, there is no certainty I can do the job. Accidents are not so easy to manage. How have you both got on today"?

Mary spoke up.

"I have spent the day with my whores finding out more concerning the gentlemen of Whitehall Palace. I have some interesting ideas that may result in greatly aiding our work, especially a Charles Beaumont."

They both looked at Raphael, who decided he should give a low-key version of his time in Whitehall Palace.

"I have secured lodgings and took the opportunity to target Robert Blake. I managed to slip into Whitehall Palace, but had to quickly withdraw It is huge building and there were a lot of people about. I was still challenged but, thankfully my reasons for being there were accepted."

"*That should suffice,*" he thought.

Michel was still bubbling with his own success and passed on any further questioning of Raphael.

"This has been a day of progress. This evening we must make arrangements for our separation. We have much to do."

Whilst they waited for "Draught Sally" to bring their evening meal, Raphael and Mary pressed Michel for further details about Robert Blake and his entourage and their preparations for moving to Portsmouth.

"I shall know more about Portsmouth tomorrow, but in terms of Whitehall, there is Blake, his Secretary Beaumont, another clerk called Turner who I will work with. There appear to be no family members, but two or three rough looking seamen, who view with suspicion anyone who gets close to Blake. There are of course visitors all the time, most of them Captains of one sort or another, complaining loudly about their problems. One Captain called Treddager seemed to be a permanent aide to the Sea General In all, there is a suite of six or seven rooms, with a kitchen and bedrooms. They all live in except for the clerk Turner who must leave in the evening."

His two colleagues were quiet for a moment thinking through the information they had just received.

"Any ideas about an early accident Michel," inquired Mary.

"Not really" replied Michel.

"But I shall think on."

Raphael pulled a face. He was not entirely happy.

"It's all very well for De Ritter to talk of accidents, but I feel sure that it is not an easy matter. My best chance of succeeding in this is with that pistol he gave you. Get close to him on the road, a quick shot and a fast horse and away. No accident, but the job is done. Also let us not forget that we have the poison, and now you are so close to him, that offers a perfect opportunity. Just waiting for the chance to affect an accident is hopeless, it may never happen."

Michel was not going to be hurried.

"I easily have the best chance with the pistol, but we must at least in these early days, look for an accident, So, I will keep the pistol for the moment."

He smiles at Raphael.

"But you remind me of the poison. Let us see if all is well with it."

He rose and strode across the cellar to his bags and bedding. He returned carrying a small green bottle with a cork stopper. He sat heavily on to his chair and so doing, the bottle slipped from his grasp and, despite his despairing grab, it broke open on the stone flagged floor. A strangled set of oaths rang around the cellar. All three looked down at the broken glass, and the green oily liquid soaking into the stone floor.

After a moment's hesitation, Mary Sharpe moved with surprising speed. From her dress she pulled out a long hairpin and dropped it into the poison. Then with a small spill of wood, she deftly secured a coating of poison on the pin. When finished she took out a not so clean handkerchief and wrapped it carefully around the pin. She looked up at the two men.

"This may come in useful."

She produced a second handkerchief and dropped it into the remaining liquid.

"I shall leave it there to take up the remaining poison, then let it dry. It may have a use. "

Her expertise in this matter quite overawed her companions.

"Well, we shall leave that to you Mary," muttered Raphael.

Any further activities were curtailed by the sound of their landlady arriving with their evening meal. When the food was being distributed, there was a further offer of help from Sally which Michel gracefully declined. He wanted to get on, but it was only after the meal had been finished and the remains taken away that he started to consider the remaining matters to be decided.

"We must not waste time we have a lot to decide before we go our separate ways."

Mary and Raphael had concerns of their own, but Michel was determined to clear away his own first.

"Now we must share out the money we have been given. Our masters have been generous."

He returned from his corner of the cellar with a heavy leather bag of gold coins. Under the steady gaze of his fellow conspirators, he counted it out into three equal piles and pushed their piles across the table towards them. They were well received.

"Draught Sally" has already been paid Oh! I shall keep the bag."

This small matter caused some short -term difficulties for Raphael and Mary, who had to improvise in the way of storage for their own coins. Michel avoided their unhappy looks and moved on.

"Michel Gauvin and Raphael de Rousse are not English names; Mary's name is English and is fine. When we separate, I shall be known as Michael Gough and you Raphael, would you be happy with Robert Ratcliffe?"

Raphael nodded.

"There may be a problem with my lodgings but I will not be there long. On the road I shall be Robert Ratcliffe."

Some of their candles were burning low and all three felt a need for sleep, but Michel had one last matter to discuss.

"We three will disperse tomorrow to follow our own plans to dispose of Robert Blake either here or on the Portsmouth road. I would welcome knowledge of any plans that have been considered."

He waited in silence for a while.

"Nothing? He said.

"Alright! I will start. In Whitehall Palace and on the road to Portsmouth I am well placed to create an accident and I hope to be successful. Only if I fail in this will I use the pistol in Portsmouth, even if it means my own death"

He looked at Mary, who accepted her cue.

"I have no immediate contact with Robert Blake, but I have something that may develop and lead to use of the poison that I have preserved. I see little hope of me creating an accident."

Michel and Mary turned to Raphael.

"I have nothing and I see little chance of creating an accident. I shall, however, purchase a horse and a pistol and I will follow the entourage as it travels South. There will be stops, Perhaps I can get into their encampment and get at Blake or, if an opportunity arises on the road to use the pistol, I will take advantage of it."

Michel grunted. One last thing had occurred to him.

"If we meet on the road, or any time let us agree that we do not know each other. No recognition. No one knows anyone else. Agreed!

Their silence was taken as agreement.

It was clear that they all felt that they had talked enough. Michel echoed their thoughts.

"Now we must sleep, I for one have had a busy day."

Chapter Six   Preparations

Ketch approached Whitehall Palace from the North, at this
doorway he was well known and was waved to go in.
However, he stopped to secure clearer instructions on how to
find Sea General Blake's part of the Palace. Despite some early
mistakes he found himself on a landing, where through an
open door he could see Charles Beaumont working at his desk.

"Hello Charles! It's John Ketch. Some years ago, we
met in Northampton and enjoyed a dinner together at the
home of Sir Arthur Hasselrig."

For a moment Charles Beaumont looked puzzled,
then he smiled in remembrance. He rose from his desk and
extended his hand to Ketch.

"Of course, Captain Ketch you provided care and
sustenance after our accident. I am delighted to see you."

Beaumont was tall, slim and handsome. His dark,
hair was full and naturally curled. In his early thirties he had
all the confidence of private money and a university
education. His meticulous dress marked him as a ladies' man.
Ketch had not been especially drawn to him on their only
other meeting, but he knew him to be clever and astute.
However, the genuine pleasure expressed by Beaumont on
their meeting was forcing him to a change of view. Beaumont
guided him to a chair and resumed his own seat.

"How can I be of service Captain?"

Ketch hesitated for a second but realised that Beaumont would have to know of his role and the possible dangers facing the Sea General. Briefly, he explained the situation facing the General from the arrival of the Spanish agents and how he, Ketch, had been assigned to provide extra protection. He showed Beaumont his letter of authorisation from Thurloe to Sea General Blake. He thought it wisest to say nothing about Tull and Holditch. Beaumont frowned but then smiled.

"So, Ketch! You will be with us until Portsmouth. I shall look forward to your company. Unfortunately, we cannot accommodate you here in Whitehall Palace, but it can all be arranged for you, on the journey South. I assume you will want to be close to the Sea General at all times; three Spanish agents you say."

Ketch did not want to create needless alarm.

"Fear not Charles, these are just extra precautions. I understand that the Sea General always has a good number of loyal and sturdy seamen around him. It seems he will not want for protection."

"Well! We are down to only two at the moment, but they are the best we have. There is his coxswain Hedges and a tough bosun called Brown. Of course, there is myself and Captain Treddager, who you know, and now yourself, that should prove sufficient. Oh! There are also his clerks, Gough and Turner, although I am not certain what use they would be.

Ketch nodded, they would all help and there was also Tull and Holditch. He had one final caution for Beaumont.

"For the moment only you and the Sea General will know of my role. This you must keep to yourself."

Ketch rose to his feet.

"Now, if possible, I would like to see the Sea General. I must give him my letter of instruction from Thurloe and brief him on the threat of the Spanish agents."

In answer to their knock, Beaumont and Ketch were invited into the Sea General's study. They found the Sea General staring out of the window. He seemed in a pensive mood.

"Damned difficult weather."

He turned to face them.

"I shall want to be away soon Charles; the fleet is almost ready"

He suddenly realised he had a visitor in Ketch.

"My dear sir, Captain Ketch! How very pleasant to see you. I hope that God continues to protect you and your family." He paused and checked himself.

" Especially from run -away carriages eh!"

Ketch laughed, he was pleased to be remembered, but he had to get on with his business.

"A pleasure to meet you sir, I hope you also are in good health but I have some important news that directly affects your person."

A moment of concern crossed the Sea General's face.

"Affects me sir! Take a seat and give me this news. Oh! Should Charles hear this?"

"Yes sir. I have taken the precaution of explaining the situation to him."

Blake waved at Beaumont.

"Pick up a chair Charles. Let us hear what Captain Ketch has to say."

It did not take Ketch long to describe the nature of the particular danger facing the Sea General and it was quickly understood.

"Is this news recent Ketch, I have already discussed my personal safety with Cromwell and he wanted to foist some of his heavy-handd troopers onto me. I told him there was no need. I have my staff and two trusty seamen to provide protection."

He gave a small laugh.

"Our Lord Protector does not like being denied."

Ketch quickly took back the conversation.

"This is a more definite and dangerous threat General. I have here a letter from Secretary Thurloe requiring me to join your staff until you are safely on board your ship in Portsmouth. Nothing too obvious and I will not get in the way. I will just generally seek to be everywhere., of course, working closely with Charles."

Ketch reached for the letter in his pocket, but the Sea General waved it away.

"I have a rule Captain that I always listen very carefully to the words of Secretary Thurloe. He is full of good sense and this is an example. I know you have his confidence and he obviously has trust in you."

He paused and looked carefully at Ketch.

"Is it just you?"

"Yes sir," replied Ketch.

He knew this was untrue and did not like it, but he reconciled himself to his lie in that Tull and Holditch embedded in the entourage may save the Sea General's life. He could not let the sensitivities of the Sea General to new faces disrupt the mission. Besides, his was the only name mentioned in Thurloe's letter.

"Agreed then, you will be an extra aide on my staff, but of course without pay."

The Sea General walked once more to the window. Ketch noticed that his limp was rather more pronounced than at their first meeting

"God willing, we shall be away soon"

Ketch was pleased with the course of events, there was no more cross-examination.

"I shall not bother you in Whitehall. I think you are safe enough here in the Palace. You will see me again on the journey to Portsmouth."

The Sea General returned to his desk. He was anxious to get on.

"Thank you, Ketch. Tell Thurloe it will be as he wishes."

Ketch took that as dismissal and left the room. He heard the sound of the Sea General quizzing Beaumont on the condition of his new maps. He was clearly not over concerned about his safety. Ketch loitered in the corridor waiting for Beaumont. There was a lot of information he needed. Beaumont when finally released by the Sea General took Ketch back into his own room. Ketch needed to know the exact composition of the group that would be travelling with the Sea General. Beaumont was happy to provide the information.

"Besides you and myself, there are two clerks, Turner and Gough, two seaman, Hedges and Brown, The Sea General has two servants and there is Captain Treddager. He counts for rations only. That matters little, he is as rich as Croesus, prize money from his sea exploits. "

Ketch next came to the date of the departure for Portsmouth Here Beaumont looked more uncertain.
"The Sea General is very keen on March 6th. That is the date on which he wishes the fleet to sail. I have worked on a five -day journey to Portsmouth so probably the day before the first of March, but there is still much to do so we will await events."

A number of further points were considered, but Ketch did not linger long and soon made his farewells and left. With Thurloe's department for Spies also being in Whitehall Palace, despite the complexity of stairs and corridors, Ketch made good time in seeking out Benson. He needed another room to put some courage into Tull and discover whether or not Holditch had made any progress.

It was late afternoon before Tull returned to work. He had spent a lot of time thinking over what Ketch was expecting of him. His mind came back again and again to the question:

What is the right thing to do? Eventually he had arrived at a definite conclusion. Benson had provided a room for Ketch to discuss matters with him. Now he must get his answers.

"Come in Tull "

Ketch had a welcoming smile on his face, but the words had hardly been uttered, when he gave a gasp of astonishment. Tull had never been overconcerned about his dress, but he had transformed himself into the complete "Independent" preacher. He wore a full-length, black coat with black shoes, trouser and shirt. At his throat was a white cravat and in one hand he held a black, wide rimed hat with a high crown, in the other a bible. For a moment Ketch could neither laugh nor speak, but he held himself in check.

"Well done Tull! This cannot have been easy for you.

"This has not been a charade for me Ketch I shall be a religious man who believes in chaplains being appointed for every navy ship at sea. I shall do this because I believe in it, and I shall seek to convince the Sea General of its merit. Thus, I can fit in with your plans concerning the safety of the Sea General."

Ketch was well pleased with Tull, who had once again proved himself to be an agent of value. He had brought with him the letter of support from Hugh Peters. He handed it over to Tull who read it carefully and then put it away.
"Thank you, Ketch. This is truly encouragement from a man I greatly respect."

Ketch was not finished.

"Another piece of information for you. You once lived in Bridgewater, well Robert Blake has been the Member of Parliament since "42". You might have been neighbours.

Tull laughed. I wondered when you would find that out. You never miss anything. No, we did not meet."

Ketch felt considerable gratitude to Tull in this and he wanted to lay out for him exactly what was expected.
"If things go well you will be the most constant companion of the Sea General. I have no doubt that whilst travelling you will discuss the words of the bible, theology, philosophy and your personal life. My only advice on this is to just be yourself. You are not acting. Just be the natural Tull, who is so strong in himself. Also, you have no need to be the evangelist with the rest of the travellers just stick to the Sea General and the need for chaplains."

Tull smiled his agreement.
Ketch is trying to be helpful, but I have thought through all this myself"

Ketch drew a deep breath and stroked his nose. He was unsure how Tull would take this final piece of advice.

"Undoubtedly some of your fellow travellers will come to you with deeply personal problems, religious and otherwise. Again, just do the best you can. After all that is what you were called upon to do anyway, when we were soldiering. But always remember your main task is the protection of Robert Blake."

Ketch leant back in his chair.

"Well, Tull that is all I have to say, just remember that Holditch and I will always be close at hand if needed, and no one will think it strange, if from time to time we converse with each other."

Tull stood up.

"Well Captain, I had better get over to see the Sea General and convince him that I am worth travelling with him to Portsmouth."

Giving Ketch a hesitant wave, he left the room.

For the first few hours of his time as second clerk, Michel or rather Michael, worked in a state of permanent nervous tension. His throat was dry, he had cramps in his stomach and started at any sudden noise. However, as time passed his confidence grew. His place of work was a hive of constant activity, with Captains and messengers constantly coming and going. The work piled high and Charles Beaumont insisted that whenever possible the day's work was dealt with that day. The work itself he found straightforward and his fellow clerk, Turner, was an amiable colleague. Between them they managed all that Beaumont required of them. Just occasionally, Turner had to explain a detailed nautical term or naval practice. What pleased Michel most was that he gained favour from both Turner and Beaumont over the clarity and beauty of his script. One morning, whilst taking a note to Beaumont, he saw Ketch and Tull going in to see the Sea General. He noticed that they were not typical of those who were normally seen by the Sea General. He would look out for those. Given the pressure and variety of his work, he found it increasingly difficult to formulate any plan for an accident He had a lot of direct contact with the Sea General but always in an office and never alone.

"I could try a pistol shot when with him and make a dash for it, but I would be caught, suffer terribly under torture and then be killed. It is too early for this."

He resolved to leave his pistol back in his lodgings. There was danger in just bringing it into Whitehall Palace. He reluctantly decided that any accident would have to wait for the journey to Portsmouth, this would produce many more real opportunities. He sighed, what really pained him was that every day information passed over his desk that would be of real value to the Spanish Government, but he had no means to pass it on. He had also noticed that since the visit of the man called Ketch, there was greater scrutiny of visitors in to see the Sea General.

Although Michel had not seen any sign of Raphael, he had in fact been busy. He had given up on trying to enter Whitehall Palace and had completely abandoned any thought of an accident, but he had purchased both a horse and a pistol. His plan, his only plan was to shoot the General on the road and make his escape.

"It is simple and direct. Admittedly, the pistol is not as good as that which Michel keeps to himself and as yet I have not gauged the full abilities of my horse, but I am a fair shot and an excellent horseman It has the best chance of success."

His initial thought was to choose the first bridge over the Thames, but as an escape was as important as actually shooting the Sea General, he decided he would take more care and find the perfect ambush for making a shot and a successful escape. Back in his lodgings, stretched out on his bed with his hands behind his head he was quite cheerful

"Yes, the food is awful, the weather is worse, but with luck, within the week, I will have completed the task and be on way home to Ghent."

Mary Sharpe was experienced in the ways of men, in particular rich, elderly, preferably widowed me. But on this occasion, she had a different target, men of the sea. Using her make up skills, she could improve her appearance and so ready herself to frequent the illicit gambling rooms, that could still be found in London. She was hoping to find admirers amongst naval officers. At this moment, prior to the fleet sailing, London was full of such men. She knew that time was short, if she was going to secure a passage to Portsmouth. To her delight it was almost too easy. On her very first night in a respectable club off the Strand, she was surrounded by potential admirers with even naval Captains well represented. She did not need to return to Billingsgate that night.

Tull's interview with Sea General Blake went well from the start. The note from Hugh Peters made a strong impact on Robert Blake His own religious convictions chimed well with those of the famous preacher and Tull's history as a soldier added to the favourable reception. The Sea General was cooperative from the start.

That you arrive at my door, Tull, at this moment with Peter's letter has a favourable wind behind it. My own belief in how battles should be fought and won fits in very well with the idea of sea chaplains. I try to infuse my Captains with the belief that they are doing God's work and they in turn raise the fighting spirit of their men, but in a fleet of nigh on one hundred ships a fighting chaplain in every ship is something to be very much desired."

The Sea General's active mind found additional benefits.

"This is not just about winning battles Tull. It is about creating a Godly ship. The curses of the navy are blasphemy, sodomy, fornication. Think how sea chaplains could press down on those. Tull, you must certainly come to Portsmouth with me."

Deep inside Tull was partly concerned that Ketch's ruse had worked so well. He disliked deceiving who he saw as a decent, religious man. He only partially soothed his discomfort with the belief that though he was a fraud, he spoke the truth, what he had really come to believe. For a further half an hour the Sea General questioned Tull about his life as a soldier, about his family and he was delighted that they had both lived in Bridgewater and surprised that they had never met there.

"We will have much to discuss Tull on the way down to Portsmouth. I must assure myself that your teachings are in line with the requirements laid down by the Lord Protector."

Tull muttered something about being honoured and looking forward to such a conversation. This he had not discussed with Ketch and he had no idea if his views were also those of Oliver Cromwell. The Sea General called for Beaumont and gave instructions that Tull was to be part of his staff. Eventually, having provided Beaumont with the necessary information, he was able to leave and find his way across the Palace to find Benson and brief him on developments. Only then was he to give a huge sigh of relief.

The days to the journey South were fast approaching and Ketch determined that he had to have a more detailed discussion with Beaumont about the details. It was true that Beaumont and his clerks were working constantly in managing such details, but he would insist and eventually a time was arranged to meet in his office. At the appointed time, as he made his way from his lodgings in the White Hart towards Whitehall Palace, he noticed the poor state of the church of St Martin in the Fields, when in the distance coming from the new building area of Pall Mall, he spied Charles Beaumont and Captain Treddager both strolling along each with a woman on their arm. The foursome was clearly having a good time, laughing and sharing stories, pleased with each other's company. Ketch discreetly took up a position, whereby he could not be seen and they passed him bye without so much as a look. He had to admit that both women were very attractive. Beaumont whispered in the ear of a brunette with a lightly tanned face and challenging, large brown eyes. Captain Treddager was obviously entranced by the cascading fair curls, blue eyes and well made-up face of his own companion. This lady was more comely than handsome but well the equal of her female friend. Ketch wondered whether or not the women were bound for Portsmouth and was Charles Beaumont going to make his meeting.

As it turned out, Ketch did not have to wait long before Charles Beaumont climbed the stairs to the landing and welcomed Ketch into his office. Ketch felt it was wisest to mention nothing of his recent observation. They got down to business immediately. The first detail laid before Ketch was definite and welcome.

"We will start on the last day of February, hopefully arriving in good time for the fleet to sail on the sixth of March."

Chapter Seven   The Journey South

The following morning Ketch strode into the Intelligence department of Oliver Cromwell's Government. As usual the Chief Clerk Benson was standing just behind the door surveying the room and checking that everybody was hard at work. Benson had many skills, one of them being that he usually knew exactly where Tull and Holditch were to be found. As a result, Ketch found both of them awaiting his arrival in one of the side rooms. After initial greetings, he got straight down to business.

"It is time to bring ourselves fully up to date on the protection of Robert Blake. I have already introduced myself to him and his Secretary Charles Beaumont. They have agreed that my identity is to be kept as secret as possible and that I have a general commission to do anything that will keep the Sea General safe. My latest news is that the convoy shall leave on the last day of February, assembling alongside Westminster Abbey at eight in the morning. We shall travel with the convoy keeping a sharp lookout for any possible threats from inside or out. It will be quite a convoy. The Sea General is taking a lot of personal possessions, including furniture, together with enough food and drink, of all kinds, to last at least six months, possibly longer. There will be quite a collection of coaches and carriages, waggons and carts. Thus, besides his staff there will be servants, drivers, grooms and casual labourers. This convoy will be slow moving as Beaumont has assessed that five days will be necessary to get to Portsmouth"

His two companions listened earnestly. It was a relief to get some details of their mission. Then Holditch jumped in with his contribution.

"Well Ketch, I have been hanging around and I can tell you it is not easy to make contact with those who work for the Sea General. I have been chased out of the Northern half of Whitehall Palace more than once. But now I know of this convoy and its assembly, I have much more hope of getting fully involved."

Ketch was mildly amused at Holditch's frustration, His friend had heard, from Tull himself, as to the West Countryman's enhanced role and desperately wanted to be just as fully into the mission. Now it was Tull's turn. His sombre outlook had not been affected by his new significance for the mission, but inside he was fully engaged with his new importance.

"I seem to have made a favourable impression on the Sea General. He is a religious man and has taken up how sea chaplains can have a powerful impact on the behaviour and fighting spirit of the fleet."

Ketch nodded his approval, but Tull had more to say.

"There is a downside to this Ketch. He wants me to share a place with him in his coach for the whole of the journey. This is going to be a strain. He has accepted my religious conviction and the letter from Hugh Peters was a great help, but Thurloe also has sent him a copy of Cromwell's requirements for ministers, curates, vicars and chaplains. He wants to discuss them with me throughout the journey. I shall need rescuing from time to time. You must require to consult with me regularly."

Ketch interrupted him.

"The main thing is Tull that as the Sea General's constant companion, you are our last line of defence. You must remember this."

The three men spent an hour discussing further the possible interventions that might be made by the Spanish agents.

The last day of February at eight o clock in the morning was gloomy, cold and thick with frost. Multiple torches and lanterns threw a weak defused glow rather than a bright light, bringing little warmth for the waggons, carts and carriages that had assembled. Many of the drivers had arrived early and when Ketch appeared, he found large numbers of servants and porters bringing the last bits and pieces of the Sea General's luggage. Great clouds of steam were coming from the horses that stood in their shafts, occasionally stamping their feet. The lights and the steam created an eerie atmosphere for normal work. He could see Beaumont and his clerks seeking to regulate matters. Beaumont was mounted and riding from place to place, trying to establish some order over the reserve of horses that were deemed necessary for the journey. Ketch rode up to join him.

"Has the Sea General arrived yet Charles? Are matters going well?"

Beaumont' face was grim.

"No sign of the Sea General yet, but we have had trouble this morning. I think every thief and bullyboy in London is here to enjoy the rich pickings they believe can be snapped up in this assembly. We have had fights, an attempt to steal a horse. Two of our carts foolishly had no tarpaulin to secure their contents. I have had to employ two extra day labourers to simply act as guards to our cargoes."

Beaumont was clearly relieved at the appearance of Ketch.

"What is the number of our transport? Asked Ketch

"We have two waggons. and three carts, all hired for the week, together with the Sea General's coach, a carriage for the clerks and servants and then I have my own carriage, which you, of course, are welcome to share, and then whatever transport Captain Treddager has arranged. "

Ketch was happy to assist Beaumont in sorting out the final preparations for departure and he was thankful that Holditch, as one of the new guards, had in some way, become involved. Slowly daylight began to assert itself, torches and lanterns were doused to reveal a new day. After half an hour the Sea General and Tull appeared together with the two seamen, who continued to look closely at anyone who approached closely the Sea General. According to Beaumont the seamen were expecting to walk to Portsmouth.

After a final look about him to see that all things were more or less ready, Beaumont secured permission for the convoy to move off.

Just at that moment, a carriage drew up in haste and took up a position at the back of the line. When perfectly still, the carriage door opened and Captain Treddager descended, followed by two women, that Ketch recognised as the companions of Beaumont and Treddager by St Martins in the Field. He dismounted and made his way to meet them. He was, however forestalled by Charles Beaumont who struck up an earnest conversation with Treddager. After a moment's hesitation, he embraced both women and shook Treddager by the hand. He escorted the party to see The Sea General and Tull, both of whom had taken up their place in the coach. Treddager and the women went into the coach and took up a conversation with the Sea general whilst Beaumont went to see that all was well with the newly arrived carriage. As Ketch went to greet them, he saw Beaumont as a man who was desperately trying not to look embarrassed.

"A slight change of plan. Our Captain has not only brought along his intended, but also her lady friend as a sort of chaperon. I had no knowledge of this. I hope we can manage their joining us without too much discomfort all round."

Ketch smiled and tied to put Beaumont at ease.

"Everything is going well. I am sure the Sea General will be delighted with the additions to our party. fact, I would quite like to meet the ladies myself."

Beaumont was still all confusion, but of course, he agreed.

"Of course! Happily, you know Captain Treddager so all should be well."

Introductions were made and indeed Ketch found the two ladies both pretty and charming. The brunette answered to the name of Sally Peters and the blonde lady was Molly Mosely. They clung uncertainly to their male patrons, showing some concern at the noise and bustle around them. Captain Treddager greeted Ketch warmly, but asked no questions as to why he was included in the party. He was fully engaged in securing the attention of his very comely partner, who was in turn making a great fuss of him. After a few minutes, Ketch left them to themselves and moved about the waggons and carts, trying to become familiar as to who was doing what. He exchanged a few words with Holditch, who was sitting high on the piled luggage of a cart seemingly on guard.

He walked about and looked on at the order that was gradually emerging. There was a sense of readiness, of a desire to be on the move.

"Well, even amidst all this activity with Tull, Holditch, the two seamen and myself, the Sea General is as safe as it is possible to be,"

The position of Michel Gauvin, alias Michael Gough was not such a happy one. The days spent clerking in Whitehall Palace had provided no opportunity for an accident. Above all he was becoming increasingly concerned at having the ornate Spanish pistol in his personal baggage. If that was found, he would be lost. He was also growing unsure about Raphael's commitment to the task and Mary had just disappeared. He knew he was required to kill Robert Blake, whatever the consequences, but he was increasingly aware that this personal sacrifice was a step closer.

At last Beaumont re-mounted his horse and gave the signal to depart There was a creaking of wheels and the shouts of the drivers as coach, carriages, waggons and carts lurched forward. A small group of onlookers gave a half-hearted wave and cheer. It had been a surprise event for such a bleak morning. Slowly the convoy began to move steadily along the appointed way, in amongst them and on foot were the two seamen, some of the loaders, day labourers and grooms. All flanked by Beaumont and Ketch on horseback.

Now that the convoy had started moving, Raphael, who had been hiding behind an abbey buttress, mounted his horse and rode on ahead. He realised that this meant the Sea General was still alive and their task remained to be completed. He had expected nothing less. He was ready to do the job. He had spent a day considering various sites for a successful ambush.

"I shall find some way of stopping the convoy and when the Se General steps out of his carriage, I will shoot him."

He, enjoyed an inward smile.

"Then I shall be away on my horse. Michel and Mary may lay down their lives for the King of Spain, I have no such intentions. This is a good simple plan that allows me to live. As my fearsome uncle used to say," The simple way is always the easiest way."

He was quite exhilarated at the moments to come. He had little doubt at the route that was being followed by the convoy. Kingston bridge was the first bridge upstream from London. There was no other bridge crossing the Thames from London Bridge to Kingston bridge. The Guild of London Watermen had always preserved their livelihoods. The convoy would remain North of the river until Kingston.

Mary Sharpe was bubbling inside with excitement. Sitting in Captain Treddager's carriage, she would have a comfortable journey and would be well looked after by Beaumont and Treddager. Underneath their seat were two wicker hampers full of food and drink. As long as she kept her beau happy, she would have plenty of time to deal with the Sea General. She would be the unlikeliest of suspects and when the moment came, she would quietly steal away. She was amused that Michel had not recognised her and he looked ill at ease and uncomfortable. She realised a grim thought. She had no intention of giving him any warning

*"When I finish with the Sea General, he had better look out for himself. ***

From time to time, she glanced out of the carriage window. She was looking for signs of Raphael but he was nowhere to be seen.

On the early part of the road from Westminster to Kingston, the Thames makes a large Southern bend and the traveller must leave the river's edge and move straight ahead, where he will meet a smaller similar exercise. Beaumont knew the road well and his first landmark was the church of St

Paul's Hammersmith, a relatively new building with classical architecture. It had been of a high church character in ritual and liturgy, but under the reforming Government a lower mode was required, hymns and prayers rather than bells and incense. Here was the place for Beaumont to give the command for the convoy to stop, and take a break. They were not yet halfway to Richmond but he judged an early halt would refresh everyone for the long afternoon ahead. He himself, after ensuring that the Sea General was comfortable and well cared for, hurried to enjoy the hospitality of Captain Treddager. The travellers at large took their ease and devoured their food. But they soon found that having finished, the deep cold soon found a way back into their bones. Thus, they were all very receptive to Beaumont's order that it was time to move on. After a few slowly travelled miles, the journey became increasingly a grim chore. The conversation and good humour of the early morning had disappeared and a heavy silence descended on them. Despite their coats, blankets and gloves they felt the icy grip of winter. As the convoy moved to the long Southern stretch towards Kingston, they returned to having the river's edge on their left. Ketch felt it prudent to swing round and join Beaumont on the right side of the convoy. The two men rode side by side but there was little conversation, each dealing with the cold in their own way.

For Raphael his thoughts were becoming as bitter as the weather.

"*I have greatly underestimated this task. Hours in the saddle have sapped my strength and my concentration. There is a weakness upon me that rejects danger, my interest in the mission wanes as I think of nothing else but keeping warm.*

He also did not want to be between the river and the convoy and so like Ketch he swung around on to its right flank, taking care to be further out, well away from its two guardians. He had experienced disappointment in that of the four possible sites he had identified for ambush, he had in the end dismissed three. Only the fourth would allow him to complete his task today and that would be reached in half an hour. He knew there were further days ahead but he just wished to get the whole affair over with, so he could leave this country with its appalling weather. He dug deep within himself. He began to improve his commitment when reflecting that those surrounding the Sea General would also be occupied with their own problems. That they as well as he would move slowly, eyes and limbs dulled by fatigue and cold.

"Come on Raphael, surely the odds are better than even, the best chance of ambush lies just ahead. Just one last effort and the job is done."

He spurred his unwilling horse into a trot and swung in an arc that took him to a spot half a mile ahead of the convoy. It was his fourth and final choice. Here with the river on its left, the road ran within fifty yards of a wooded rise on its right. This provided a wide view of the road. It had a small copse with a large wooded area at its back that stretched away into the distance. In his earlier reconnaissance he had spotted a wooden horse trough by the side of the road. He had time to attach it to his horse and drag it into the middle of the track This was not enjoyed by his horse who made it a more difficult exercise than it should have been. Nevertheless, finally it was done. The convoy would have a choice, to go around it, by moving closer to the wooded rise where Raphael would be hidden, with pistol ready. Or it would stop and remove it, possibly providing an easier shot into the Sea General's coach. It would also be a possibility that this would encourage everyone to leave their coach or carriage to stretch aching limbs. Ready for any eventuality Raphael rode up to the copse at the top of the rise. He, himself, had to make a choice either to dismount and get a steady shot, or to fire from the saddle, thus easing a speedy withdrawal. The winter cover from the trees was not perfect and he opted for a speedy getaway. He was annoyed that his horse was unsettled, gently moving from side to side. In response he forcibly tried to relax for the convoy had finally come into view and drawn up before the horse trough. Beaumont and Ketch rode up to the front to investigate why the convoy had chosen to stop. They worried that passengers had taken to leaving their coach and carriages to converse and ease and stretch their legs. Ketch looked about him. He looked at Beaumont.

"This has been planned. There is danger here."

Raphael was annoyed that the coach passengers had dismounted on to the river side of the track and that the driver and horses were partly obscuring his view. But two men had left the coach and he deliberately fired at the smaller figure. It was a good shot, for at the moment of firing his horse had remained still and his pistol had worked. But it was not the result he had hoped for. The driver of the coach twisted in his seat and then fell to the ground. The smaller man was unharmed. There was no time for him to see any more. He turned his horse and rode away into the forest as fast as he was able.

"I will not veer left or right. I will keep straight and make all the distance I can. There will be pursuit but those in following will not want to be away to long from their convoy."

Beaumont had stopped to have a word with the Sea General when the shot rang out. He looked around in dismay. Ketch reacted quickly. He guessed that the shot had been fired from the wooded rise and thought he heard hoof beats. But at this point the driver had fallen to the ground and the coach's horses began turning towards the river. They were an obstacle in Ketch's way. Desperately he rode around them but he had lost valuable time. He rode swiftly up to the wooded rise, but the marksman and the sound of hoof beats had gone. He was annoyed that he had let the assassin escape. The woods were a formidable obstacle for pursuit. There were sounds of confusion behind him. he turned his horse and could see that down in the convoy people were milling about, drawing swords and looking for pistols. He decided to return to the convoy. On arrival he dismounted and made certain that the Sea General was unharmed.

"He got away," asked Beaumont.

"Yes," admitted Ketch.

He knew there would be a loss of confidence in him. He turned his attention to the fallen driver. He was surrounded by Tull and the seamen looking for the wound. There was a lot of blood and it was Captain Treddager who announced that the pistol ball was in the driver's thigh. Treddager took charge.

"Beaumont look after the ladies, take them back to my carriage., feed them food and drink but rescue any clean napkins and the salt barrel and bring them to me."

He turned to the two seamen.

"Lift this man into the Sea General's coach. The sooner this ball is out of his thigh, the better. I will cut it out and you will hold him down."

He motioned to Ketch.

"It would be helpful if you could provide a short leather strap>"

Ketch gave him an inquiring look. The Captain's retort was sharp.

"I have watched pistol balls being cut out of shoulders, backs and legs a dozen times Ketch and I suspect, so have these two men. It is a common feature in naval warfare. I doubt any here can do better,"

When what was required from his carriage was delivered, Captain Treddager and the seamen entered the coach.

Ketch turned to Beaumont, who was still looking uncertain.

"Get the women back to their carriage, but first move this crowd away, we do not want them hanging around the coach."

As Beaumont began herding people away, Ketch stepped past Tull with a supporting nod, and up into the coach.

"This is going to be bloody and noisy, but Captain Treddager seems confident."

The groans and the screams that came from the Sea General's coach had a sobering effect on the company and with standing still in the icy cold a few minds turned to just leaving and getting back to London. Ketch tried to find something to raise spirits but nothing came to mind. He was surprised after but half an hour Treddager descended from the Sea General's coach with his shirt and britches covered in blood.

"Well, he made an awful lot of noise Ketch, but it is often the big ones who squeal most. It is out. Yes! A bit of blood, but I have seen my surgeons face worse. Blake's coach will need to be well cleaned."

Ketch asked the central question.

"He is alright then, he can travel?"

"Put him in my carriage with the women, they will fuss him back to good humour."

Ketch still looked uncertain.

"Oh! He is a lucky man. His heavy clothing in part lessened the ball's force. Yes! It broke the skin and hit the thigh bone. But that did not crack or break, rather the ball followed its line for some inches. We couldn't find it at first, but once located it came out soon enough."

Captain Treddager climbed back to his patient. Beaumont remounted his horse and called out to Ketch.

"I shall ride on to tonight's stop, the Good Shepherd Inn. It is but three years built, I have commandeered the whole place. So, we shall be comfortable tonight. Ketch watched him ride off into the gloom Instinctively he took command and waved people back to their transport and places. It was time to move on. The convoy returned to its slow trudge forward. The cold did not relent and although the light was beginning to fade, horses and people began to sense that they were not far from the end of their journey. After an hour Ketch saw something in the distance that caused him to ride on and investigate. Standing in his stirrups he had a good look into the distance. He called back to any who could hear.

"I see lights ahead, many lanterns and torches. I think Mr Beaumont is signalling us a welcome."

Chapter Eight   Poison

The Good Shepherd inn was a new building made of brick and enjoying plenty of glass windows. The landlord was there at the front door to welcome the travellers. Beaumont introduced the Sea General and his guests and then hurried away with much to do on room allocations, finalising the parking of transports and ensuring that only essential baggage was unloaded. The landlord ushered the Sea General and his party into the lobby where coats, hats, scarves and gloves were hastily removed and placed on a long row of hooks. The landlord guided them towards the public room

"Leave your cold and wet clothes here, I have some warming drinks available for you all. Please follow me. When you have recovered, I will show you to your bedrooms."

He guided them to a long table on which were laid out mug and glasses together with a bottle of brandy, jugs of hot water, a bowl of sugar and a tureen of mulled wine. There was grumbling from the clerks, servants and drivers when they were directed to another part of the public room, but this ended when on a long bar, hot soup was available with plates of fresh bread.

Warmth and good humour began to surface as the events of the day were discussed. Beaumont began the task of directing the working travellers to their sleeping arrangements. Some had been given the smaller rooms, others were in the kitchen and the rest were found places in barns and stables. Ketch was pleased that Holditch had managed a place in the kitchens. The wounded driver was found a room at the back and a doctor was sent for. The Sea General had insisted on the best of treatment for him.

Ketch found himself standing next to the Sea General and Captain Treddager. Tull had the much more challenging task of entertaining the ladies. His new role and his natural uncertainty with women made it a conversation for which he was very ill-fitted. A man who had boldly faced the charges of Prince Rupert's cavalry was hopeless at small talk in the company of women who, in their view had narrowly escaped death and now needed the re-assurance from expressing their feelings. The Sea General, Ketch and Captain Treddager discussed the same events but in a less dramatic fashion.

"Well Ketch," spoke the Sea General.

"Thurloe was right. This is going to be a journey with danger in it. That ball was clearly meant for me and I think that will not be the end of it."

Captain Treddager had understood the Sea General's concern.

"The Sea General's safety is your responsibility, eh Ketch! My God you must make use of me. You seem short-handed for this."

Ketch eyed the Captain carefully. A range of thoughts crossed his mind.

"A man of action. Yes! He seems to have sound judgement, but seemingly able to be led by a pretty woman."

That note of uncertainty lingered on but he determined to follow his instincts and see Treddager as a valuable ally. He allowed himself a wry smile.

"There is after all a likelihood of plenty of danger ahead".

He made up his mind"

"Frankly Captain, I am not alone in this. I have other men with me, but you will be a welcome addition."

The Sea General interrupted.

"You have more men here with you? That is not what you told me."

Ketch became most uncomfortable.

"Lies come back to haunt you, however, you dress them up."

"Yes, General I was not completely open with you. For me your safety was worth risking your displeasure and I am sure Thurloe would say that your dislike of instructions should not put the nation at risk."

Ketch held his breath. How would the Sea General respond?

The Sea General grimaced, but Captain Treddager had the nerve to slap him on the back.

"Cheer up Robert. Don't blame Ketch. He is only following orders to ignore your wishes. You must take it up with Thurloe and Cromwell."

Ketch made a weak smile and moved away to join Tull and the two women. When he was out of hearing Treddager turned to the Sea General.

"That man will do all he can to keep you safe, Robert. You should fall in with his wishes. Yes! He deceived you. Yes! He missed the marksman, but he will be very anxious not to make another mistake."

The Sea General did lighten up and looked at Beaumont joining the group with Ketch. He grunted.

"Tell me about this new woman of yours Stephen. Where did you meet her and have you brought the other one for Beaumont? He is going to be far too busy for her."

"No! No! Robert you have the wrong idea. I have quite taken to Molly Mosley and as you know, this is going to be my last time of going to sea. If she waits for me. I hope to settle down with her. I have known her barely a week so I really must get to know her. As for Beaumont, Sally is Molly's best friend and had already taken up with him, so why not bring them together. When we leave, they will be company for each other?"

After a while the landlord suggested that the Sea General and his guests would like to be shown to their rooms and their evening meal would be on the table in half an hour. He had arranged a private room. Led by the Sea General the travellers collected their cloaks and hats and took possession of their accommodation. They had been allocated all the rooms in the corridor at the top of the stairs leading to the first floor. The Sea General had the furthest room, then came Beaumont and Treddager sharing, then the two women also sharing. Tull had been given the next room on his own. He was enjoying his new found status. His place, normally, would either be

113

sharing with Ketch or in the kitchens with Holditch. Ketch's room followed Tull's. He was also on his own. He was very satisfied with these arrangements. His room was next to the top of the stairs. Anyone threating the Sea General would have to pass by him. A full night's vigil would positively safeguard the Sea General.

The Sea General and his guests were soon downstairs sitting expectantly awaiting their evening meal. The landlord's hearty welcome had given them all hope for an exceptional dinner They were not to be disappointed. Bowls, tureens and dishes were brought, full of meats and vegetables of all sorts; pies and savoury tarts filled the gaps on the table. When finally empty they were replaced with puddings, tarts and cakes, fruits and nuts. Besides beer there was wine, brandy and port throughout the meal. The Sea General took special note that his "crew" as he called them were also well satisfied with their fayre. Dinner passed as a pleasant affair, perhaps more gentile as ladies were present, but the experiences of the day had left most of the party ready for their bed. Out in the large public room it was quiet with a few other travellers and one or two locals. However, Holditch, Michel, Hedges and Brown were having a few final drinks before retiring. Their conversation was made up mainly of stories from Hedges and Brown of their experiences at sea, but Holditch in the conversation was finding out more about Michel and his life. To Holditch it was all pretty boring especially when compared to his own career, but on that he kept himself in check. The only item of interest that he gleaned concerning Michel was that he was Dutch and had dealings with the sea. Not that he had been to sea, but had worked in dockside warehouses handling, bales, boxes and sacks of many different commodities, including wool, grain, spices then recording them in and out. Bosun Brown became a little aggressive when he heard this.

"It's not a year gone that we were fighting your lot at sea and giving you a real beating."

Michel was wise to agree.

"You're right Brown but that war is over and two good Protestant countries should never have fallen out anyway." At that moment Michel's defence was interrupted by a small swarthy man who had emerged from the back of the inn. He looked about him and then moved towards the four men.

"Would you lads care to see something you have never seen before For a few coppers you will be amazed, if you can bear to look and for a few coppers more you can touch."

The two seamen laughed and Hedges spoke their mind.

"Me and my mate here, have seen so much of the world that there ain't nothing you can show us that we haen't seen before."

"Money back and doubled if that is true," was the quick reply.

Michel and Holditch were not much interested, but eventually the four agreed that they would see whatever it was that would amaze them. The man led them to a lean- to shed at the back of the inn. Inside he took up a candle lamp and stood by a table with a tarpaulin covering something bulky.

"It's nothing to do with women then," muttered Hedges.

"Now then," announced their host.

"For a few coppers I will remove the cloth. You must prepare to be shocked."

A few coppers were produced and when there was enough, with a flourish the tarpaulin was removed. The effect was instantaneous on all four.

"Sweet Jesus! Bloody Hell! "were the cries of the seaman.

Holditch felt a surge of bile in his throat and turned away. Michel cried a despairing oath.

" Spiritu Sancti "and crossed himself.

The stranger was delighted with their reaction.

"It is as I said and for just a few more coppers you can touch."

On the table was a dried corpse of a human baby, perfectly recognisable from the cunning application of colour, but with two heads and three arms. The four men staggered out of the shed. They did not stop to take up his second offer. Feeling ashamed at their interest and disgusted at what they had seen, each man with his own thoughts went to his bed. Only Holditch ha gained anything from the event.

Throughout the night upstairs, Ketch once or twice heard faint footsteps, but on opening his door, by the light of the lamp at the top of the stairs, he saw nothing. He thought there might be some visiting but nothing that affected the Sea General. Unfortunately, early in the morning he found that, at some time in the night, he had dozed off and was woken by a chamber maid with hot water. He was not pleased with himself but he found consolation in the fact that all he could hear was the sound of guests rising, dressing and preparing for breakfast. He ventured down to break his own fast. Not everyone was up and about. Beaumont was busy but there was no sign yet of the remainder of the party. Before eating he saw Holditch across the room attracting his attention. He sat down beside him.

"Last night Ketch, I witnessed some behaviour by that clerk called Michael that concerned me. Never mind the exact details, but then he behaved to a shock by crossing himself and swearing an oath in Latin. Rather suspicious I thought. We must keep an eye on him."

Ketch gave Holditch's news some thought.

"Not enough to accuse him of anything but you are correct. He will require careful watching."

Not wishing to reveal their cooperation Ketch whispered a well done, and went to breakfast. As the late comers arrived and completed their meal, Beaumont began asking everyone to be ready to move on.

"The transport is ready; drivers and grooms are in place. Come on everyone, there is now no time to waste. "

Guests still remaining hurried to their rooms for their coats and cloaks. Ketch was in his own room when he heard a roar of pain from the Sea General's room and a second and

117

then a third. He rushed down the corridor fearful of what he might find. On opening the door, he found the Sea General on his feet, twisting and turning trying desperately to remove his top coat.

"Get this off me Ketch! For God's sake, get it off!"

Ketch grasped the coat by the shoulders to help pull it off. There was another cry of pain.

"Careful, God damn you. There is something sharp,"

"Stand still General," demanded Ketch

When the Sea General was still, very gingerly, lifting the coat as much as possible from the Sea General's body, he managed to remove it. There was another grunt of distress. He dropped the coat to the ground and looked at the back of the Sea General's right shoulder. There was a widening patch of blood on his shirt. Bursting buttons both men ripped of waistcoat and shirt. The Sea General turned his head to see the source of his pain. He tried to feel with his hand.

"What is it Ketch?" He demanded.

Ketch was describing what he saw when Treddager and Beaumont entered the room.
"There is a hole, a small hole, but it is bleeding badly and there are deep scratches on your shoulder and the top of your arm. It looks the work of something sharp, perhaps a large pin or needle."

It was in my coat," groaned the Sea General

Ketch turned to Captain Treddager.

"Go downstairs and bring some clean clothes and hot water. It is painful, but does not look life threatening."

Treddager left and Beaumont picked up the coat. He held it up while Ketch carefully examined it. He was conducting his search when the two women came into the room. On seeing the Sea Generals shoulder and arm, they immediately produced an array of clean handkerchiefs together with soft consoling words. Eventually Ketch found the source of the wound, a long lady's hair pin. He held it up for all to see. The two women were quite chastened by what was before them.

"It wasn't us", cried blonde Molly Mosley. We have pins, lots of them but not like those. Look! You can see, I always have my hair down>" Sally Peters blurted out her thoughts.

"And I use only combs to put up my hair"

The Sea General could see that the two women were quite distressed.

"Of course, it was not you ladies. You have been nothing but kindness on this journey. Any rogue or villain could have interfered with my top coat when it was hung up in the lobby Be content, you are amongst friends."

The Sea General, rather shaken, sat on his bed. Captain Treddager undertook a more detailed examination of the Sea General's wounds.

There is some sort of dark stain, like brown molasses mixed into this. It might be poison"

He put his nose close the site of the oozing blood and stain.

"I cannot smell anything. I think plenty of warm water and a clean bandage should be sufficient for this, but it must be cleaned daily.".

Ketch took the pin across to the Sea General for him to examine.

Nasty thing, hurts like the devil."

Ketch could see that Beaumont was hovering outside with what looked like a glass of brandy and hot water. He waved him in and made the Sea General drink it slowly. After one or two sips of the liquid the Sea General looked up at Beaumont.

"I am fit to travel Charles. We must not let this hold us up."

Beaumont stood silent for a moment and then looked around him.

"I think a little time for you to recover is in order,"

He turned to Ketch and suggested a quiet word downstairs. They left the Sea general in the hands of Captain Treddager and sat down stairs in the public room.

"I had an interesting conversation with the landlord whilst waiting for your arrival yesterday. We may want to take advantage of it."

He looked about him to ensure they were not being overheard.

"He was very informative about recent works up- river that link Weybridge on the Thames with Guildford. As Guildford is our next destination, I was immediately interested. Further questioning satisfied me that we have an alternative route for the Sea General to be taken to Guildford whilst the convoy continues in the normal way. Given the recent attempts on the Sea General which, if you allow, you have been unable to prevent, a boat up the River Thames and then a trip along the new watercourse from Weybridge to Guildford, becomes an attractive idea. Of course, he would need some trusted companions, but you can arrange that, my post must be continuing with the convoy. What say you to this?"

Ketch stroked his nose. He ignored Beaumont's mention of his failure but he saw much merit in his suggestion. A full day in the coach being bumped and thrown about would not be help the Sea General's condition, whereas a water born trip would certainly be smoother. It would also throw into confusion any further attempts to harm the Sea General planned by Spanish agents. It would be a day free of immediate worry.

He looked carefully at Beaumont.

"If any man had a chance to harm the Sea General, it is Beaumont. So, we can trust him completely and his idea is a good one. If it is possible now, with transport being available, we must take it."

He looked into Beaumont's serious face and laughed.

"It is a fine idea and we must try and make it happen. Two key matters, I must go with him and who can provide the transport?"

Beaumont was ready with an answer on transport.

"The Guild of Watermen's monopoly of river transport ends at Kingston. Two brothers are already trading between Kingston and Guildford on this new route. They have their own boat and at the new lock at Weybridge, on a regular basis their goods are transferred on to boats and taken to Guildford. They brothers are both here in Kingston looking for cargo and passengers. They can transport up to four passengers to Weybridge and then easily arrange the hiring of transport to Guildford where the convoy will be waiting. The landlord is happy to act as a factor in making all arrangements, but I need a decision on this Ketch now!"

"I am with you on this Beaumont, but we must assemble the whole of the Sea General's party here in the public room and let the landlord spell out the details."

Sat around a large table the travellers assembled to hear the words of the landlord. He was a large, heavy set man with a clear face and brushed back hair. He looked relatively honest, but Ketch, nevertheless was on guard whilst he spoke.

"I have been talking to Mr Beaumont and he mentioned his concerns about securing the safety of Sea General Blake and how he was shot at and now we have had this unpleasantness this morning. He remarked that you were heading for Guilford and that it would be an uncomfortable coach ride for the Sea General."

The Sea General was not happy.

"I'm not unable to travel, damn your impudence, Sir!

The landlord held his ground in the face of the Sea General's displeasure.

"I put what I hoped was a helpful suggestion to Mr Beaumont who has discussed it with Captain Ketch."
"And what is this suggestion," interrupted Captain Treddager.

"Go on landlord," demanded Ketch.

The landlord took a deep breath and began his explanation. "The Sea General can have a safe and secure journey, comfortable and free of danger. Upstream at Weybridge there is a new waterway from the Thames to Guildford. It is fully working with plenty of barges and other traffic There is a boat, the Skeleton, run by two brothers Frank and Jethro Osterly, who could today, take you up on the tide to Weybridge lock, where at the Old Swan tavern you can hire transport into Guildford, arriving late afternoon, to early evening. It is also possible to get food at the Old Swan."

Having delivered his suggestion, the landlord retired to sit on the edge of a table.

"What do you know of these Osterley brothers?" asked Captain Treddager, suspicion written all over his face.

"Honest as any other river trader," offered the landlord.

"How much will this cost?", inquired Ketch.

Beaumont intervened at this point.

"Not unreasonable. We have discussed this and it can be accommodated."

The landlord had something to add.

"Mr Beaumont does not yet know this but when they heard the name of their passenger, they were prepared to provide their boat for nothing. The very idea that they could boast for their whole lives that they had sailed with Sea General Robert Blake was recompense enough. They could not believe that such a chance could come to them. The Sea General Blake laughed. "And I would not deny them either.

I see merit in this Ketch. A bit of quiet and an absence of this constant plodding is something I would welcome."

He turned to the landlord.

"How many passengers can the Skeleton take?"

Waiting for instructions the landlord answered.

"They say four would be comfortable.

"I will go with the Sea General," asserted Ketch.

" I also," interrupted Treddager." I will not leave the Sea General's side."

Ketch was a little annoyed by this pre-emption by Captain Treddager, but he was the oldest and most constant of the Sea General's aides.

"And I suppose that the fourth will be that pretty woman of yours, eh! Treddager!" Voiced the Sea General.

"She will not be parted from you and Beaumont must manage the convoy so his lady will remain with him."
At the beginning of the landlord's suggestion Tull had looked unhappy. He was uncertain about the change, but Ketch's obvious support, eased his fears.

The news that the Sea General was travelling by river to Guildford quickly spread amongst the rest of the convoy. They had enjoyed having the famous man amongst them, but they were re-assured when it was made clear that Mr Beaumont would continue with them and that the Sea General would re-join them at Guildford. Before departure, Ketch had time to emphasis to both Tull and Holditch that despite the Sea General's absence, they still had to be on the lookout for signs of the Spanish agents. Tull expressed considerable satisfaction that for a day he could relax and be less of an earnest minister. Holditch also had a smile on his face.

Gathering what they needed for the day, the four travelling by river were led down to the riverside and introduced to the Osterley brothers. Frank and Jethro were obviously brothers, both middle aged and tanned from working on the river. One, Jethro, was slightly older than the other and the nominal Captain of the boat, Skeleton. This was a thirty- foot London lighter with sprit sail and leeboards. The Sea General obviously was looking forward to the trip and both brothers could hardly stop grinning at their delight in such a passenger. Charles Beaumont and his lady, the two clerks, Tull, Holditch and a few drivers and grooms watched the embarkation and prepared to wave them on their way.

Michael Gough or Spanish agent Michel Gauvin also looked with interest at the sailing party and then looked very sharply again. He was amazed, uncertain and then certain again. Molly Mosley, Captain Treddager's lady friend was actually Mary Sharpe, the English born Spanish agent. He experienced a moment of confusion.

"Perhaps here is our best chance to kill this English Commander. What an opportunity. None of us must die if Mary can manage to destroy him on her own."

He still found the reality difficult to accept. How had the world- weary slattern with her stained clothing and greasy hair, who had captured Captain Treddager, transformed herself into blond, bubbly Molly Mosley. Now he knew who it was, he began to see how convincing wig and expertly applied make up could transform a woman. Michel filed away this knowledge It had been a cautionary tale which he obviously much needed.

He watched closely as Captain Treddager held her hand to help her down into the boat. Once she had her balance, she looked back at her audience and her eyes met those of Michel. She smiled and gave a hint of a nod just for him. She now knew that he knew. Michel turned away well satisfied, to complete his arrangements for leaving Guildford. His new knowledge had put fresh heart into him.

The departure of the Sea General created a change of mood in the convoy. It felt less stressed but more sombre. In such an atmosphere, Charles Beaumont led the collected transports over Kingston bridge and onto the road to Guildford. Personally, he was greatly relieved that for one day at least, England's greatest living naval commander was not his responsibility

Chapter Nine   Spanish Agents

Raphael de Rousse known in England as Raphael Ratcliffe, was most unhappy. He was not only upset because his best shot missed his target, but also because of the surge of naked fear he had felt as he had seen those rushing to take him. His departure back through the woods had not been controlled. In a panic he had just spurred his horse away in any direction. Both horse and rider lacked any control. They just blindly fled searching for their safety. The woods had been soon passed, large, open fields were trampled over until a winding track produced a gradual reduction in pace, the result of sheer exhaustion. Slumped on his horse, Raphael came to a halt. Man, and beast, still shaking with fear

An amount of time passed that was not measured, but only concluded when Raphael began to take stock of his situation. He dismounted at least remembering some care for his horse.

I have no idea where I am or what direction to go in. I need to return to shadowing the convoy, which means finding the road to Kingston.

With such musings, he walked his horse until its shaking subsided. He remounted and looked about him. There was no one or any habitation in sight. He was soaked in perspiration and his horse was still giving off clouds of steam and the cold was once more taking a grip on them. The heavy cloud that had come up heralding a thaw, now hid the sun and there was no guidance from it. At last, he determined that his only option was to go back along the track from whence they had come. He had to hope that in that direction lay the town of Kingston. Riding along he looked left and right across the fields for signs of life. Finally, he decided that at the next track he crossed he would follow until at last he found someone, anyone. It was a limited strategy but eventually he sighted a village. Not wishing to create concern he dismounted and walked his horse into the centre of the village. He surmised that exactly as in his own country, no one was going to be helpful to a lone man riding in amongst them. As such, with this gentler approach, he was stared at and received a number of suspicious looks, but no total antagonism. Looking ahead he could see at the far end of the main street was a forge. In the failing light of the cold afternoon its fire burnt bright and a number of children were huddled at a respectful distance seeking to enjoy its warmth. They were careful to shuffle away when a look from the blacksmith warned they were too close. Raphael's fear and uncertainty had finally given way to a re-awakening confidence. He hailed the Smith.

"Good sir! You find before you a weary traveller who is lost and searching for the road to Kingston. Are you able to help in this matter?

 The Smith straightened up from his work, spat in the fire and handed his heavy hammer to his assistant. He carefully wiped his hands and approached Raphael. The Smith like many others had to be the largest man in the village. Not in height, for he was barely six feet tall, but massive arms and shoulders matched by a heavy stomach and bulky thighs that clearly marked his profession.

"Your name sir would encourage an answer as would a small coin. I would also suggest that as you have little chance of reaching Kingston before nightfall, you require more than words. You and your mount need a refuge for the night"

Inside Raphael gave a sigh of relief.

"Raphael Ratcliffe is my name, Smith, and this coin is for your answer and your advice."

Raphael tossed a silver coin in the air that the Smith caught expertly:

"My cottage could provide a restful place for Raphael Ratcliffe and we have a place for his horse. If he could wait but half an hour here in the warmth of the forge that could be arranged."

Raphael was delighted at how easily his fortunes had changed. He had lost the rest of the day, but he had hopes of receiving clear directions tomorrow.

The following morning after a country breakfast. Raphael was all action. He paid handsomely for his lodgings and was set on the road to Kingston. It took him only an hour to reach the Portsmouth road and spy Kingston bridge in the distance. On arriving in the town, he was amazed that the Sea General's convoy had only recently departed. Despite his breakfast, he found the smell of cooked food from the inn mouth- watering, It was enough to persuade him that he could enjoy an hour of its hospitality and still catch up with the object of his purpose.

 The two Osterley brothers expertly navigated "the Skeleton" to gain the maximum benefit from the tide and with a favourable wind, a speedy passage up to Weybridge was assured. Shafts of sunlight competed with dark clouds and for some minutes the passengers enjoyed a play of the sun's rays falling upon the water and highlighting the green woods growing down to the river bank. The cold, however, would not be denied and the four soon took advantage of the protection offered by a small self-built cabin. It lacked windows, there was little room for four people and thus the passengers were tightly packed inside., with only each other to look at.

Despite his attempts at humour, the Sea General was clearly in pain. His face was grey and there was a dullness in his eyes. As best as they could, the others tried to give him some extra room. The atmosphere became very warm for all the party were well dressed for the cold with maximum use being made of wool and fur. Captain Treddager regaled the party with tales of the Sea General's exploits at sea and Ketch once more had to go through the battle of Naseby. It was not long before this talk and body heat made the cabin unpleasantly stuffy. Treddager and Ketch left the cabin to let in some air. They stood side by side, smoking their pipes and watching the Surrey shore. Captain Treddager broke their silence. He kept his voice low; he did not want to be overheard.

"You know this is only a temporary respite Ketch. Two attempts have been made on the Sea General's life. This is not ended; he remains in peril and something must be done. You are responsible for his safety. You work for Secretary Thurloe; that is why you are here. You are regularly moving about and amongst us and you have other men here with you, but it is not working you cannot save him from harm. "

Ketch meant to intervene but the Captain needed to get his concerns out squarely in the open.

"He is not a well man Ketch. His leg is getting worse, he suffers from cramps, there is a general weakness about him. He has declined terribly since you saw him in Northampton. He is more vulnerable than ever. I fear this will be his last voyage. He is more vulnerable than ever and current arrangements are not keeping him safe."

He paused but he had still more to say.

"This is not entirely your fault, Ketch. Thurloe has given you an impossible task. There are just so many people involved in this convoy, drivers, grooms, servants, labourers. Any one of them could be poised to destroy him. You do not know them all, you cannot control them all."

He sighed.

"You are the only man I trust, Ketch. I just hope you realise all this."

Ketch did not take well to criticism, but in this case, he knew Captain Treddager was right. In fact, they had been extremely lucky that the Sea General had not been shot and, if the truth was told, he was still struggling with what appeared to be attempted poisoning.

"He should have taken Cromwell's offer of troopers. Give me twenty of them and he would travel in a ring of steel, but the Sea General was stubborn. He would have his way."

Captain Treddager made to speak but this time it was Ketch who had more to say.

"This convoy arrangement is of no help. After Guildford Captain, there will be changes. We are not going to lose this Sea General."

Whilst Ketch and Treddager were debating security, back in the cabin the Sea General had fallen asleep and Mary Sharpe was looking carefully at him with narrowing eyes.

"Here now! He is at my mercy. I have my knife well hidden amongst my silk and lace. One stroke across the throat and he is dead."

She had an inward smile.

"But Mary dear. There would be the most unpleasant consequences. You would not live to enjoy your triumph or collect your rewards. You would die in a very unpleasant manner. Besides he may yet succumb to the poison. No! You must wait. They all trust you and if necessary, there will be other opportunities"
Despite these cautions she was pleased with herself.

"Raphael has missed and Michel has done nothing. It is I who now faces a defenceless Sea General."

Hidden deep within her, however, was an uncertainty, a knowledge that although her cleverness had created an opportunity, she had never killed anyone directly before, man or woman.

"Oh yes! I have destroyed men and women, but never in such a way as to see their last moments."

She curled up her toes at the thought of such intimate deaths. She cast a look at the Sea General. He was certainly looking worse and there were little whimpers of pain in his sleep; and she had plans to hurry him along to a final demise. She leaned back in her seat and awaited the return of Ketch and Treddager.

It took three hours to arrive at the Old Swan, a time that gave great satisfaction to the Osterly brothers. They manoeuvred the "Skeleton" alongside the quay, that lay immediately downstream from the lock.

"Here we must leave you," said Frank.

"We have a cargo to unload, but no permit to travel down to Guildford. However, you will easily find a barge willing to give you passage on your way.".

The travellers thanked the brothers for their efforts and were surprised at the genuine amiability of the Sea General's response. It heartened them to see that he still had spirit. A set of stone steps led up to the Swan and whilst Frank led the Sea General, Captain Treddager and so called Molly Mosel up to the front door, Jethro took Ketch around to the right side of the inn down to where the boats travelling to Guildford were to be found.

"I think we will all benefit from some hot food and drink together with a short period of rest before moving on." Smiles all around indicated their consent. The landlord gave them a hearty welcome and led them into a snug parlour where a generous fire was giving off considerable warmth. Outer clothes were shed and positions taken to enjoy the heat. Captain Treddager quietly mentioned to the landlord the name of his significant   guest, and within a short period of time, they were informed that at their leisure there was a modest board of fayre for them to enjoy. There was no delay in their acceptance and they moved with some enthusiasm into the private dining room that had been provided for them. They found laid out for them hot beef stew, roasted potatoes together with a range of other vegetables. There was beer and cider and warmed wine to accompany the meal. The landlord was profuse with apologies over the limited nature of the fayre, but he was heartily assured that it was precisely what they themselves would have chosen on such a day with such a journey. The company pulled up their chairs and made the most of what had been provided. After some twenty minutes, the silence that accompanies serious eating was broken by pleasant social conversation on the merits of the journey so date. There was some laughter and a general feeling of good humour. Mary disappeared to re-arrange her toilet, the Sea General opted to return to the snug parlour and Ketch and Treddager decided that a turn outside with their pipes would be very attractive. Ketch, when he had finished his pipe strode down to the waterway quay were a series of boats of various sizes were to be found. Eventually after a number of conversations, he secured passage to Guilford on a barge whose original living quarters had been turned over to passenger accommodation. This was very different to their experience on the "Skeleton". Padded seats, windows with curtains and a small wood stove promised a much more comfortable ride. Ketch was also intrigued to find that motion was to come from a strong looking shire horse pulling the barge by rope; something he had never seen before.

Captain Treddager when his pipe was finished, decided to return to the dining room to check on the Sea General. On finding the room empty he passed into the parlour. To his surprise he found Sea General Blake sitting on a chair with his top coat off and his right shirt sleeve rolled down. His wounded shoulder was being bathed by Molly Mosleyl.

"What is this?" He demanded coldly.

It was the Sea General who replied.

"My shoulder was stiff and painful Treddager. Molly suggested some simple bathing with cold water would bring some ease and indeed it is wonderfully cooling."

Mary smiled sweetly at the Captain.

"It is just cold-water Captain. It will only help."

Mary did not tell him that the handkerchief she was using was that which had moped up the surplus poison from the floor of "Draught Sally's "cellar. She kept it tight in her hand, but she had noticed that the water in the basin had begun to turn murky. Fortunately, Captain Treddager was too busy looking at the Sea General's wound to look into the basin. She rose to remove it back to the kitchen. It was at this point that Ketch entered the room and had to stand back to allow Mary out of the room.

"You have cleaned away some dirt there, Molly," he said.

Mary smiled and moved around him on her way.

"Come and look at this Ketch," exclaimed Treddager.

The Sea General's wound was damp from the bathing and there was an unpleasant puffiness around the shoulder and a dark centre at the actual puncture. Gently, Treddager with his forefinger wiped away a film of murky water and there was an unhappy grimace on his face, when he saw that the skin around the wound was an unhealthy red. "We will keep a close eye on this Ketch. You must have a doctor look at it in Guildford."

The Sea General grunted and restored his clothing.

"It is all the Lord's work,"

Back in the kitchen Mary was elated; she had soaked the Sea General's wound for some time. She had high hopes of further infection.

Raphael's hour in the "Good Shepherd" had restored his spirits completely. The time he had lost through his excessive desire to avoid capture was forgotten. He was confident that it could soon be made up. For the moment he was sitting enjoying the buzz of conversation of people eating and drinking and generally enjoying themselves. He rose from his chair it was time to go. Within ten minutes he had left the warm room of the "Good Shepherd" and was back on the road battling once more with the cold. He pushed his horse into a gentle canter and within half an hour he could see the Sea General's convoy ahead. He reduced the distance between them and then moved out onto the left, entering a large field. With a short sprint he was able to get ahead of the convoy and watch it pass. He was concerned that he could see no sign of the rider who had previously flanked the convoy and had given him such a shock with his speedy reaction to Raphael's shot at the Sea General. He also felt he good detect a lighter mood amongst the travellers. There was some laughter and individuals looked less grim. The other man on horseback was still there leading the convoy, but there seemed to be a man and a woman missing. He continued on his parallel course and as the morning wore on, he realised that he had seen no sight of the Sea General. Raphael was bemused.

"If he is no longer here. Where is he and what are we doing here?"

He began to give some serious thought to the state of the mission when, with some relief, he saw Michel leave one of the carriages.

"I must talk to Michel. He must know what is going on. He does not seem disturbed because the Sea General has disappeared."

Michel in fact was enjoying his walk His fellow clerk was an amiable fellow, but had little conversation other than their clerical duties, the Sea General and his own family. He found it pretty dull fare. His mind was much more aglow with the thoughts of Mary Sharpe being Molly Mosley, captain Treddager's companion. He had high hopes that from this vantage point she could fashion the demise of Robert Blake. Despite the cold and the showers of their journey, he felt good.

Raphael was determined to secure a conversation with Michel. He had noticed that in many of the villages small crowds and well-wishers would come out and wave and cheer and march alongside the convoy. He decided to ride on well ahead to select a village large enough to provide a sizable crowd. He would settle his horse, encourage news of the Sea General's arrival and then mingle with the crowd and find an opportunity to have his conversation with Michel.

Raphael was able to secure a short conference with Michel. He was relieved to hear that the Sea General would be returning to the convoy at Guildford and was full of admiration for the efforts of Mary Sharpe. What heartened him the most, however, was Michel's optimism. He could not help responding to the idea that all was well and that they would complete their task and get away in good order

"I may even try something myself this evening," was Michel's parting remark as they separated

They would not have been so buoyed up with the thoughts of success if they had known that at that moment Sergeant Holditch had observed them together. He had developed some firm opinions about Michel

"I think the Captain and I need to give that clerk some more of our time. I think he needs to answer some questions and I would like a look at his baggage."

He resumed his place perched on a cart packed with furniture It had been a boring and uncomfortable position. But now he had something useful for the Captain.

Chapter Ten   The Hospital

It was the party that had travelled by boat to Guildford who first arrived at their destination. The short quayside was welcoming with lanterns that kept the gloom of a dying March afternoon at bay. They had passed a stoic afternoon on their Wey river barge. The accommodation had been comfortable but dull, the scenery that was visible was dull and eventually the conversation became dull. The condition of the Sea General became an overpowering influence. It was a relief to finally arrive. The passengers were allowed off first and it calmed a few anxieties when they saw that Charles Beaumont was waiting to welcome them.

"Your possessions, General, are but half a mile away. They will be with us very soon, but I ventured ahead in case you arrived first. There is time for me to escort you to your rooms for the night."

"Well done, Charles," enthused the Sea General. Although I am a man of the water, I was damn pleased to be off that boat. The Thames gave us a splendid journey and the "Old Swan was everything that was promised, but a gloomy afternoon in a slow-moving barge was an endurance."

There was a general affirmative grumble from his fellow travellers who were largely spending their time stretching their limbs and stamping their feet.

"Miss Morley has need of warmth and access to her room."

It is not far General," assured Beaumont.

"Tonight, the party will rest in Guilford Hospital, a fine charity building recently constructed but undergoing repairs following a fire in one of its wings. We have full use of the areas that were untouched. It is handsome accommodation."

"Lead on man!" Demanded Captain Treddager.

"Less talk"

Beaumont leading the way with a lantern had them soon at the front steps, where a well wrapped- up man was awaiting them. Beaumont quickly introduced each member of the party to Governor Halsey. Halsey was a large man, who under his coat, scarf and hat seemed an energetic fifty-year old. He had silver hair pushing out from under his mole skin hat, which topped a ruddy face. His amiability and genial appearance gave hope of a comfortable stay.

"A pleasure to meet you General and your companions. Come in! Come in! First some hot drinks and food and then we shall talk room arrangements."

Beaumont, his job done, made his excuses and left to bring in safely the arriving transports. Governor Halsey led his guests into an expansive, well- lit hall with a high ceiling and large windows along one wall.

"Our main dining room,"" he declared. "Or rather so when we were fully operational. You see tables and chairs in sufficient number for feeding all your party and it may become the sleeping area for as many of them as you wish."

. The darkness of the evening outside made the dining room a haven of good cheer for all who saw it

The Governor broke off from his introduction to the facilities as he noticed both the limp of the Sea General and that he was favouring his right arm.

"Are you alright General, or have you had a fall."

The Sea General grunted and made to speak but Captain Treddager intervened.

"The Sea General's leg was damaged in one of his battles and from time to time the pain returns, but at present more concerning is a wound to his shoulder. It has not healed and needs attention"

"At once," replied the Governor.

"I know the importance of the Sea General and the great tasks that face him. I shall secure a doctor immediately, but first please take up this food and drink."

He pointed to a table at the end of the room alongside a large fire. It was laden with meats, cheeses, winter fruits. What was immediately attractive to those who had experienced such a cold journey was a tureen of hot soup. As one the party moved to satisfy their appetites. The Sea General was placed in a chair at the centre of the table, where food and warmth were in ample supply. With promises to return soon, Governor Halsey disappeared to find a doctor.

Apart from sighs of content, the four travellers said little, but as food and drink began to go down, convivial conversation developed. There was much concern for Molly Mosley by the Sea General. Captain Treddager was happy for him to have the greater part of her attention. Ketch, however, was thinking hard about their female companion until his mind moved on to what might be the sleeping arrangements for the Sea General and how secure they would be.

It was not long before Beaumont and the rest of the convoy arrived and there was the usual noise and bustle of the coach, carriages and carts securing places in the hospital courtyard. Horses were being removed from their shafts, fussed over and gently led away. Drivers, grooms, carters and the rest were taken to the dining room. Sally Peters and Beaumont quickly re-joined the Sea General and his guests and there was much conversation about the merits and difficulties of their respective journeys. The two women were wrapped together in themselves and their conversation was largely kept low between them. As they all found their personal comfort restored, they began to survey their temporary home. Charles Beaumont came up to Ketch and took him aside for a private conversation.

"I know you retain grave concerns for the Sea General's safety, but here in the hospital I think we can keep him secure from harm. I have had a discussion with Governor Halsey about arrangements, but we feel your approval in necessary."

"Thank you, Charles, this is re-assuring, but I would like to bring Captain Treddager into our conversation for he also is most concerned for the Sea General, especially after the two attempts on his life He greatly fears there will be further dangers ahead."

Beaumont called Treddager over and the three men left the dining hall and moved into the large open space that was the main entrance of the hospital. He paused at the foot of the grand staircase and outlined his proposals.

"This staircase leads to the first floor where there are five rooms. Three are to the right- hand side and are locked and unoccupied. They are full of furniture and equipment Their windows are both locked and barred. "

He looked expectantly at Ketch and Treddager but they had as yet no comment to make,

"At the far left is a room which is especially reserved for patients who, for whatever reason, have to be kept in isolation, some for fever or say for madness. It also is a secure room with windows locked and barred. I propose that we place the Sea General safely into that room. The other room on the floor is next to The Sea General's but has no access to the corridor. Its only door connects with that of the Sea General. It will have washing and privy facilities for him alone. It also is fully secured. Furthermore, I am suggesting that the rest of the company, including ourselves, sleep below. The ground floor has sufficient accommodation for us."

Again, he waited for comments.

"What about the floor above?" Asked Ketch.

"Thank you," replied Beaumont.

"That comes next. The floor above is totally occupied by servants and kitchen staff in two dormitories. They have a separate staircase, that goes down to the first floor, which is only occupied by the Sea General and then on to the ground floor. The Governor has given the strictest of instructions that the occupants of the top floor are only to use their own staircase, no short cuts down the main staircase from the first floor. For them the first floor is totally out of bounds. All these people are well known and of good standing. I believe that with these arrangements we can sleep easily tonight, knowing the Sea General is secure."

Beaumont had finished and it was now time that Ketch or Captain Treddager to make a contribution.

Treddager waited for Ketch. He himself thought Beaumont had done a good job. He could see little fault with it. Ketch stroked his nose. He thought it seemed appropriate but the Sea General could be vulnerable to anyone going up either staircase and straight in to the Sea General's room. "If I could make two suggestions Charles. First, I would like to sleep in the room closest to the bottom of the main staircase and secondly that we station one of the Sea General's own seamen to sleep outside his door. Other than that, I can think of nothing else that can be done.

"Capital!" Cried Captain Treddager.

"Those seamen would die for him, either of them would suffice. I shall make the choice myself."

Beaumont's face was all smiles.

"Well gentlemen, we are all agreed."

In fact, such had been the squabbling as to who should undertake that duty, its resolution required the Sea

General to have two protectors sleeping on the floor outside his room. As his security arrangements had been agreed the Sea General tried his best to join in with the post dinner conversation, to play the role of the host. Beaumont grew concerned that he would have difficulty getting the Sea General to have an early night. It was the arrival of the doctor that finally produced change. Governor Halsey had rousted out his senior doctor, Doctor Belpin. He took the Sea General into a side room and insisted that only Beaumont and Ketch together with Governor could be present at the examination. Once the Sea General was seated the doctor carefully exposed the wound. There was muttering and some shaking of the head.

"Nasty, painful but not serious, eh! Doctor," suggested the Sea General.

The doctor ignored the remark and took from his bag a small jar of cream that was applied to the damaged shoulder.

"This salve is messy, but try to keep as much in place as possible. This is a serious wound, You, must have rest if it is to heal. Certainly, no carousing through the night. If further infection is encouraged there can be no going to sea.

The Sea General remonstrated strongly with the doctor.

"Not carousing, just some light hearted conversation with friends".

The doctor was not to be bullied by any patient.

"You have a long and demanding journey ahead of you. Ignore my advice if you wish. I will not be responsible for the demise of England's General at Sea. "

The Sea General was not used to being denied, but he did listen to the strongly explained dangers he faced. As a result, he kept his post dinner conversation short, although there was some grumbling and mumbling about "force majeure" Beaumont, with feigned deafness, ignored his complaints and soon had him to the first floor, where he was finally, as Beaumont put it. "stowed away."

By the time Beaumont had returned, given Hedges and Brown their instructions, the atmosphere in the dining room was one of contentment. There was general agreement amongst drivers, grooms and company that as an overnight stop, the Hospital had met the bill. As the evening wore on some got up and moved amongst the tables conversing with friends and colleagues Ketch took the opportunity to catch words with both Tull and Holditch.

"Well, Tull, you have had a pretty easy time of it. True! You have been shot at, but that apart, all that has been required of you has been to sit in the Sea General's coach for two days."

Ketch's remark had just sufficient truth behind it, that Tull felt bound to lay before Ketch the real nature of his efforts.

"True enough for today Ketch, but all day yesterday, for the most part I was subject to religious cross-examination. The Sea General fully knows his bible through and through and we spent most of the journey examining his favourite texts. The

147

only change of topic was how do we transform seamen from sinners into god-fearing men. I tell you Ketch, I have never known such pressure. At every moment I felt in danger of being exposed as a fraud.

Ketch gave Tull a slap on the shoulder.

"Well, Tull, you are still with us as Chaplain Tull and the Sea General seems to have really taken you to heart. He tries to include you in all his conversations."

Tull would not be mollified.

"Quite so Ketch. I have no respite. How will I last to Portsmouth?"

Tull did not get an answer for Ketch wandered away and sat down next to Holditch, who had in turn moved away from his usual associates, on the excuse of having trouble in lighting his pipe.

"Anything to report?" Asked Ketch.

"Well Captain, I have kept my eye on the clerk, Michael Gough, you remember the Catholic. We have to face it Ketch that these Spanish agents will all be Catholics."

"Yes Holditch," replied Ketch.

"But not all Catholics are Spanish agents."

Holditch was not convinced.

"Ah! Well! There was something else about this clerk. I saw him walking and chatting with some local when we were passing through one of the larger villages. He may have been giving or receiving instructions."

Ketch just shrugged.

"I expect you have walked through a village yourself, taking up conversation with the locals."

Holditch had to agree, that he had from time to time done that, but he wanted to move on to another matter that he wished to recount.

"Something I noticed this evening and I am surprised that it escaped your attention."

He waited to make sure he had Ketch's full attention "That Captain Treddager brought that attractive woman, Molly, with him and everything was lovely and friendly at the start. But he has spoken very little to her this evening. She has spent her time with the other one, Sally, laughing and flirting with the drivers and grooms. I think they may have fallen out."

Ketch was surprised at the acuteness of Holditch's observations. He had himself seen this change, but he was very unsure as to the reason, but he did not want to question all Holditch's report to him.

"Add her to your list of people to watch."

He left Holditch to find Charles Beaumont, he wanted to see where exactly he was to spend the night. As the evening wore on parts of the dining room were converted into sleeping areas for all but the Sea General's guests. Ketch had his room close to the bottom of the Grand staircase, next to that shared by Beaumont and Treddager. Molly Mosley and Sally Peters shared the next room along the corridor. The final room had been intended for Tull, but at the last moment he was moved into the dining room, so that Governor Halsey could sleep on

149

the premises. It did not take long for the fatigues of the day, warmth and good food, to lead all the travellers settling down to a relaxed sleep.

Whilst the travellers had been enjoying their evening, the hospital and its courtyard had been under observation by Raphael. In their brief discussion, Michel had advised that as the Sea General that day was no longer with the convoy, he, Raphael, should ride on to Guildford and find lodgings close to the hospital. He had also been anxious to advise that it would be useful if such lodgings enjoyed a clear view of the hospital.

Raphael had enjoyed a ride without pressure and indeed found lodgings that met Michel's suggestions. From his bedroom window he had watched the arrival of the waterway party and the subsequent arrival of the convoy. He especially took note that the man who had initiated the rush towards him before Kingston was once again amongst the travellers. He was relieved to witness the arrival of Mary. Michel had told him that there were only two women amongst the Sea General's guests and that she was the blonde one. He relaxed fully when the convoy arrived and he had sight of Michel himself. He felt they had all done well and were present together at the key moment. He watched with diminished interest Beaumont showing everybody into the hospital demanding "no unnecessary unloading of baggage."

Chapter Eleven   Michel and Mary

Ketch awoke in the dark to a loud crash and scream. He could
not immediately remember where he was. He stumbled out of
bed, desperately searching for his flint and steel. After a few
moments he found a candle and with some fumbling managed
to light it. He carefully opened the door of his room to find
Governor Halsey looking down at a body of a man. The
Governor was holding a lantern and Ketch cursed himself for
not having similarly prepared for night time danger.

"Surely not! It was impossible."

His felt sick with concern as to who was there and
what had happened. He heard footfall behind him as others
emerged from their rooms. He knew they also would want
answers. He moved up close to the Governor and looked
down. The combined light of candle and lantern clearly
showed the body and face of a man who was a stranger to
him.

"I'm afraid he is dead, Ketch, broken neck."

Ketch could not help but be engulfed in a flood of
relief. It was not the Sea General and, as far as he could see, it
was not one of their party. The Governor continued softly.

"It is one of my young servants. He has not been with
us long. Why did he disobey my orders?"

Ketch did have some idea and slowly the answer
came to the Governor. Ketch's candle light, lifted high,

revealed a broken, ceramic chamber pot. There was a heavy smell of urine on the stairs. The Governor sorrowfully shook his head.

"He was probably bullied to get rid of it. An unhappy accident."

Ketch was looking uncertain.

"Possibly Governor, but there may be other explanations."

By now the Governor and Ketch had been joined by Beaumont and Captain Treddager and the corridor behind was full of men and women anxious to know what had happened.

"Get them back to their rooms Beaumont," demanded Ketch.

"Tell them an unhappy accident, a hospital servant slipped and fell when carrying a chamber pot."

He looked for confirmation to the Governor, who readily agreed.

"Yes! That's probably the best explanation."

He lowered his voice.

"You have other ideas. If so, please sort this out quickly."

By now there were lights at the top of the stairs. The two seamen, Hedges and Brown, who had slept in darkness, had finally managed to light their candles. The Sea General had opened his door, but his two guardians had respectfully ordered him back.

"Stay where you are," called out Ketch.

"Do not come down the stairs."

He turned to the Governor.

"May I request that once Mr Beaumont has cleared the corridor, yourself and Captain Treddager remove the body and then return with as much light as you can find. Then we may examine the staircase.

He then called back up to the seamen.

"Do not allow any of the servants on the top floor come to the head of the Grand staircase. Explain this is the direct order of Governor Halsey. If necessary, they must use their own staircase."

At that moment the Governor and Captain Treddager were carrying away the body of the young man, but Halsey was able to nod his agreement to the order. Ketch had a moment whilst he waited for more light and Molly Mosley and Sally Peters opened their door and timidly called out.

"What has happened, are we in danger?"

"Just an accident," replied Ketch.

"No need to be concerned, it would be best if you remain in your room until we call you to breakfast. There is no danger."

Ketch felt that he should really assure himself of the Sea General's safety. He called out to the seamen on the floor above and was relieved at the reply, that all was well with the Sea General in his room. Waiting for the Governor to return he found Tull at his side.

"An accident is unlikely Ketch. This was meant for the Sea General."

Ketch could not help but agree.

"I suspect some trip wire or similar device on the stairs We must check it and safely get him down here amongst us."

Tull thought it was important to mention another key point.

"This murdered young man must be a victim of one of our party, Ketch,." and that means that at least one Spanish agent is amongst us."

Tull's statement was true but obvious and Ketch found it irksome. It was not his usual behaviour. He had long valued Tull and Holditch as both military comrades and fellow agents. His failure to protect the Sea General was getting at his normal good humour.

"I must get back on track, grumbling at Tull and Holditch is not helpful and Captain Treddager will be enraged."
The Governor arrived with two more lanterns and some candles and, by their light, Tull and Ketch slowly crawled up the wooden stairs, with hands outstretched to detect any obstacle or trip wire. It was an unpleasant task for as they rose up the stairway, they found the quantity of urine increased. Watched by the Governor from below and the two seamen above, they pressed on ignoring both the odour and their discomfort. It was four steps from the top where Ketch found the evidence of murder, a thin length of rope tightly stretched across the stairs.

"I have it," he declared.

He looked up at the two seamen above him.

154

"I want one of you to descend just above me where you will find a length of rope stretched across the stairs, cut all of it and bring it to me."

He and Tull stood up and stretched their backs.

"I will wait until that seaman has collected the evidence. I need you with the other one, to collect the Sea General and his belongings and take him to my room. You had better find Captain Treddager and get him to sit with the Sea General and re-assure him that all is well."

It was seaman, Brown, who brought the rope to Ketch for inspection. They had barely started when Governor Halsey joined them.

"I must have that Ketch. A man has been murdered in my hospital. The coroner must be informed and a cause of death declared and matters of responsibility decided. This rope is critical evidence."

Ketch and Brown had an initial examination and Brown handed it on to the Governor. At that moment Ketch noticed Captain Treddager talking to Molly Mosley who moved away to the dining hall. Ketch beckoned him over.

"The Sea General is on his way down. I am putting him into my room. I'm relying on you and chaplain Tull to keep him safe."

The Captain looked grim faced and tight lipped.

"I'll keep him safe Ketch."

It did not take the Sea General too long to arrive at the top of the stairs and limp his way down to the safety provided by Treddager and Tull. Ketch noticed his slow gait down the stairs and the evident favouring of his right arm. He also found that seaman Brown was at his elbow with the thin bits of rope still in his hand.

"Begging your pardon sir, but Governor Halsey agreed that I should show you this ."

Mary Sharpe entered the dining hall and sat down beside her fellow Spanish agent Michael Gauvin.

"Michel, it is time for us to go. The dead man on the stairs was you're doing, she asked.?"

A raised eyebrow from Michel confirmed it was so. "Captain Treddager has grown cold towards me and has started asking me questions about the Sea General's wound. He is growing suspicious and Captain Ketch always seems to be close by me. Our efforts so far have not succeeded but if we get away now we can try again."

"Then we must go now Mary whilst there is still some confusion about the murder. I have managed a word with Raphael. He should be close by looking out for us and I still have hopes that your poison will work."

They both rose to their feet. Mary took Michel by the arm

"Come to my room Michel. I have some things I must collect.

Michel was concerned about this. He also had things to collect. Now the decision had been made he was anxious to get away. Nevertheless, he followed Mary to her room.

Captain Treddager was sitting in silence alongside the Sea General and chaplain Tull. After a long-drawn-out sigh, he turned to Tull.

"This is no good. Three attempts on the Sea General's life in two days and no one apprehended. Every day Robert looks more uncomfortable, the pain is clearly getting worse. " He lightly touched the Sea General on the knee.

"You are looking in more pain Robert. You need to see that doctor Belpin again."

Tull was surprised there was no resistance from the Sea General to the idea of a doctor, He obviously was suffering.

Captain Treddager spoke harshly to Tull.

"We must get him away at once, your man Ketch has been unable to protect him and he needs a doctor."

Tull, responded quickly.

"My man Ketch," he exclaimed.

Treddager was adamant.

"Well, you could have killed the Sea General a dozen times and besides, Ketch would not be on his own in this. You have been the Sea General's best protection throughout."

Tull was becoming concerned at Captain Treddager's rush of energy.

"Well, Treddager, what are you proposing?"

Treddager lowered his voice to a whisper determined that what he had to say was for Tull only.

"We need to move him away from the convoy to a place of safety. That is urgent. He needs a doctor. That is urgent. So, now we take him in his coach to a doctor, Doctor Belpin.

Last night I questioned Governor Halsey about Belpin. He was fulsome of his medical skills. Apparently, he is infrequent in his attendance at the hospital. He prefers his rural practice, around his home in the village of Wendover Parva. It is a fair haul from here, being but two miles North of Hindhead; but if we go now the horses are rested, the coach is waiting outside. There is nothing to stop us getting away."

He looked at Tull with a hard determination in his eyes.

"Can you handle a coach and horses?

This was a big moment in Tull's life. Always Ketch had been there taking the decisions as soldier and agent. He had. of course, worked on his own, but he had always been told exactly what was required. This was a decision he had to make on his own. He caught the eye of the Sea General who just looked at him…… waiting. Tull did not dither, but he gave the question a long moment's thought.

"Treddager is no more a danger to the Sea General than I am. The Sea General needs both safety and medical attention and Ketch has a body on his hand and Spanish agents at large. He will understand what we are doing.

He reached for the Sea General and looked at Treddager.

"Yes, I can manage horses. Help me get him into the coach.".

Michel and Mary went straight to the room occupied by Molly and Sally Peters. They found Sally sitting on her bed fearful of the events in the corridor.

158

"Molly what is happening? Who has been killed? We must go back to London. I do not like it here."

She stood up from the bed and moved to comfort Molly with a hug. Over Molly' shoulder she was surprised to see Michel.

"Sorry Sally," whispered Molly.

She released herself from Sally's arms, drew back her fist and gave Sally a mighty blow to the head. Sally fell back on to the bed pole- axed. Michel looked astonished.

"Did we need to do that Mary>

"Yes Michel! We have no time for explanations or to seek cooperation. There are things I need. I am wearing a pretty white dress and I am a golden -haired harlot. I will be seen leaving."

She reached into a cupboard and pulled out a leather case.

"New and different clothes, but for later."

She laid the case on a side table and returned to the cupboard. There, she drew out a large dark blue cloak that she had worn for the river journey. It entirely hid her dress. Next, to Michel's astonishment, she pulled off her glorious blonde wig and threw it on the bed beside Sally.

"A present Sally. It is saying sorry."

She turned to Michel.

"I am going. Are you coming with me.?"

Michel was amazed at the transformation from the removal of the wig. Golden haired Molly Mosley had become the greasy slatern of Billingsgate with her dark, thick hair hanging in clumps.

"You go. I must also get some things."

First Mary stepped out into the corridor where she saw Ketch and the Governor examining something closely. She attracted no attention and made her way to the dining hall. No one recognised her or spoke to her as she walked through to the kitchens. A servant girl directed her out to the privy.

"It's pretty nasty. Are you sure you want to go?"

Mary nodded and waved a hand and stepped out into an alley way. To her left she saw a privy door and to her right a double bolted, high wooden, gate. Easily released she found the alley was a side exit from the hospital and led into its courtyard. She headed for the road.

Ketch had initially tried to push seaman Brown away, but his persistence would not be denied.

"Well! What do you want? He said, anxious to get on.

Brown held the strands of thin rope that he had cut from the sides of the stairs.

"You ought to know sir that there is something unusual about the knots used to fix the trip wire. Englishman, never use this one. For a good safe knot, we prefer the ordinary bowline, so do most of the world's sailors. Both these knots here are a bowline with an extra half hitch. The country that uses these is the Dutch merchant marine. They like to tell the world that it is better, safer. These knots were tied by a Dutchman. Does that help sir?" The Governor did not take my meaning."

"By God, Brown. This is important, I think both you and I know someone with that background. I think Governor Halsey will now have a story for the Coroner."

Telling Brown to keep the bits of rope safe, he sped off to find Holditch. He was in the dining hall.

"Holditch! The clerk Michael you are suspicious of him?

"Yes Ketch. He is a Catholic, and in my eyes a possible Spanish agent."

Ketch wanted confirmation of the conversation held by Holditch, Brown and Michael in Kingston.

"You said he had worked in and for the Dutch merchant marine. Well, the knots on the fatal trip wire are commonly known as Dutch knots, mainly used by those with that experience. I think that is enough to question master Michael. "

There was no sign of him in the dining hall or the main corridor. They hurried into the main entrance and then out into the courtyard. Here there was early activity as members of the convoy prepared for departure. There, fifty yards away, astride the top of a cart was Michael, struggling to undo the ropes of a tarpaulin. As soon as he saw the two men coming towards him, he jumped down from the cart and ran towards the courtyard exit. Two figures appeared to be waiting for him.

"Stop!" Cried Ketch. He reached into his pocket for his pistol. It was a reflex action and he cursed when he realised it was futile. It was not loaded. It was rarely used and then only when danger was certain.

"Come Holditch! We can catch him! They began running towards the exit when the Sea General's coach crossed their path with a heavy momentum, they only just avoided serious injury. Gathering speed, it lumbered on towards the exit.

"Sorry Ketch," cried Tull from the driver's seat.

"We must get on."

Ketch and Holditch were bewildered by events.

"What was Tull doing? Where was he going"

He was equally confused when Captain Treddager's head appeared at the coach window.

"It's alright Ketch. Do not worry."

For a few moments Ketch and Holditch just stared after the coach as it rolled away. They realised that all hope of securing Michael was gone. The exit on to the road was now empty.

"I sometimes think I am in some strange world," muttered Ketch.

"Come on Holditch let us see what Michael needed so desperately."

The two men got on to the cart and began to release the tarpaulin. They found a number of bundles that contained property of some of the travellers. They began to lift and feel for things other than clothing. They opened a few that felt unusual but found nothing of interest. Then they picked up a bundle that was much heavier than the others. They found clothes, some quill pens, a book and at the very bottom, wrapped in rags a gilded, wheel lock Spanish pistol. Holditch stroked it admiringly.

162

This is lovely Ketch. The finest I have ever seen."

Ketch just grunted. He had other thoughts.

"Well! We have definitely identified one of the Spanish agents. "

Chapter Twelve   Explanations

Clutching the Spanish pistol, Ketch retraced his steps to the hospital entrance. At their top he handed it to Holditch.

"Here, you take this Holditch. It is a fine gun. Look after it and if I were you, I would collect from his bag in the cart pistol balls and any other bits and pieces. You may need to use it before we are finished with these Spanish agents."

Holditch was delighted.

"Thank you, Ketch. I shall value this. Such a pistol gives a man confidence,"

Ketch was pleased at the pleasure Holditch found in his gift.

"Never mind that. Do not let it lead you into trouble. Now, get your things together and find yourself one of the spare horses. I will inform Beaumont that you are working for me. We have got to catch up with Tull, Treddager and the Sea General."

Having seen Holditch heading for the cart, he moved off towards the dining hall. The hall had the colours of early morning light when dawn and candles came together, with small areas of bright light competing with a wider greyness from the high windows. Despite the accident on the stairs, for many of the convoy it was just another early start to the day. There was breakfast to be eaten, belongings to be secured and horses to be prepared. Ketch felt tired and unbalanced. He had been woken less than an hour ago in pitch dark. He had examined a body, searched a staircase, consulted on knots, re-assured a Sea General, chased a Spanish agent and it was only first light and breakfast. He looked across to the table where the night before the Sea General and his guests had dined together. This morning only Beaumont and Sally Peters were settled there. Beaumont looked bemused with a distant air and his particular lady friend had her head pulled down to hide her damaged face. They looked very forlorn, but at the sight of Ketch Beaumont brightened.

"Ketch, thank God you are still here. What has happened? The Sea General has left with Treddager and that chaplain fellow, Tull. I have no instructions, no idea what to do. I am missing a clerk and Sally's companion Molly has also disappeared. For no apparent reason she struck Sally such a blow that she was knocked down unconscious. She has taken her belongings and left a stupid wig."

There was a strong emotion in Beaumont's words of having been badly done to and Ketch had to admit to himself that he had cause.

"I have been abandoned also, Charles, , left behind to explain matters to you and Governor Halsey. So! I am going to join you for breakfast and then if you can arrange Sally in some comfortable spot, I will find the Governor and explain all I know."

Over breakfast, Ketch kept the conversation focussed upon moving the Sea General's stores to Portsmouth. Beaumont took the opportunity to outline to Ketch some of the changes he was making to the composition of the convoy.

"I cannot believe that my clerk has run off with Molly Mosley, but nevertheless, he is missing. As a result, I shall move my other clerk Turner into my carriage and send Sally back to London in the clerk's carriage. It was hired for fourteen days and the driver and groom are most amenable to the change. Frankly, Sally just wants to go home. At the moment, that leaves Captain Treddager's carriage empty, but for now we will keep it with the convoy. It is not my responsibility, Ketch. He will have to deal with it. "

Ketch was happy to confirm that he thought Beaumont was acting in the Sea General's best interests. When all had finished breakfast, Beaumont escorted Sally to her room and suggested that she rest on the bed.

"I will lock the door Sally and have a seaman stationed outside. You will be quite safe and when I have finished with Governor Halsey and Captain Ketch we will discuss all the arrangements for your return to London."

Sally was broken in spirit and acceded to all Beaumont's suggestions.

The three men met in the Governor's office. Ketch had two priorities. He wanted the Governor to feel satisfied that he had the full story of all recent events, so that the Coroner's court would be satisfied. Then he wished to be away as soon as possible to catch up with Tull, Treddager and the Sea General. He immediately took up his account.

"Governor, three Spanish agents have been seeking to kill Sea General, Robert Blake, on his way to take command of the fleet at Portsmouth. His intention, a mistaken one as it turned out, was to travel with all his necessary stores and equipment in a convoy of coach carriages and carts. Mr Beaumont was to manage the convoy and the Secretary to the Council of State, John Thurloe, required myself to manage the Sea General's security, given that he had refused the Lord Protector's offer of a troop of Ironsides."

Ketch could sense that, at this point, Beaumont wished to intervene but he motioned him to be silent.

"From the start, this has been a poor arrangement, it has provided ample opportunity for the Spanish agents to infiltrate amongst us. Already there have been three attempts on the Sea General's life, a pistol shot, a stabbing and the incident on the stairs last night, that led to the death of one of your servants. We have identified two of the agents, one of whom, masqueraded as one of Mr Beaumont's clerks. He was known to us as Michael Gough and was responsible for the death on the stairs. The other was a lady friend of Captain Treddager's ,one you have met, called Molly Mosley".

The Governor could not hold back his astonishment.

"You mean that attractive young woman with golden hair was a spy, a killer."

Ketch grimaced.

"Yes Governor, we were all deceived."

He returned to his explanation.

"Unfortunately, they have both eluded capture but these are the facts as we understand them. Out evidence for the clerk is that he was an undisclosed Roman Catholic, familiar with the unusual knots used on the trip wire and in possession of a

Spanish pistol. When all this became known he fled. The woman all along has been in disguise, the Sea General was stabbed by a poisoned ladies hairpin and she regularly, unknown to us, bathed his wound in a dilution similar to the poison found on the pin."

Ketch leaned back in his chair. He had given all he could to the Governor as fast and as clear as he could. Governor Halsey had listened with widening eyes.to Ketch's account.

"I have no doubt that this will frighten our citizens, Ketch. Three Spanish agents at large in our town is not a story they will want to hear, but I am sure it is enough for the Coroner. May I presume to give him only what is necessary. Keep the concerning details to a minimum."

Ketch was pleased at the Governor's discretion. He had no wish to frighten the citizens of Guildford.

Charles Beaumont felt that he just had to speak.

 "Yes Ketch, all this I understand, but what has happened to the Sea General? Has Captain Treddager gone mad, what about this chaplain Tull? As far as I can see, he and Treddager have kidnapped the Sea General. What do you know of this Ketch."

These last words were accompanied with heavy undertones of both complaint and accusation. Ketch was not surprised. He would have felt the same.

"Charles, let me assure you that I know absolutely nothing of this. The Sea General's coach nearly knocked me down and helped the clerk escape from me. I am not at all happy about this. You must remember that to the powers in the land, I am the person who is responsible for the Sea General's safety. I do not want him out of my sight. However, in two matters I can give you some consolation. I believe that Captain Treddager's actions are born of a deep concern for his friend. He has been gravely upset at the number of attempts on the Sea General's life in such a short period of time. I think he is trying to get him away from a most dangerous situation."

Charles Beaumont again wanted to reinforce his concerns but this time Governor Halsey intervened.

"Let him finish Charles."

Ketch, threw a thank you look to the Governor.

"The second point Charles is that Chaplain Tull is one of my agents and has been from the start. To succeed it had to be kept a secret from the Sea General, Captain Treddager and yourself. It has been my consolation throughout, that he has been constantly by the Sea General' side."

Beaumont was all surprise.

"But he was a very religious man, an honest man, he knew his bible as well as the Sea General."

Ketch gave his first laugh of the day.

"All that is true. But he does work for me"

Beaumont sat back in his chair, for the moment bereft of speech. Governor Halsey then leaned forward to make his contribution.

"In the matter of Captain Treddager, the Sea General and chaplain Tull, I believe I can be helpful. You remember that I called in Doctor Belpin to tend the Sea General's wound. Let me first tell you something about him."

The Governor wrinkled his brow, gathering his thoughts.

"He is not one of our regular doctors, but we do use his outstanding services for very special cases. Last night he was available as a result of visiting friends in Guilford. As a favour to me he agreed to tend the Sea General. He normally only practises from his own home in Westonville, a small village, two miles North of Hindhead, off the Portsmouth road. He is very wealthy, takes few patients and sees himself as more of a scientist than a rural doctor. Well, when he was administering to the Sea General, he mentioned that he could have been more useful had he been at home in his own surgery with his own equipment."

At this point the Governor broke off and gave an apologetic gesture.

"Much of our own equipment was destroyed in our recent fire. Well, in the evening Captain Treddager inquired about Doctor Belpin's actual address, which I obviously gave him. I anticipated that later today he would in fact seek a second consultation."

He looked reassuringly at Charles Beaumont.

"I would be very surprised if that was not his destination."

Both Ketch and Beaumont were content that Treddager and Tull's dramatic leaving was now not such a danger to the Sea General. Governor Halsey continued the conversation.

"I believe that we each must now get on with our own particular tasks. I have no doubt Ketch that you will want to follow the Sea General. Beaumont, you have a reduced convoy to take on to Portsmouth and I have my own sad duties to perform.

Raphael ushered both Michel and Mary up to his room in the lodging house. He gave them strict instructions to stay away from the window, for his lodgings faced directly on to the hospital courtyard entrance. He placed them both on his bed and himself took up the only chair in the room. Michel, as their nominal leader, thought it his task to review their performance and start thinking about what to do next.

"When De Ritter first outlined to us our central task, he stressed that each one of us should act as individuals quite independently of the others. He was firm in his view, that our success may require three or four attempts to succeed."

He paused for a moment. There were encouraging nods of agreement

"Well, we have followed our instructions and managed three attempts and to date we have failed."

He checked himself.

"I am sorry, Mary, the wound you inflicted may yet kill him, but we cannot be sure of this."

He waited and looked to them for a response. None replied. They knew Michel had more to say. He continued,

"We could leave matters there, hope for the best and return home. But if Robert Blake recovers, we may not come out of this very well. In fact, De Ritter could charge us with deliberate inaction. So, I say we go on and finish this job, once and for all, but not as three individuals, but as a team, a group working together, using our skills in harmony."

This time there was a response. Raphael was the first to speak.

"I agree Michel. I find it difficult moving about this sorry country with its dismal weather. I miss the support and advice of others and to date my only contribution has been a single pistol shot."

Raphael was never pleased to discuss personal weakness, but he was certain that any further contribution he would make, to be successful, would require the support of his companions. Mary Sharpe looked at both men. She was not impressed.

"They are not very promising. Michel has a good brain, but is physically weak and frightens easily. Raphael is rash and only good for riding around the country, shooting at people. But he is the only one amongst us whose face is not known to members of the convoy. This may be the only advantage we have,"

Trying to be cheerily positive, Mary agreed to Michel's proposal.

Having decided this issue, Michel thought that his own and Mary's experiences required somewhere more pleasant and comfortable than Raphael's room.

"Are we safe here, Raphael. I feel uncomfortable this close to the hospital and we have much to discuss. Is there a tavern or inn, where we can find a private room?"

Despite Mary's doubts, Raphael in this matter, proved to be an excellent partner.

"I dined at the "Lamb and Cross" last night. It will meet our needs I am sure."

Anxious for greater safety and comfort, within half an hour, they were in a snug room, sitting around a fine table with food and drink laid out before them. Once more Michel led off the discussion.

"What are we going to do now? How are we going to kill this Sea General?"

Chapter Thirteen   Dr Belpin

The unexpected departure of the Sea General's coach took place in the early dawn of a March morning. As such there was very little wheeled transport on the road and Tull was able to move the heavy coach up to a respectable speed. Midst the clatter of horses' hooves and the rattling of the coach Tull could hear the groans of the Sea General. Tull hated being the cause of such suffering but he remembered the words of a white-faced Captain Treddager as they lifted the Sea General into the coach.

"I am fearful of his death Tull, fearful for the navy and fearful for the country. We must succeed, we must find this doctor."

Captain Treddager sat in the coach next to the Sea General, holding him steady against the leaps and bumps as the coach hurried along. He abandoned his position only the once to stick his head out of the window, and shout out Doctor Belpins address. He repeated it until Tull in turn, returned it accurately back to him.

"Tull! At the village of Wentonville take the right fork and after two hundred yards turn right again and there on the left is a large, double fronted house. Go straight into its courtyard."

Tull knew there was a day's journey ahead of then, but as the hours passed he began to lose any firm grasp of time and distance. He just held tightly in his mind....

"The right fork at the village of Wentonville."

Through gritted teeth, he cursed each disappointment. As a rider Tull was good with horses but his experience as a coachman was limited. Of course, he had seen it done, but that was all. On this journey prayer came very easily to his lips, as did words of a stronger nature. It was also proving to be a long day for the horses and every few hours, to Captain Treddager's dismay, stops for rest and water were required. Both Tull and Treddager had expected to hear the sound of Ketch riding to join them but as the fork of Wentonville finally came into view, there had been no sign of him.

Tull was happy to slow the coach's pace at the fork and prepare carefully for the right-hand turn. The prospect of missing the turn was not to be considered, for he knew that successfully reversing coach and horses was beyond him. However, all was achieved and the large house on the left was soon in sight. He felt an enormous relief when he could enter the courtyard and draw the coach to a halt outside the house with its name board "Larch House." He stumbled down from the driving seat and with heavy legs stepped up to the front door and hammered loudly in a manner he hoped would definitely summon its inhabitants without annoying them. A manservant came to the door and in a tone lacking all courtesy, demanded to know who was bothering the doctor. Tull was in no mood for uppity servants. He grabbed the young man by the shoulders and shook him.

"Tell Dr Belpin that Sea General Robert Blake is at his door and in serious need of medical attention.

"Captain Treddager was gently easing Robert Blake out of the coach, but on hearing the servant's words, gave such a roar of rage that the servant fled back into the house. Dr Belpin came to the door with a frown on his face. He did not recognise Tull at all, but on seeing Captain Treddager struggling with the Sea General, he understood the situation at once.

"Ah! I thought I might see you again, but not quite so early. Please bring him inside. We will go into my back room, the one I call my laboratory."

Dr Belpin was a lean man, thin in face and body. His clothes were dark, but across his waistcoat was a fine gold chain that disappeared into a waistcoat pocket, hinting of a heavy gold watch within. This hint of colour, encouraged the eye to observe a well powdered wig and shoes sporting silver buckles. His manner was one of confidence and kindness. Tull could see that his very presence was a comfort to Captain Treddager.

"I suggest you two gentlemen go into my parlour and take your rest whilst I examine the Sea General."

Captain Treddager felt he had to establish an important point with the doctor.

"Dr Belpin I value your help enormously, but I must know of any treatment. There will be those that, whatever happens, will want to know that all possible has been done for him."

Dr Belpin, looked marginally amused.

"I know he is a great man, but do all our own lives, rest on his? Nevertheless, fear not Captain, after my examination which you can watch if you will, if there is need for treatment, I will explain it to you. "

Tull was quite happy to leave matters to the doctor and made his way to find the parlour. The doctor and Captain Treddager gently led the Sea General into his laboratory. This was a large well-lit room with benches and tables around all the walls. On these were a range of instruments of brass and wood, together with an array of glass jars and tubes. A quick glance from Captain Treddager convinced him that he had no idea as to what activities were undertaken in this room. It did, however, reassure him that the doctor was a learned man and a man of science. The two men removed the Sea Generals coat, waistcoat, shirt and undergarments. The wound looked puffy and red but the same as the night before.
"Well, the salve has done its work and eased the infection and I hope the discomfort, but the poison is still there and untreated, It will get worse. We have still much to do."

Captain Treddager, in the form of a question, dared a medical suggestion.

"Will you cut and hope to drain it doctor?"

Doctor Belpin frowned.

"I am not ready for that Captain."

Both men were surprised when the Sea General spoke. For Captain Treddager his voice for the last two days had largely been for the registering of pain.

"Go ahead doctor. Do what you have to do and Treddager, out!"

Captain Treddager looked about him, hoping the doctor would insist that he stay. But no such help arrived. Giving a mournful look he left the room, like Tull looking for the parlour. Dr Belpin smiled.

No General, there will be no cutting and draining. There will be pain, but not that of the knife. Have you heard of White Clay?"

Ketch stood with Holditch in the centre of the hospital courtyard. watching Beaumont organising wagons, carriages and carts, drivers and carters for the departure to Hindhead. The start day of their journey, back in London, had been frosty with deep cold and hard roads. Today a thaw had well and truly taken charge. A fresh wind with rain blowing erratically seemed to be the weather to be endured on the convoy's third day of travel. There could be mud ahead. Beside Ketch, Holditch continued to examine his Spanish pistol.

"This is beautiful Ketch, such craftmanship. I have never had anything so fine. This means no more misfires and real accuracy. It is worth a fortune."

"Yes! Yes! Holditch! Stop waving it about. You risk drawing the attention of those who would quite happily relieve you of it."

Holditch mumbled something about they could try, but he followed Ketch's advice, stuck the pistol into his waistband and buttoned over it his leather coat.

"I must have a word with Beaumont," said Ketch.

"He has a new host of worries."

Beaumont was on horseback giving instructions and seeing that they were being carried out. But a wave from Ketch drew his attention.

"Charles, a word please, best that you dismount a moment."

With Beaumont by his side, he outlined some concerns about the overall state of affairs.

"Your convoy is very different now. You are without the Sea General's coach, your clerk's coach you are sending back to London and Captain Treddager's coach is empty. You have lost a clerk and both women. This all reminds the convoy that you are on your own your supporting figures of help and authority have disappeared. You are without the Sea General himself, Captain Treddager, chaplain Tull and if I leave, along with Holditch here, in pursuit of the Sea General. There are always plenty of opportunities for dissent to break out that can always lead to outright rebellion. You may find fresh problems of discipline arising. The two seamen may protect your person, but I suspect not much else. In these wagons and carts there is much of value, furniture, naval stores of food and drink, guns and munitions, together with the Sea General's personal effects. We have some hard men amongst us who may see you as the only man preventing them from enjoying them."

"Well Ketch", snapped Beaumont.

"What do you expect me to do?"

"I want you to know Charles that Holditch and I are not chasing after the Sea General. I am confident that I know where he is. We will remain with you as part of the convoy, but

Holditch will need a horse. I think three men riding together with Hedges and Brown on foot will be enough to maintain the good order we have enjoyed so far."

Beaumont's whole body seemed to relax.

"Thank you, Ketch, this is a great weight off my mind I shall be most grateful for your assistance. I believe the Governor also mentioned to you, the full address of Doctor Belpin, Westonville, just short of Hindhead?"

"Yes. I hope we can be there at about mid-afternoon. If all has gone well, the See General will be on the road to recovery when we catch up with him."

. Having agreed on the immediate future, together they moved the convoy out on to the Portsmouth road.

The fact that the convoy was leaving without the Sea General was soon known all about the town of Guildford. Raphael decided that it could be worthwhile to watch the convoy leaving. He was surprised that he could report back to Michel that Captain Ketch, the man responsible for the Sea General's safety, had not gone on after him. Thus back in the Lamb and Cross the three Spanish agents felt they had time to plan their next move. Although all three had committed themselves to a team approach, each had their own ideas as to how much they would personally risk to see the Sea General dead. Raphael had put his name forward for the mission out of boredom and a wish to impress his uncle the General. When further details were explained to him, he saw how great would be the honour and reward for success., even if Mary or Michel had performed the final deed. However, he had no intention to secure the ending of the Sea General's life at the expense of his own.

Mary Sharpe's involvement was of a more practical nature. She had been promised freedom from imprisonment, money and the return of her daughter. She deeply cared about these things and would risk much to secure them but, as with Raphael there was no question of her sacrificing her own life.

Michel Gauvin was the Deputy Head of the Spanish Intelligence service in Southern Flanders. He had served it faithfully and successfully for some five years. He was dedicated to the forces of Catholic Spain. Though it would be hard, he hoped he had the heart to give his life in its service. None in the room understood the degree of commitment to securing the Sea General's death felt by the others. Against this background Michel began their deliberations.

"I believe that Captain Ketch has only two options. He has witnessed already three attempts on the Sea General's life. He must see that the current travel arrangements are not working. Placing the Sea General in a slow- moving convoy amidst lots of strangers was a poor decision. He will not risk this anymore. So, his first choice is to recover the Sea General from wherever he is and then choose his fastest carriage and with a few trusted companions, make a fast run straight to Portsmouth leaving the convoy to find its own way. Quick and simple. The Sea General would be in Portsmouth after a day and a half, possibly sooner."

Mary was concerned at Michel's words. It was plausible plan with a chance of success. "And his second option," she inquired.

"It is possible that the Sea General is so wounded that such a journey cannot be undertaken. In such circumstances, I would change the nature of the convoy. I would place the Sea General in his coach at its centre surrounded by wagons of armed men. Amongst his stores I have no doubt there will be guns and swords. I would break out these weapons and distribute them amongst the known trusted men. I would seek to find veteran soldiers and sailors to sign up for the journey. Such a company would see the Sea General safely to Portsmouth. It would move slowly but be formidable."

There was something of a gloomy silence in the face of Michel's analysis. It was Mary who took up the conversation.

"Do we have a chance of success with these options, two men one woman and Raphael's pistol? It is hard to see an achievement of our desired outcome."

"What we do have Mary is a significant amount of money. There are some things we can do to improve our chances."

Both Mary and Raphael were pleased that Michel had more to say and after a moment's thought he went on to outline, what he thought were the necessary actions to be taken.

"Whether the Sea General moves quickly or slowly to Portsmouth, it is vital that we can shadow his movements. So, we must first buy horses for myself and Mary. But that is not enough. There is not always going to be a comfortable tavern when we need one. We must secure better clothing, blankets for ourselves and our horses, saddle bags for food and drink. If possible, we must purchase pistols, although we must be careful about this. It is perhaps best left to later."

"We must be quick", added Mary.

"Remember the Sea General has been spirited away and this Captain Ketch and the convoy has already left. We must keep up with them."

Michel was brisk in his instructions.

"You have two hours to purchase what you need. I shall meet you outside this building in two hours. You must be ready to move".

Chapter Fourteen   Reorganisation

Sea General Robert Blake was a solitary figure sitting in a chair
in the middle of Doctor Belpin's laboratory. The doctor could be
heard in a side room preparing his patient's treatment. Captain
Treddager was out in the lane attending to the coach and horses
and keeping an eye out for Ketch, Beaumont and the convoy.
Only Tull was with the Sea General and there was an
uncomfortable silence between them. The Sea General was
hunched into himself and stripped to the waist he portrayed a
small and damaged figure. He made small gasps of pain and
could find nowhere to put his hands. At times, his left hand
moved to grasped his right shoulder, but the touch was never
welcome and returned unsettled. His face was grey with a sheen
of perspiration and his torso seemed an unhealthy white. He
was a man without comfort.

"So Tull," he said.

"You are not any kind of minister, you are one of
Thurloe's men, part of Captain Ketch's force. Well! I have been
well fooled by you all. There was no truth in our hours of talk,
everything was an act. Our conversations were meaningless.

Tull felt very hollow.

"Yes, General there has been some deception. I can only
hope for forgiveness in that it was to preserve your life. You
should know that I meant every word in our discussions
together. Yes, you have discussed your innermost religious

thoughts with me, but I have been much affected by you. I have looked into my own life and questioned my purpose. I have learnt much that was new."

The Sea General swayed with uncertainty.

"I have been sadly disappointed. For me, I thought we had a strong bond, that our convictions and our search for God's grace were the same. Our discussions on creating a godly host of Captains and men, that one day would sail into battle singing hymns and psalms, were all false. No Tull! It has been cruel of you.

"General you have taught me that such is a worthy future to strive for. When you are safe amongst your Captains and men, had I been with you and a man of the sea, I would truly have wished to be with you, your chaplain, their chaplain. That has been your impact on me"

The Sea General gave Tull a sideways look, but it was not hostile. At that moment Doctor Belpin entered the room.

"I am ready. I think it would be helpful to have your companions here with you. My experience tells me it gives a patient comfort. Where is Captain Treddager?"'

"He will be here in a moment," answered the Sea General.
Doctor Belpin turned to Tull.

"Perhaps you can help me. In that side room is my assistant, he will provide you with clean cloths, towels and basins, together with bandages and leather gloves. Bring them all here and place them on that side table."

Tull happily undertook his commission and then Captain Treddager entered the room.

"Coach and horses happily stowed away, but no sight of anyone."

He looked about him but no one seemed interested in his news.

Doctor Belpin took charge.

"With such an important patient, I am not such as most of my fellow physicians in that I will tell my patient what is going to happen."

He eyed the Sea General for any objection The Sea General sat impassive. The doctor pointed to the side room.

"In there I have an assistant preparing a poultice."

The Sea General and Captain Treddager knew about poultices as a standard treatment on both land and sea. The doctor ignored their frowns.

"Oh yes! Bread poultice, mustard poultice even comfrey poultice are all very good in their way, but limited. The poultice that is being prepared here is many, many times more effective. It is a clay. Yes gentlemen!, a clay dug up from the earth, mainly in Cornwall. It is white and its key property is that it can hold great heat for a time. Bread and mustard are fine but no comparison to what I shall use today."

He gave the Sea General what he hoped was a look of reassurance.

"Great heat means some pain and frankly General you will just have to bear it. It does not compare to what your sailors suffer under amputation, but it will be uncomfortable. After you will rest, preferably sleep and then we shall see how you have done. Are you ready sir!"

Tull and Captain Treddager made as if to hold the Sea General, but both doctor and patient waved them away. The doctor then placed himself behind his patient and on his command a young man entered gingerly carrying, a large pot of boiling water. Placed in the water was a metal tin containing a slowly bubbling white substance. This was all placed on a side table adjacent to the patient. The doctor drew a leather glove onto his left hand and had his assistant place a much-folded clean cloth on to it. With his right hand he took up a large spoon and used the back of the spoon to extract a quantity of the white substance which he placed onto the cloth. When he was satisfied that he had enough he covered the substance with another piece of cloth. Quickly, he placed the poultice on the Sea General's wound. A loud bellow filled the room followed by a string of nautical oaths, unknown to all but Captain Treddager. The Sea General was grievously hurt and pushed hard into the back of his chair. The doctor took that moment to bind the poultice firmly into place.

"We have done our work. I hear you are a godly man General and you are certainly a brave one. I will now take you upstairs to a bedroom in which you may sleep. Something I suspect you have not managed for some time."

When Dr Belpin returned downstairs, he moved Treddager and Tull back into the parlour. There were armchairs and a couch for their comfort. Once they were seated, he gave them a brief account of the state of his patient.

"It took him a while to get comfortable on the bed but sleep came very quickly. His last words to me were "" hot and throbbing doctor."" That, gentlemen, is what I hoped to hear. If we have avoided scalding him, all will be well. And now we must wait."

The doctor disappeared back into his laboratory and Tull and Treddager took their rest in the parlour but after an hour sitting, they decided to walk back down the lane to the main road to see if there was any sign of Ketch, Beaumont and the convoy. Tull in particular was anxious to see Ketch. He felt he had some explaining to do over the high- jacking of the Sea General.

The March afternoon light was beginning to fail as the convoy came into sight. It remained the dour spectacle it had been from the start. Both Ketch and Beaumont made straight for Tull and Treddager. Tull decided that it was best if Treddager explained what they had been doing.

"It was force majeure, Ketch. Three attempts on the Sea General's life in two days was one to many. I could not stand by any longer. I had to get him somewhere safe and where he could receive medical attention. I had previously seen Doctor Belpin attend to the Sea General. He was obviously a skilled physician and I secured his address from Governor Halsey. I bullied Tull to join me and he thought it was in everybody's interest to come along, As I later surmised, he was one of your men all along, I felt more comfortable about our actions."

Ketch smiled at Treddager and gave Tull a slap on the shoulder.

"It was because Tull was with you and I was told by Governor Halsey of your interest in Doctor Belpin, that I felt happy about not immediately charging after you. So, given Beaumont's need of support with the convoy I remained with them."

Tull made to speak but Ketch waved him away. "You did the right thing Tull. I had full confidence in you that yours was the right decision."

He clapped his hands, "Enough of that, where is the Sea General now?"

Treddager again took up the conversation and quickly described the journey to Doctor Belpin's house and the subsequent operation.

"Apparently, the Sea General has received a draught that will allow him to sleep through till tomorrow."

The Captain was quite pleased with his eloquence and how his activities had received everyone's approval. Ketch laughed.

" Indeed, we had some excitement of our own this morning. The trip wire was the work of the Sea General's new clerk, Michael Gough, who was undoubtedly a Spanish agent."

Ketch could not easily supress an unusual pleasure.

"It also appears that your lady friend, Molly Mosley is also a Spanish agent who had gained your confidence with makeup and a clever wig and went on to deliver poison to the Sea General by a lady's hair pin."

Captain Treddager's face twisted into disbelief, concern and then embarrassment.

"Good God Ketch!"

He turned to Beaumont desperate for some helpful comment, but none was forthcoming. Treddager was enraged with the news.

"By heaven, I hope you have the pair of them."

Ketch thought it was best that Beaumont explained how the unexpected rush of the Sea General's coach through the hospital courtyard had eased the escape of the Spanish agents. As Beaumont provided the full story, the shoulders of the Captain slumped and he appeared to loose a little of his energy and confidence.

Ketch wanted to get on.

"Enough of this, we have important decisions to make. We have our convoy here waiting and getting cold, needing instructions. Now I am clear in my own mind as to what we must do and frankly gentlemen I expect you to agree with me."

He looked at the three men as they waited for his words.

"Somewhere not far from here will be three Spanish agents seeking to execute the Sea General. We have enough evidence that they are determined and dangerous. As a result, I think that from now on all four of us must be armed and ready to use them at all times. Myself, Tull, and my third colleague Holditch have our pistols but I suspect that you gentlemen are unarmed."

Beaumont and Treddager admitted that was the case. Ketch spoke specifically to Beaumont.

"I imagine there will be arms amongst the Sea General's stores. If so, we must break them out and provide you both with pistols."

For a moment Beaumont looked uneasy at this breach of privacy, but whatever his thoughts, he saw the merit in what Ketch was saying. He moved towards the convoy, but Ketch was not yet finished.

"I think it would be prudent to arm both Hedges and Brown, each man with a cutlas, at the very least they will help in the protection of the Sea General's stores. Now, before we do all this there is the matter of protecting the Sea General and managing the convoy. The convoy must start now. It has barely two miles to finish today's journey. I am of the opinion that you Beaumont and you, Treddager, stay with the convoy and together with Hedges and Brown, see it safely to Portsmouth. Tull, myself and a porter who has been with us from the beginning called Holditch will get the Sea General to Portsmouth."

Ketch looked about him he spied Holditch standing alongside one of the carts. He pointed to him.

"That is the third man of my team Sergeant Holditch. "

He waved Holditch to join them. He was pleased that Holditch had come as a surprise to Beaumomt and Treddager and felt that consequently his own expertise had been enhanced.

Captain Treddager, however, was most unhappy.

"I will not leave the Sea General," he announced. "I have been with him too long. I am his right-hand man."

Ketch was not going to accept dissent.

"No Captain! I and my men have a direct charge from John Thurloe Secretary to the Council of State to take charge of security arrangements for the Sea General. Our position is not one based on friendship but of following and executing a state order. We will be held responsible for any failure. As the Sea General's particular friend, you can serve him best by making sure that the convoy arrives safe and sound in Portsmouth."

Treddager was not convinced, but the memory of Molly Mosley and the confusion he had caused in the hospital courtyard hung heavily upon him and reluctantly, he remained silent.

Ketch looked about him.

"I suggest we secure our arms and you begin immediately. Once the Sea General has fully recovered, we will join you for the last leg of the journey. We must then decide how best to get him safely into Portsmouth. "

The conference broke up and the parties moved off to take forward their decisions. They were totally unaware that they were being carefully watched by three riders some half a mile away. The three Spanish agents had acquired their horses and caught up with the convoy. Raphael had the best eyes and he reported what he could see.

"They appear to be gathering some stores from one of the carts and sharing them out. Oh Michel! They are pistols and cutlases."

There was an uncomfortable silence in which no one wished to comment. After a moment Raphael continued with his observations.

"Three men, one of whom is that Captain Ketch, have moved away on foot. It is not clear where they are going and now the transports are moving again."

The three agents felt it was worth a moment to discuss this new information. They found a lone copse of trees, settled themselves and their horses. They began their conference by agreeing that their decision to work together had been successful. They had achieved a certain harmony and a confidence in each other. The buying of horses and supplies had been a pleasurable common experience. Mary had surprised them when with clothes from a leather bag and much cutting and combing of hair she had transformed herself into a young gentleman. One who could ride as any other. But they had not as yet formed a collective view as what to do next. Michel felt he had to draw attention to a major problem.

"We are now better prepared to take on our main task, but we have just seen arms have been distributed amongst the leaders of the convoy and those three men who have some other task. I suspect the Sea General is nearby and those three will be protecting him as he recovers from the wound from Mary."

Mary received an approving smile from Raphael. Michel continued.

"Our problem is that we only have one pistol between us and as such in no position to take on a heavily protected Sea general."

This unpleasant but realistic remark hung in the air before them. There was a feeling of some discontent.

"We have been badly prepared for this venture Michel", voiced Mary.

"You were given a pistol but it has been left behind in Guildford. Raphael managed to buy one but that was back in

London. We have no other support and it was we ourselves who decided we should best work together."

Michel felt he had to say something encouraging.

"Well, we have been provided with plenty of money and this gives us the opportunity to purchase pistols."

"But!" interjected Mary.

"Where will we find these pistols, and when that is done, how will we track down the Sea General, who by then may have recovered from his wound?"

Michel's mind raced with the problems facing them. After a few minutes he nodded to himself and smiled.

"There is one fact we do know. The Sea General is going to Portsmouth by the Portsmouth road. He may travel light and fast or slow, strongly protected. At the moment we can travel swiftly ahead of him and arrive in Portsmouth first. He would then be coming to us. In Portsmouth we can most certainly obtain pistols and ball. Thus,armed, we can lay an ambush on the Portsmouth road in the most preferable positions. It would be our last attempt, but one with a high degree of success."

He looked at them both.

"What say you?"

Chapter   Fifteen   Disagreement

Tull, when leading Ketch and Holditch to Larch House, explained the drive from the hospital and the treatment that Doctor Belpin had provided for the Sea General

"His shoulder looked very ugly, Ketch. If seen on a battlefield you would say there was no hope. Anyway, all was done that needed to be done and the Sea General is upstairs sleeping, and that is about all I know. I am sure it will be a long sleep."

They arrived at the house and entered by the main door to find the doctor coming down stairs. Tull hurriedly introduced him to the new arrivals.

"Well gentleman your Sea General is still sleeping. I hope he will sleep through the night. If he does stir, we will take the opportunity to see if the poultice has done its work. Perhaps a light meal and then more sleep. That is, of course, if all has gone as we hope. "

Although the doctor's remarks were guarded, Ketch was relieved at Belpin's manner. He was obviously competent and in control. They all moved into the parlour and settled on the couch and chairs. Doctor Belpin looked about him.

"I have high hopes of a recovery, certainly some improvement by the morning. But you must also realise that his overall health is not good. His leg is a problem. There is usually no pain but the occasional collapse is dangerous. He has laboured breathing. Sea air may be healthy but months of damp and cold are not. We shall know more tomorrow morning. For the moment I suggest you make yourselves comfortable Unlike other members of my profession I like to spend time watching my patient. I feel I can sometimes will their recovery."

He laughed.

"Probably nonsense, but what is certain is that I cannot watch him from now until tomorrow morning. You must take your turn."

All three recipients of the doctor's words immediately indicated their wish to be of service and he had but to outline what was required.

"It is all quite simple. You watch over the patient. See that the dressing stays in place. If he calls out, gets too disturbed or awakens, you call me."

Ketch and his companions indicated that they understood what was required and that, when the doctor was ready for his own bed, they would establish a series of watches.

Doctor Belpin was pleased with their cooperation.

"For the moment it is probably best that you remain here in the parlour. There is food and drink in the kitchen, my manservant and my cook are at your disposal. However, under no circumstances are you to enter my laboratory."

With these final words the doctor left them to settle themselves amongst his armchair and couches.

"Well, this is very fine indeed," announced Sergeant Holditch. A dry, extremely comfortable billet with a cook at our disposal. This is a rare opportunity for us to enjoy a time of real comfort. I shall explore the kitchen at once and make friends with this cook."

Ketch gave Holditch a hard look.

"Do not annoy the doctor by abusing his hospitality. Remember he may have the Sea General's great gratitude if all goes well. You would also be wise to consider that three Spanish agents may not be so very far away."

Both Tull and Holditch accepted the need for vigilance and for the moment Holditch forbore to visit the kitchens. Nevertheless, they continued to enjoy the comfortable parlour.

Ketch awoke to the chiming of the mantlepiece clock. He looked at Tull and Holditch asleep in their armchairs. His eyes flashed around the room. He was relieved that the parlour was unchanged. They had not been attacked. He was disappointed at their joint failure. Old comrades from time past would have jeered at such failings. He rose to his feet and kicked the boots of his two men. As they stumbled out of their sleep, it was seven o clock and totally dark outside. They were both apologetic and a little ashamed.

"Sorry Ketch. Very wrong, tired but no excuse."

Ketch waved aside their explanations but thought it best not to mention his own slumber. He looked at the clock. At that moment the doctor entered the parlour.

"I did not want to interrupt your rest gentlemen but I now need a little respite. I would welcome one of you taking a turn of a couple of hours with the Sea General."

At once Ketch spoke up.

"I will take the next watch doctor and then followed by my two men; we should see him through to the morning."

The doctor nodded approval and then gave his parting instructions.

"It is possible he may wake at any time. If that happens or he becomes particularly restless call me at once."

Ketch joined the doctor on the stairs and once on the landing the doctor directed Ketch towards the patient's room and indicated that he was sleeping next door. Ketch entered the sick room and sat down watching the Sea General. For the moment all was quiet. Downstairs Tull and Holditch looked quizzically at each other.

"Had Ketch been sleeping?"

The Sea General did not sleep through to the morning. Towards midnight he began restlessly turning and Ketch grew concerned at the danger that posed for the wound. He felt compelled to waken Doctor Belpin.

"The draught is wearing off, we must wake him, make him comfortable again and return him to sleep. I am worried about his lack of strength. As a man he has been weakened by a life of continued hardship."

Ketch could see that Doctor Belpin was not entirely pleased at his patient's progress.

To wake up in flickering candlelight is difficult, the mind is uncertain and looking for familiar things As Ketch and the doctor eased the Sea General up into a sitting position, he was clearly unaware of his surroundings. He looked about him in bewilderment. His hair was stuck fast with sweat to his head and his mouth was open. A thin stream of saliva was on his chin. He had slept in linen trousers but from the waist up his naked torso was covered in sweat. The doctor spoke to him very softly and carefully sought to protect the damaged shoulder. After a few seconds an understanding entered the Sea General's eyes. It was a relief that he knew where he was and what had happened.

"Now then," said Doctor Belpin.

"Let us have a closer look"

He expertly untied the bandages that held the poultice. On a side table was a basin of water. He dipped a cloth in the basin and began to moisten the cloth protecting the wound.

"Now hold still General let us see how you have behaved."

He began gently tugging at the bandage to uncover the wound itself. At each movement the Sea General gave a gasp of pain. Belpin was quite unsympathetic.

"Not so much fuss, General, you must have dealt with much worse."

Finally, the dressing was removed with the Sea General bearing his discomfort. It looked very unpleasant. A nasty, yellow puss lay thick upon it and the dressing itself was very wet.

"Good! He remarked.

He then threw it into the basin and took a closer look at the shoulder's skin.

"The poison has been drawn, but all is not well."

The Sea General looked sharply at him and then turned his head in a vain attempt to look at his shoulder.

"I feel better. I can move my shoulder without pain, but stiff, not fully part of me. Has it worked doctor?"

"Not quite, "replied his physician.
"The poultice was very hot and there is a nasty blister next to the wound. This has burst and creates a chance of infection. It needs cleaning."

The Sea General began to make further comments on his recovery, but Doctor Belpin waved them away.

"A clean dressing, another draught, more sleep and we will see how you are in the morning, but we will start with some clean clothes."

He turned to Ketch.

"Join your men downstairs. If the patient behaves, we may have better news in the morning. My concern, however, is his continuing overall weakness."

As Ketch returned to his men downstairs, he was struck by the overall enormity of what was happening and the responsibility it had placed on Doctor Belpin. Should England's naval Commander in Chief fail to recover the consequences would be grave for the doctor and all concerned.

After a night spent in an armchair, Ketch woke to the sound of movement on the stairs. As he rose to his feet, he met Doctor Belpin and his manservant carefully ushering a pale Sea General down to the parlour. The chair slept in by Ketch was placed close to the fireplace. The fire had been regularly tended during the night providing much comfort. The doctor's patient was placed there, wrapped in a woollen dressing gown. The manservant poked the fire into a brighter flame and the Sea General leaned forward to enjoy its warmth. After eating a breakfast of eggs and toast he seemed to regain some of his vigour. Tull and Holditch were enjoying a rather more substantial breakfast in the kitchen. So, when the manservant had cleared away there was only Dr Belpin and Ketch sitting with the Sea General. The Sea General turned to Ketch.

"Hopefully the convoy will have left Hindhead by now and be well on its way to Petersfield. With luck we can catch up with them to enjoy that town's hospitality and then enter Portsmouth the following day. Our timetable will be met and the fleet will be away in good time."

He had spoken in a whisper but in a determined tone. There was an explosive sound from Dr Belpin.

"Nonsense! You are in no fit state to travel you need at least another day's rest. You are far too weak."

The Sea General gave the doctor a look of pity mixed with amusement.

"I am sorry, Doctor Belpin, you have done well and I am most grateful but I must be able to get the fleet away on the sixth of march."

Dr Belpin rose to his feet, a ferocious look on his face.

"You propose to be thrown about in a carriage for the next two days. This is madness. Your physical condition is very poor. You are not robust and you are recovering from being poisoned. The wound is not fully healed and what you are considering is utter folly. Should infection set in you would surely not survive and if you did reach Portsmouth some poor physician would not be treating your wound, he would be examining your corpse. I utterly forbid this madness."

The Sea General's face betrayed his dismay.

"But the fleet must sail on March the sixth"

"Well, if you do not rest it, the fleet will sail without you. Besides, I do not believe in the sanctity of such a date in sailing matters. You could arrive in Portsmouth and find wind and storms delaying you for weeks. This is pure deceit. As your physician I insist on saving your life."

Ketch was shocked and quietly amused at Dr Belpin's spirit. He was defying a military man who had but to stamp his feet and ten thousand sailors would do his bidding. But it was a measure of the truth of Dr Belpin's diagnosis that the Sea General was too weak to argue any further.

As the convoy of transports led by Beaumont and Captain Treddager made their slow progress to Petersfield and the three Spanish agents found their way to Portsmouth, a day and a night was spent by the Sea General and Ketch at Larch House. It was a day of gloom courtesy of heavy cloud and rain. Ketch, Tull and Holditch filled the time with books and quiet conversation. Dr Belpin had ordered silence amongst all his staff whilst he nursed the Sea General, who was once again upstairs sleeping.

The following morning was very different a West wind had blown the clouds away and it was a bright, if still cold morning. Since early light Ketch together with Tull and Holditch had been up ensuring that the Sea General's coach and horses were fit and well for the days travel. All of Thurloe's men were ready to take on the day.

Tull had a difficult question for Ketch.

"The convoy with the Sea General's stores and equipment will at this moment be heading for Portsmouth. It will arrive late on the fourth of March. If we allow a day for unloading then the fleet can leave the following day. We are a couple of miles North of Hindhead and we also have to be in Portsmouth today, if the Sea General's plans are to be fulfilled. That is a very tall order Ketch. It must be close to a thirty- mile journey. What do we do?

Holditch, who had been listening with interest to Tull's view as to the day's problems, had one of his own to put forward

There is also the matter, Ketch that there are three Spanish agents out there somewhere just waiting for us to come by. If they have pistols, a slow -moving coach with only two outriders does not seem such a challenge for them."

Ketch was able to answer in part the questions from his colleagues.

"If we leave now, we will have some eight hours of light, and with fair weather, it can be done. As for the Spanish agents, that needs more thought. "

At that moment the Sea General entered the room dressed ready for travel. There was no sight of Doctor Belpin. There was a silence in the room. The Sea General looked pale but his posture and movement were considerably improved on yesterday.

"I am ready to travel", he said.

"With or without Doctor Belpin's approval,"

Tull went in search of Doctor Belpin, whilst those left in the room began their final acts of preparation for the road. The two returned to the room and the doctor took a hard long look at the Sea General.

I see you are leaving whether or not I approve. I do not think you should go. You are stronger from your rest but another day would see even more improvement."

The Sea General snarled at him and then shook his head.

" I apologise Doctor Belpin. You have done me great service, probably saved my life. I am indebted to you and I do not approve of my behaviour yesterday, but with my thanks comes my good bye for I really must be away at once.

"I cannot prevail on you to stop for breakfast?" Asked the doctor.

"No!" Was a firm reply from the Sea General?

The party was moving out towards the front door where the Sea General's coach was waiting with Tull in the driver's seat and Holditch now mounted, when Ketch thought of another reason for delay. He turned to Doctor Belpin.

"I would be most grateful doctor if before we settle the Sea General in his coach, we fill it with as many cushions, pillows, bolsters you can find Those from your armchairs and couches would be most useful. It would aid the Sea General by protecting him from the inevitable jolting actions of his coach. Let us place him firmly in a womb of comfort and it may even offer a measure of protection against pistol shot. "

The doctor took a deep breath and agreed. He summoned his servants to gather as much of the desired items as were available. Such was the response that there was far too much available. It ensured, however, that the Sea General was well buried in comfort for his journey. They made their final goodbyes and settled the Sea General as best they could in his coach. As he sought to position himself amongst his pillows and cushions the Sea General called Ketch over to him and Ketch climbed up into the coach with him. He sat up close to the Sea General, who spoke quietly to him.

"You ought to know, Captain, that today is the fourth of March and if my deadline is to be met, at this hour Charles Beaumont will be leading the convoy out of Petersfield and on to Portsmouth. To make up the day that we have lost, I need you to also get me to Portsmouth today. Can it be done?

Ketch pulled an uncertain face.

"If we have good fortune with the weather and the horses remain fit, and stops are kept to a minimum, we may be in Portsmouth after nightfall. That is not my key concern. There remain three Spanish agents out there somewhere seeking your life. We are a small party to face such a danger.

The Sea General smiled.

"I see you have good men about you Captain and I have my pistol at the ready. We shall have an exciting day Let us get on with it."

At the door of his home, Doctor Belpin turned to Ketch.

Ketch's annoyance at the delay was obvious, but he could not refuse Doctor Belpin

"Unlike many in my profession Ketch, I do send bills to the great and mighty in the land when I treat them. To whom should this bill be sent. I understand the Sea General will be away for six months"

Ketch gave a wry smile. He was not a man of commerce, he understood, however, that in the midst of military peril there were always such matters to settle. He thought for a moment.

"Send it to John Thurloe, Secretary to the Council of State care of Hampton Court Palace. I shall remind him of it when we meet."

Leaving Guildford behind them Michel, Mary and Raphael were in good spirits. But for the lack of pistols they felt fully equipped for the task ahead and they were growing a collective team sense. Their purpose was to get to Portsmouth in two days, arm themselves and prepare to ambush the Sea General either within the convoy or alone out on the road. They rode the Portsmouth road at a steady pace, from time to time enjoying easy conversation. Michel could not totally throw off his loss of the Spanish pistol.

"If I had had your shot with that Spanish pistol, I would not have missed Yes, Yes! I know it was cold and you had to be quick but that pistol would have done the job for you."

Raphael just grunted. He was not convinced, but he did not let Michel's comments spoil his good humour. Raphael was more interested in how Mary had wounded the Sea General with her hair pin.

It was not so difficult, Raphael"

She called across as they passed a wagon on the road.

"When we arrived at the "Good Shepherd" we all hung up our outer clothes in the public room. It was easy to find a moment to lodge the pin in the Sea General's coat. After the meal we all collected our clothes and retired for the night. Nothing happened and I feared it had been found or fallen to the floor. But next morning after breakfast, there was such a buzzing around the Sea General that I knew I had succeeded."

"Yes! Interrupted Michel

"That was our best effort. Mine was also a good idea and but for a stupid servant, he would have broken his neck " Raphael inwardly smiled. He was not too unhappy that Michel had lost his bright shiny pistol

They made good progress out of Guildford and fairly soon passed the convoy, leaving it to plod on to Hindhead. They had taken care, from a safe distance, to look for the Sea General but it was clear that he had as yet not re-joined it. Beaumont and Treddager were giving the orders. Eventually they reached that point where the road forked with the road to Portsmouth on the left and the village of Westonville on the right. They had no idea that at that moment the Sea General was resting from the beneficial ministrations of Doctor Belpin. With barely a glance they carried on, and themselves reached and passed through Hindhead aiming to reach Petersfield before dark. Their horses needed a rest and Hindhead common provided water and grazing. All three dismounted and Mary had an issue that she felt had to be discussed.

"Where is this Sea General? Raphael has told us that back in Guildford early this morning, Captain Treddager, my so-called beau, with a coach, carried away the Sea General. It was at the time, Michel, we were making our escapes. Back there on passing the convoy we saw Treddager and Beaumont but no sign of the Sea Genera. So, Raphael's account was accurate. Therefore, I ask again. Where is the Sea General? Has he been spirited away or has that Captain Ketch somehow got him away onto the road to Portsmouth ahead of us.?"

An unhappy silence descended upon them. It was Michel who broke into their musings.

"When Captain Treddager carried him away, the Sea General was suffering from Mary's poison. He could not travel far or fast. You agree Mary?

Mary nodded her agreement and Michel developed his argument.

". Treddager is devoted to the Sea General. I think his actions were a desperate search for medical help. We have seen that Treddager is with the convoy. So now, it is that Captain Ketch who has the Sea General and somewhere under his protection, the Sea General is recovering or dying. If he were dying Treddager would be with him, so the likelihood is that he is recovering. If he were fully recovered, he would be with the convoy for protection, but he is not. My final conclusion is that the Sea General is well behind us. Our plan is still the right one. We need to secure arms and then prepare an ambush on the road for when he does reappear."

All, including Michel himself, were heartened by his words.

"Let us get on," he cried.

"We shall not make Portsmouth tonight but we shall tomorrow.

Midway between Hindhead and Petersfield there was a collective decision to find a place to stay for the night. The convoy would be soon arriving in Hindhead and they were now well ahead of it. Tomorrow they would be in Portsmouth with the convoy heading for Petersfield. The Sea General would eventually be coming towards them.

To their distress, three people on horseback appeared to be too many to easily secure lodgings on the road, but eventually an inn, The Green Man" happily accepted them. It was a large establishment, well patronised and a little too public for Michel's wishes. He felt they were too conspicuous. In fact, it was well that such a choice had been made for as they slept in their room, they could hear the rain lashing down outside. In Larch House that same rain failed to disrupt the sleep of the Sea General bearing his poultice. For the convoy, the overnight stop in Hindhead was the only occasion when Beaumont had been unable to secure dry accommodation.

.

Chapter Sixteen   The Ring of Steel

The morning of March 3rd not only witnessed the confrontation between Doctor Belpin and the Sea General over his need for a day of rest, but also was the setting of a confrontation between Charles Beaumont and the drivers, grooms and labourers who made up the convoy. In Hindhead a cold, wet night, and the absence of the Sea General had planted seeds of unrest bordering on mutiny. Preparations to move out were not happening, rather fresh fires were being lit and groups of men around them started loud conversations about extra money and returning to London. The discontent increased when Beaumont and Captain Treddager stepped out form their cold, but dry carriage, followed by Turner, Brown and Hedges from the clerks' carriage.

"There is trouble here Charles," murmured Treddager.

"These transports are in danger of being pillaged"

He turned to Turner, Brown and Hedges.

"Arm yourselves, there is danger here for us and the cargo."

Beaumont had other ideas. In an authorative voice he ordered.

"Keep them hidden and do nothing, just wait for me."

He climbed back into his carriage. Under a bench seat, screwed to the floor was the money box, full of coins, for the journey's expenses. This, however, was not the object of Beaumont's purposes. Under the opposite bench seat was a similar box, but not of money, but containing a bottle of Claret, a bottle of Port and two bottles of Brandy. He climbed down from the carriage holding one bottle of brandy aloft with the others tucked under his arm. Those he handed to Captain Treddager and Turner. He strode over to the fires.

"A miserable night lads. In our last stop today in Petersfield we shall be snug and warm, but for this morning we have a tot of something to help us on our way. Find your mugs and Captain Treddager and Clerk Turner will see you right."

He turned to Brown and Hedges.

"Keep your cutlas by your side and see that each man gets something"

Initial looks of suspicion changed at the prospect of drink. Men started scurrying around to find their drinking vessels and Brown and Hedges managed to ensure that distribution was orderly using a few hard glances and an occasional push. It did not seem to matter as to who got what to drink. It was all swallowed gratefully. At just the right moment, Beaumont began quietly issuing orders for the resumption of their journey. Horses were managed into their shafts, bags and baggage were stowed away and slowly the convoy moved off Hindhead Common back onto the Portsmouth road.

On this same morning Michel, Mary and Raphael were treating themselves to a substantial breakfast in the "Green Man." They were all sitting satisfied with their meal and musing on the day ahead. Michel felt that a few words would be useful.

"Today is fairly straightforward. Our destination is Portsmouth with the object of purchasing pistol and ball. On the way we must seek out the best position for our ambush, but what are we going to be faced with? Has the Sea General recovered enough to re-join his convoy? If he has, then the task before us will be very uncertain. I am sure that Captain Ketch will surround him with protection that will be difficult to penetrate. I do not like thinking we must try something in Portsmouth. At the very least we must fire a volley at the coach and then ride for our lives. As our best hope is that the Sea General is unable to re-join the convoy that must then proceeds without him on to meet whatever is its timetable. As such he will be on the road; a single coach with probably only three men to protect him. We will need to seek out a good position for a serious fight to kill him. He paused and gave a short snort.

"Of course, the very best outcome is that Mary has already killed him. Praise God for such an outcome."

Raphael felt he had something helpful to contribute.

"I think that tomorrow we must make an early start, ride from Portsmouth North towards the convoy. We must discover if the Sea General has joined them at Petersfield. If so, then we must return South to choose a site that allows a volley and run, But, if he is still absent then he will be travelling South to join them. Thus, our chosen place must be North of Petersfield ready for a real fight."

His two companions took a moment to think through his proposal. Speaking slowly Michel tried to understand the meaning of Raphael's comments.

"So, North of Petersfield we should look out for a place for a real fight and South of Petersfield somewhere for volley and run."

"Bravo gentlemen," exclaimed Mary.

"I think we can do no more planning than this. Now we should get ourselves to Portsmouth we have pistols to buy."

On the morning of the 3rd of March when the Sea General had reluctantly agreed to remain at Larch House for an extra night, Ketch knew that they had lost any hope of securing protection for the Sea General from the convoy. On that lost day the convoy would reach Petersfield. The Sea General would be ready to re-start his journey on the morning of the 4th March, but the convoy would at the same time be staring its final leg to Portsmouth. Ketch began to understand the consequences.

"Our party of Thurloe's three men with Tull up in the driver's seat, the Sea General cocooned inside the coach and myself and Holditch as outriders will be travelling at a known time down a known road opposed by Spanish agents able to choose the time and place of their attack,"

He grimaced, looked about him, waved to Doctor Belpin and gave Tull the order to move on.

As the coach began its short journey to the Portsmouth road, Ketch had a possible idea on improving their odds of arriving in Portsmouth safely

It was not long before they reached Hindhead Common where they stopped and looked at the rubbish strewn about by the convoy two nights previously. Ketch dismounted, Holditch followed and Tull was called down from the driver's seat, and

213

all three men crowded around the window of the Sea General's coach as Ketch described to the Sea General what he thought they should do next.

"We have a long day ahead of us. We wish, no we must, be in Portsmouth by the end of the day. That is a hard drive in a heavy coach when we will be on our own. No support from the convoy. The Sea General is in considerable peril."

The peril was felt by all his listeners but Ketch wanted it to weigh even more heavily upon them. He turned to Robert Blake.

"With full respect sir, I think it is clear, that it was a mistake for you to reject the Lord Protector's offer of Ironsides and the ring of steel they would have provided. I think our only hope is to create our own. I believe we must go into Hindhead".

Beaumont and Treddager led the convoy through the centre of Petersfield to its Southern edge. There adjacent to the road to Portsmouth stood two large, empty timber warehouses. The current demands of the navy had left them with nothing more than a few stacks of green timber and some large saws. But as Beaumont had promised they were watertight and wind proof. The promised warmth had come from the Town Mayor who had provided two brasiers in each warehouse and two janitors to tend them. In addition, on his own initiative he had secured the services of two traders whose stalls had been set up in the slightly larger of the two venues, one for bread and cakes and another for beer and cordials. A beaming Mayor had joined the convoy as it distributed itself between the two venues. He had arrived for the second substantial payment to be provided by Beaumont. After receiving his money and a decent interval of conversation he left them to settle for the night. As he wandered off into the night Beaumont shrugged and grumbled.

"He has done very well out of us and I have no doubt that the two traders will have been charged for their presence with us. "

"Money well spent," replied Treddager.

The two men looked about them as horses were looked after, candles were lit and brasier warmth began to spread. The whole atmosphere in both warehouses was so different from that of the rain- soaked morning in Hindhead.

"Well, Beaumont, I think you will get them to Portsmouth and complete your commission tomorrow. They seem happy and content with tonight's stop."

Beaumont, was always happy to receive praise, but some less pleasant thoughts, at the back of his mind, could not be resisted. He guided Treddager to a quiet corner of their warehouse.

"I am concerned that we have no news of the Sea General and if we arrive in Portsmouth without him there are going to be some serious questions thrown at me. I have lost the Commander in Chief. What am I going to do? If we are to meet his deadline to sail on the sixth, we must arrive tomorrow, unload on to the Naseby the following day, and all would be ready. But we can't do this without him."

Captain Treddager was himself beginning to realise that he also would be seen as culpable in losing the Sea General.

"It's all down to Ketch and his men. I left the Sea General in the care of Doctor Belpin, with Ketch there providing protection. If all goes badly wrong and the Sea General does not survive, then the full wrath of the nation will not only fall on us, but also on Captain Ketch and his men. But he is able enough, he will do everything to get the Sea General to Portsmouth on time. So, Beaumont we must just carry on as normal putting our trust in first Doctor Belpin and secondly in Captain Ketch."

The three Spanish agents had a comfortable ride to Portsmouth, only stopping to more fully examine possible ambush sites of the sort they required. As it was already mid-afternoon when they arrived, Michel thought that it would be best to immediately complete their main task of securing suitable firearms.

"I think we should make our purchases in one shop only. This is a town of sailors and soldiers, purchasing pistols will be quite a normal transaction and if we buy as a group, with a common story, it may lessen any suspicion. As we only require two pistols, this is modest enough for travellers risking the highwaymen of the West Country."

All went well with their purchases and they easily enough found themselves lodgings on the outskirts of the town. Although the day was ending, they used the remaining hours of light to find a vantage point to view the English fleet in the harbour. They counted over forty large ships and many smaller boats moving to and from the land carrying goods and people. The whole harbour was a mass of unending activity.

216

"This is magnificent to see," exclaimed Raphael,

"But also frightening. Who can hope to oppose such force and power?"

Michel added to his concern.

"Each will have thirty to forty cannon and as many as three to four hundred men and along this coast there will be three or four harbours with the same number of ships. We may have some five hundred cannon and forty to fifty thousand men. This is an army at sea, all under the command of one- man Sea General Robert Blake. You see the importance of what we must do."

Whilst Michel and Raphael spoke of what they could see and what they had seen elsewhere, Mary remained silent, but when their talk began to dwindle, she gave them one thought

"Michel, I will do all that I can to kill this Sea General, but I would very much like to then return safely home. The two men looked at each other and exchanged a sigh. It was their hope also. As they walked back through the streets of Portsmouth, Michel struck up a conversation about the place of their ambush. He kept his voice low, but he was confident it would mean very little to anyone who heard pieces of what they were discussing.

"Of the sites we have examined, I rather prefer that which was some four miles North of Petersfield. The road dips and then rises again. My assumption is that we will be facing the Sea General's coach and a small escort. There are hedges along each side where we can position ourselves. There are large grassy fields either side, ideal for an easy and quick

217

escape. Should we be facing the Sea General protected by the convoy, we will hold our fire, regroup and try a volley South of Petersfield."

"It is tomorrow?", asked Mary.

"We must be up early," replied Michel.

"We must take up our positions and await events."

It took but a few minutes for the Sea General's party to reach the town square of Hindhead. A covered market usually filled the square on Tuesdays and Thursdays but this morning the square was empty apart from one or two hot food stalls. Ketch had not as yet told the Sea General the full nature of his plan.

"Keep a sharp lookout both of you, I want a word with the Sea General."

He climbed into the coach and for a few moments they were in conversation. For the length of their journey Holditch had never heard the Sea General laugh, but to his surprise that was what he was hearing, Followed by…

"You can try it Ketch. It's a gamble but it might work."

Ketch left the coach, the Sea General and his companions in the square and disappeared into a large building that had all the appearance of the Council House. There was a long moment when nothing happened, then Ketch emerged with a smiling, prosperous looking man. His new companion was of average height, plump and with a definite air of self-confidence. He was well dressed and carrying a bell. Ketch escorted the visitor up to the carriage door.

"Sea General Blake, Holditch, Tull this is Martin Hosley, the Mayor of Hindhead, he has agreed most keenly to take part in our plans."

There were bows and murmurs of welcome and then the bell was handed to Ketch. At the centre of the square was a large stone cross with an equally large plinth. Ketch jumped up onto the plinth, grasped the stone cross with one hand and began energetically ringing the bell. Within minutes the square was full of men, women and children wondering what Mayor Hosley was doing allowing that man to make so much noise. When he was satisfied that the square was full, Ketch placed the bell beside him, stood up straight and in the silence looked out at and then addressed the crowd.

"Men of Hindhead he declaimed", and paused.

"Yes ladies, it is to the men of Hindhead that I must speak."

He smiled and threw up his hand, pointing at the coach.

"In that coach is Sea General Robert Blake, England's finest sailor and hero. You will have heard tales of him. He beat the Dutch three times in battle. In the Mediterranean he bullied the French and bombarded the Turk to release Christian slaves. Prince Rupert and the renegade admirals, he chased to the Indies and destroyed them."

There was a murmur of approval. They all knew him. "He is here now in Hindhead, wounded, but ready to take command of the fleet. It must leave in two days, for the Spanish treasure fleet is already at sea. That means he must be in Portsmouth in one day."

A buzz of interest and concern ran around the crowd. Ketch continued.

"Why is he here in Hindhead wounded?

He paused. He had everybody's attention.

Three Spanish agents have shot at him, stabbed him and tried to break his bones. They have tried to kill him three times and they are still out there waiting on the Portsmouth road with their pistols loaded."

He looked down on the faces looking up at him. He was getting to the heart of his message.

"One day to get to Portsmouth and take up his command and who is there to protect him? Only myself and two comrades. Hindhead, it is not enough! We need the men of Hindhead to step up and protect England's great Captain, to see him to his command and to get the fleet to sea. I need men, men and horses who will ride alongside me as a screen of protection, an irresistible force that no Spaniards can halt. Now is the moment for the men of Hindhead to write a page in England's history. A chance that will not come again, something that children and grandchildren can hear with pride, when tales are told of these times."

At that moment Mayor Hosley leapt up onto the plinth.

"I am with these men, Hindhead. Who will ride with me?

A loud cheer greeted the Mayor's words and a forest of hands went up.

Ketch had to shout out his instructions above the commotion.

"Men with horses ready to ride, here in this square in one hour."
He jumped down from the plinth and faced the Sea General at
the window of the coach.

"It seems we will have our ring of steel after all."

The square began to empty and within a few minutes there
were only a few women and boys hanging around to see what
would happen next. Ketch was surprised to find the Sea General
standing next to him.

"I had to get out of that damned coach Ketch. It is soft and
comfortable but very warm and so short of air, I can hardly
breathe. Anyhow, that was a stirring speech you gave, how
many do you think will respond?"

"Well General, I would be happy with six men on good
horses. They would give us a company riding ahead of you in
the coach that could shield you and sweep away those intending
harm. More of course would be even better."

The Sea General nodded his approval and turned away
to talk to Tull who had remained sitting up in the driving seat.

"Could you come down a moment Tull, my shoulder
will not allow me to spring up beside you?"

Uncertain of what was in store Tull slowly stepped
down to the ground. The Sea General's face was not unkind.

"I have enjoyed your company on our travels Tull. Our
time together and our talks were not only a pleasure but they
gave me an insight into myself that strengthened my religious
beliefs and calmed my uncertainties. I found someone who
believed and yet struggled as I did. I made you a friend Tull. I
encouraged you to think hard on your future."

The Sea General stopped for a moment seeking for the right words.

"You were right to resist my enthusiasms for you to actually become a sea chaplain. It is a life of continuous uncertainty and general disappointment. You do important work with Captain Ketch and Thurloe would never forgive me for taking you away. But I will keep you in mind as the standard for the future sea chaplains we will undoubtedly appoint."

Tull was lost for words. He had been avoiding the Sea General, concerned that he would be the object of cold words It was a great relief not to have upset such a man he so admired.

"I have valued your company sir" were the only words that came to him. He gave the man, who for a short time had been a friend and confident, a look of thanks and climbed back up into the driver's seat.

Chapter Seventeen A day of Action

Whilst Ketch was addressing the men of Hindhead, Charles Beaumont and Captain Treddager stood side by side watching the early mist swirl around the two warehouses, where the convoy had spent the night. Their experience told them that it would soon be burnt away to reveal a bright, sunny, but cold day. At that moment, they held an unspoken common thought that they should be getting the convoy underway. The mist could no longer justify delay. This was the last leg of their journey. This evening they should be settled in Portsmouth. But the problem of arriving in Portsmouth, without the Sea General, was a step that neither could easily accept. However, it was Beaumont who voiced the most compelling case against delay.

"After yesterday's unpleasantness, not to arrive in Portsmouth tonight would not be well received by the men. Another night out in the open and I am not sure we can control events. There is no more drink readily to hand and the Sea General's bottles would be too much of a temptation and would just increase disorder."

"You would need a damned good reason to keep this convoy out of Portsmouth," agreed Treddager."

Beaumont could not help but notice that Treddager was giving him the full responsibility.

To be helpful Treddager mused aloud.

"I have considerable confidence in Captain Ketch and his men. It really is a question of time. He will bring the Sea General to Portsmouth but it has to be sometime today."

He stood silent for a moment and then voiced another thought.

"Of course, at sea, convoys are held up for all sorts of reasons, lack of water, men gone missing, but most often it is the unseen breakdown of equipment. Such an event here would be seen as most annoying but understandable."

It was Beaumont's turn to muse aloud

"Yes! That would be most unfortunate, but understandable. "

The two men looked at each other and then began to walk back towards the warehouses. They could delay no longer; the convoy must be got underway.

Michel, Mary and Raphael were up, breakfasted and away from their lodgings well before Beaumont and Treddager were reluctantly moving on the convoy. Their journey North to Petersfield also started in mist, but after an hour they had ridden the slowly rising road that led up to the base of the South Downs. Here the sun had broken through to reveal a frosty countryside and a road with few travellers on it. They decided to give their horses a rest before the climb to the top. Michel took the opportunity to review their plan of action.

"We stop just short of Petersfield and wait for the convoy. If the Sea General is amongst it we volley and run, hoping for a final, desperate, later opportunity, If he is not present then we ride North of Petersfield to the site we have chosen as giving us the best chance of getting close and finishing the job. Then we will wait until the Sea General's coach arrives with his one or two guards."

"Clear and understood," said Raphael.

Mary indicated her agreement with a smile, but both had noted the new introduction of "later opportunities," but said nothing."

The climb to the top of the Downs was long and arduous such that the horses were adjudged to deserve another rest. Raphael could not let the matter of "Later opportunities" go undiscussed.

"Michel! What are these "later opportunities" that we may require?

Still breathing hard from the climb, Michel waited a few moments before replying.

"Today, we intend to kill Robert Blake. This is our best chance. But if we should fail, he may yet be vulnerable where he would feel safe in Portsmouth. I have no plan, I only sense there may be opportunity. That is all, but let us not think on this now. Let us concentrate on success today."

Mary intervened.

"He is right Raphael. Let us keep firmly to what we must do today."

After their brief discussion they rode on towards Petersfield and within the hour Raphael had spotted the on-coming convoy. Michel took charge.

"Raphael, hide your horse and get down into the undergrowth and watch out for the Sea General. Mary, slowly trot-on towards them, smile and wave as you pass and keep a lookout for him, but remember, you are a young man., I will go back half a mile and find a place where I also can see if he is there. When the convoy has passed, come back to me and we will determine what we are to do next."

In half an hour the convoy had passed on its way to Portsmouth. At their conference each was sure that the Sea General was not present. Neither he, nor his coach nor his guards, could be seen. They had to move on to their main site. No action was required here.

They rode on past Petersfield and returned to their selected site on the Hindhead-Petersfield road. They stopped, hobbled their horses and rediscovered the advantages they had previously identified for their ambush. Each found an individual position that would give them a clear shot as the road dipped and then rose towards them.

They returned to their horses and made themselves comfortable to await the arrival of the Sea General's coach. Michel had issues to discuss.

"Finding a good spot for a shot is one thing, but there are other matters to consider. Try not to be tense and do not rush your shot. You have the advantage of surprise. I will take the responsibility to shoot the coach driver, leaving you both to try for the Sea General. Are we agreed on that?

They agreed and Michel continued.

" After that whatever happens depends on events. We would then face possibly a dead Sea General but at least two other guards to deal with and of course, there may be other travellers on the road. It may be possible to follow up with our knives or not. The important matter is to remain calm and follow my instructions.

At one point, I will give the order to leave and we must escape quickly. We will keep our horses close by ourselves and escape in different directions, meeting up back at the "Green Man" and then heading straight back to London."

Mary and Raphael were beginning to understand that managing an ambush was more complicated than they had considered.

"Michel." Exclaimed Raphael.

"We cannot plan for every possibility, but you have given us a good basic plan. You shoot the driver. Then in a calm way you give us our instructions and then when ordered we escape individually, as best we can, to the "Green Man" and then on to London."

Michel was cheered by Raphael's comments.

"Excellent Raphael."

He looked at their third member.

"You are happy with this Mary?

Mary had made enthusiastic responses to all that was said, but her concerns about what was expected of her were growing. She was not especially good at violence. Nevertheless, she gave the expected response.

"Understood and ready Michel."

By the time the hour was up Ketch found Hindhead central square full of men and horses all seeking to secure a position close to the coach. It was as he expected a group of astonishing variety. Ketch had quite a doubt about many of the volunteers. There were cart horses strong but very slow, overweight farmers on tired looking mounts looking very uncertain, young men desperately controlling horses that wanted little to do with them. He was relieved, however, to see a number of calm featured men sitting quietly on well trained mounts.

"Will you weed out those that are of no use?" whispered Holditch in his ear.

Ketch was curt in his reply.
"No! They have stepped forward. They all deserve to take part. They may drop away but they have shown that the men of Hindhead have courage."

Ketch mounted his horse and stood up high in his stirrups.

"Men of Hindhead, in a moment we shall leave, but what do I want from you?"

He waited and then answered his own question.

" Together we shall act as a shield to the Sea General in his coach. We shall ride down or chase away his enemies. But be assured they will not shoot us; they wish to shoot him. They will not waste powder and shot on us. It is the Sea General they wish to kill. They will not want to give away their positions. So, should you come upon these Spaniards ride them down or chase them away. If you have a club or whip use it. Do not be afraid."

A cheer went up from the assembled host., but there was a change of tone in Ketch's voice.

"One very important matter. Do not! Do not ride down honest English men and women. They will be travelling the road on their own private business. Leave them alone. I trust you to know our own people, be worthy of that trust. Not one to be hurt. Remember this is not a race. We will not be moving fast. Our pace will be set by the Sea General's coach, a steady trot or canter, no faster. We are to ride in a line some fifteen yards ahead of the coach filling the road and the fields on either side. In parts it will be difficult, gates and hedges will get in the way. But persevere, keep the line if you can. Regretfully we have no provisions for you, no accommodation. The aim is to get yourselves and the Sea General into Portsmouth by nightfall. Finally, some of you will not make it to Portsmouth. You may exhaust yourselves. Your horse may lose a shoe. If you are not with us at the end, you have my thanks, my respect and that of the English navy, for your efforts to protect their Commander in Chief."

With these final words Ketch gave a wave of departure. Mounted men and the coach slowly moved out of the square gradually gaining momentum. The first hour was a very discouraging experience. Men and their horses were unable to avoid each other. There was anger and occasional blows as individuals tried to establish a settled position in the line, that Ketch was hoping would emerge. The numbers began to reduce and as the weaker horses and riders dropped out a greater order began to emerge. At their first halt there were some twelve good horsemen upon whom he could rely and at the restart he had the advance protection that he had hoped for. With him leading on the road, Holditch alongside the coach and half a dozen men each side of the road, only the need to respect other travellers proved a problem. A regular pace was established that was not over- demanding for the coach, but was one that gave hope of arriving in Portsmouth at the appropriate hour. As they moved along travellers stepped aside and cheered, others waved. They did not know why, but it was a surprise spectacle and they enjoyed it.

Michel had so arranged their positions that they were not visible to each other but he moved amongst them with words of encouragement.
"Try not to be tense and do not rush your shot. Yiu have the advantage of surprise. Whether you are successful or not, that surprise will give you a head start for your escape."
.   Raphael and Mary heard his words, but each had their own thoughts about their shot and their escape. Not one of them was prepared for what they saw when the coach came into sight. They were expecting a lone coach with a couple of outriders, instead they were presented with a line of horsemen across the road and adjacent fields with the coach coming along behind. For a moment Michel stood mute, he did not know what to do.

As a Spanish spy, Michel had many thoughts but he was not dull of thought. As the coach and its escort approached the rise towards them, he shouted out new instructions.

"Quick, scatter on to the road or field! Split up! Be single travellers! Clap!, Wave! Cheer! Hide your face Mary. Let them pass."

The cavalcade swept past, no one paid any attention to any of the single persons waving and cheering. Once it was past, the three agents quickly re-assembled. Mary and Raphael had no sense of what to do next. It was not what they were expecting. Michel also had been surprised but he had seen at once how they could respond.

"Listen to me. This is not what we have planned for but we can still turn this to our advantage. If we split up and follow them, we can slowly in our own way mingle amongst them, smiling, being cheerful, joining in the adventure. At the same time gradually bringing our mounts up close to the coach. Eventually one of us will be close enough to the coach to shoot into it and kill the Sea General. There will be confusion, but the other two will be in a position to support their escape. None of these riders appear to have arms that threaten us."

Michel could not help mumbling his last few words. Raphael and Mary just looked at him coldly. Escaping unscathed seemed highly unlikely. Michel turned to remount.

"Come on! This will be our last chance on the road and it is a good one."

It was with a surprising energy that Mary and Raphael mounted their horses. It was an emotional response. A last final effort, a do or die moment. It was not so long before all three had managed to get in amongst the riders. Raphael on the track itself and Michel and Mary in the adjoining fields. Of the three,

Raphael had the most immediate opportunity. He was a fine rider and he had a willing mount and there was a harmony in their physical movement. As he neared the coach it was, unluckily, that his easy riding style drew the attention of Holditch. He also had been riding on the road behind the coach. It was as Raphael cantered past him that he recognised the riding style of a cavalryman.

"*That is no clerk or farmer,*" he thought.

"*That is no lawyer or squire's son. That is a man who rides horses daily.*"

Holditch kicked hard and tried to close the gap between them

As Raphael began to draw alongside the coach, he drew his pistol and aimed at the coach's open window. A shot was fired. Raphael shuddered and pitched forward off his horse. The smoking pistol was held by Holditch. His Spanish wheellock had not let him down. The unmistakable report of a pistol brought the cavalcade to an untimely and confused halt. Up at the front Ketch halted, wheeled his horse and galloped the few yards back towards the coach. Around the coach, horses and men collided as they tried to avoid each other, Raphael's horse and his broken body. This noise and confusion around the central cortege aroused great concern amongst those in the fields alongside. There were not supposed to be shots fired. No one was to be hurt. Many of them felt the wisest course was to move away to a safe distance. Michel and Mary were amongst these. They edged about trying not to be drawn into conversations, but trying o behave as others. Mary was full of rage and anger when the news came of a failed attempt on the Sea General's life, when the assassin was killed . She began edging towards the road. Michel was beginning to feel at risk. He was the object of a number of dark looks Two riders were openly pointing at him and looking for Ketch and Holditch. He was an ungainly rider and his somewhat ugly face did not inspire confidence. The scrutiny became too much. He began edging away and then turned and took off in a steady canter into a large field where he raised his pace, to gallop away. Two of the men from Hindhead looked to their fellows to join in a chase, but a lack of heart and determination lost the moment. Michel managed to scramble away. But he had seen Mary fall

Ketch knelt down by Raphael's dead body and was joined by both Tull and Holditch. Ketch turned to his two companions.

"It was not the shot that killed him. It was a broken neck from his fall, You say Holditch, that he pointed a pistol at the coach."

"He did Ketch and although I do not know him, I could see he was riding like a cavalry officer."

At that moment Mayor Hosley passed a pistol to Ketch.

"Found by one of our men by the body."

Tull had opened the top of Raphael'shirt and pulled out a gold chain. On it was a small gold cross together with a gold medallion.

"There are words of Spanish on this Ketch. I think it is clear he is definitely a Spanish agent."

Ketch rose to his feet. He was unsure what to do. An additional horse he could manage, but what could he do with a dead body when time was so urgent. . He moved across to examine Raphael's horse and saddlebags. He only half observed a young man edging his horse passed him. He began undoing the saddlebags when instinct told him something was wrong. In sudden alarm he spun around and cried out a warming. He saw opposite the coach window Mary with her outstretched arm, holding a pistol, pointing into the coach. There was another loud retort and a long cloud of black smoke issued from the coach window. Mary was hurled from her horse to the floor. A stunned silence followed,

".Holditch stand ready, ordered Ketch Draw your pistol Tull "

A great wave of fear ran amongst the men of Hindhead. Again, they scattered away, leaving Ketch, Tull and Holditch standing alone defiant, determined to defend the Sea General.

The coach door opened and the Sea General limped down to the ground.

"I was prepared Ketch. After that first shot, I was ready. Let us look at my assailant." The Sea General and Ketch moved across to look at the fallen Mary. It was an uncomfortable sight. Her true gender had been revealed by her long black hair which had been shaken loose. It spread out on the ground above her fallen body. The Sea General's shot had hit her full in the chest and her shirt and doublet were soaked in blood.

"War is not a matter for women," said the Sea General.

234

"It breaks my heart to see one struck down in this way."

He looked about him.

"Well Ketch, what are we going to do now."

Ketch felt the pressure of several decisions requiring immediate solutions, He looked at the two bodies of Raphael and Mary.

"What am I going to do with these?"

He recalled that Mayor Hosley was amongst them. He beckoned to the Mayor for help.

"Mister Mayor, I have two dead bodies on my hands what can I do with these?"

Ketch's question did not trouble the Mayor.

"We must get them to Petersfield. I know the Mayor there well and supervising arrangements for the dead is a matter, like me, he deals with. There will be costs, but may I suggest that these could be met if we also transfer to him their horses and saddlebags."

Much relieved, Ketch was all thanks.

"That solves a problem for me. However, I would wish to investigate their saddlebags before handing them over."

The Mayor agreed and took over the task of securing the bodies of Raphael and Mary to their horses for leading to Petersfield. Ketch summoned Holditch.
"Get those saddlebags Holditch, we must see what information they reveal, especially about the agent that is still out there. Take them to the Sea General and go through them with him"

Holditch grimaced, he was not used to conversations with Commanders in Chief , but he steeled himself for the task he had been given. Ketch, ever conscious that time was was being lost and Portsmouth was still miles away had to secure what information he could about the missing agent. He called the Men of Hindhead around him.

"We are going to stop in Petersfield to deal with the bodies of the Spanish agents, but did any of you get a good look at any third agent that may have been with them?"

There was a general silence but then after exchanging rather sheepish looks two men raised their hands.

"We saw a man who no one seemed to know riding close by. Rather ugly in the face and ungainly on his mount. When the first shot rang out, he saw we were watching him and he rode away as fast as he could. I doubt that you will see him soon."

Ketch thanked the two men and in his own mind ticked off a problem that did not require his immediate attention. Returning, to the coach he saw that everyone was standing around looking at him, waiting for instructions.

"Gentlemen, we are going straight to Petersfield . There we will re-assess our drive to Portsmouth."

The Sea General returned to his coach. Tull climbed back into the driver's seat. Holditch remounted his horse as did the men from Hindhead. When all was set Ketch issued his instruction.

"We can now all ride on the road and it is straight to Petersfield. "

Chapter Eighteen   New Plans

It was the deaths of Raphael and Mary together with the dark looks and pointed fingers that produced the uncontrollable fear that had driven Michel to abandon his fellow agents. His mind filled with no other thought than that he had to get away to safety. All sense of direction was lost, anywhere would be a refuge. He barely guided his horse, but used all his energy in ensuring its maximum effort to race away.

As distance widened and there was no immediate pursuit, the weight of fear began to lighten. He eased his horse down to a slow walk. His first returning sense was one of relief. Relief that he had not been taken that he had reached safety. It did not, however, last long as his primary emotion. He began to feel cold and a deep sense of shame swept over him. His thoughts turned to his comrades, their deaths and his betrayal of them. He began to replay again and again the events that had produced his abandonment of them. Then he began to feel a great tiredness. His whirling emotions were too much for him.

"I have to rest. I have to get warm. I must sleep."

He dismounted and to his surprise, vomited uncontrollably. For a while he just stood bent forward looking at what he had done and then with a groan he straightened up. A new rationality filled him.

"I have not done well.

He wiped his face with a handkerchief, coughed and then relieved himself beside a hedge. He began to think more clearly about what to do next. He walked his horse to a nearby wood, made a fire and wrapped in his blanket ate some food. Physically he felt better. He began to make plans for the future. There were thoughts of revenge in his plans but most of all there was a burning desire to complete their mission. The two deaths could only have any meaning his shame could only be absolved by the death of Robert Blake. He was resolved. He would sleep and then ride on to Portsmouth. He was now clear of purpose

On arrival at Petersfield's central village green, Ketch happily handed over the problem of the agents' bodies to Mayor Hosley.

"We will wait for you until the matter of the bodies has been settled and I will discuss with the Sea General on what we are to do next, but be as quick as possible, for time is hurrying on. Stress the importance of getting the Sea General to Portsmouth today."

Hosley chose four of his men from Hindhead and they led away the bodies of Raphael and Mary on their horses, Ketch climbed up into the coach to have his conference with the Sea General.

Tull and Holditch stood around with the remaining men of Hindhead conversing and trying to keep warm. Ketch found the Sea General holding the saddlebags of Raphael and Mary.

"I have been through these Ketch and I have found nothing that may interest Thurloe. There is food, various bits of clothing, flint steel and tinder, pipes, razors and in the female's saddlebags various jars of cream and ointment. However, they both contained purses quite heavy with gold and silver. I think it reasonable if we confiscate this. I have a use for some of it."

On this basis the two men discused the immediate future. They agreed that Mayor Hosley and the men of Hindhead could stand down either returning to Hindhead or remaining the night in Petersfield. The Sea General then gave Ketch an inquiring look.

"Nothing so pleases men who have volunteered with no prospect of reward to be actually rewarded. Unexpected money is always welcome. I think it perfectly acceptable that a little of this Spanish gold and silver finds its way into the pockets of the men of Hindhead."

Ketch was happy to agree.

Having settled this, they went on to discuss arriving in Portsmouth by the end of the day. Ketch expressed certain doubts, but the Sea General was still demanding that it be achieved. Having concluded their discussion both men descended from the coach. Unhappily once again the Se General stumbled and required quick supportive action from Ketch. They found that Mayor Hosley had returned with his task safely concluded. After the Sea General had examined and approved the details, he called everyone around him.

"Men of Hindhead we have come to the end of our time together. Our enemies have been killed or scattered. And you have completed your task. You have delivered the

Commander in Chief of the English navy to a place of safety where he may continue unhindered his journey to Portsmouth." He paused for a moment so that there was time for his audience to make the first adjustment to their plans. There was a broad smile on his face as he continued.

"You expected no reward for your efforts, it was inspired by a sense of duty. However, circumstances are such that there is a sum of two gold and a silver coin for each man. It allows those who prefer to spend the night here in Petersfield to do so, rather than risk a night time return to Hindhead."

For the moment the buzz of self- congratulation filled the air. The Sea General's words were well received. Then a slight twinkle came into his eye.

"There is more, gentlemen. We men leave house and home on our adventures. On our return we are welcomed and feted by our women, our wives, mothers and daughters. The glow of these exploits may last long in the drinking house but rarely so around the domestic hearth. Our women are less interested in just stories that may have resulted from considerable inconvenience to domestic arrangements."
His audience laughed as he hoped they would.

"A man returning from his exploits bearing gifts is another matter, especially if the gift is one desired by women. Of course, money is good but there are other things".

Male laughter turned into a certain puzzlement at his words. For a few more moments the Sea General enjoyed his mystery.

"I have in my coach for both my comfort and protection a quantity of fine cushions, blankets, pillows and bolsters. Enough for you all to take away for your
womenfolk that will be a permanent reminder of your support for me today. Above all they will hopefully be enjoyed as both useful and in praise of your efforts."

The Sea General made each man step up to his coach to receive one of the pile of items inside. Ketch was totally bemused. Such a careful thought never crossed his mind. What made the Sea General's actions so strange was that he was not a married man. His life had been totally that of soldier and sailor. He had to admit to himself, however, that the gifts had been well received by the men. As they mounted their horses there was much talk of treasures to be well received by their wives and mothers. There were many hands shaken and words of farewell, but finally the Men of Hindhead broke away to their several destinations.

Tull and Holditch had their own view of the consequences of the Sea Generals gifts. Holditch was quite forthright in his opinion.

"I have no doubt, Tull, that the many Sea Captains of the future, in the next hundred years, travelling between Portsmouth and London will in their various lodging places, hear of the deeds of the men of Hindhead. Furthermore, they will have explained to them in detail that the very blanket, pillow or cushion, they are sitting on, was a personal gift from Sea General Robert Blake."

"Yes, replied Tull. It is a good story and for the next hundred years they will purposely avoid the place."

"Let us get on, "cried the Sea General from inside his coach. "Tull, Holditch, Captain Ketch, we have a journey to complete. " Thurloe's men hurried back to their stations. Tull cracked his whip and the coach's' horses began their apparent unending task, of pulling the Sea General to Portsmouth. Back on their horses Ketch and Holditch took up their positions either side of the coach as its outriders. Ominously mid-afternoon clouds were blowing in from the West and the light was just beginning to fail.

Some ten miles ahead the convoy was slowly arriving at the head of the escarpment that led to a steep descent and a long flat road into Portsmouth. The day had seen a series of small equipment failures. Loads had shifted, reins and traces had broken, These had all required halts in the convoy's progress. Beaumont had insisted that two of his carriage's wheels were heating dangerously and needed removing and heavily greased. This alone had cost half an hour.

As they approached the steep decline the convoy had to halt yet again. The two wagon masters had approached Beaumont.

"We feel sir, it would be very unwise to try this descent in poor light. We are fully laden and will probably need to use the extra horses for a controlled descent. It is a sorry request with Portsmouth being so close, but we feel any descent will be at your responsibility."

Beaumont was happy to accept the wagon masters' advice. It was clear that Portsmouth could not be reached that night. The wagon masters received a quantity of abuse from the rest of the convoy, but Beaumont felt he had to stand firm. Captain Treddager was in full agreement.

Tull's whole body felt numb with cold He had been driving the Sea General's coach since early morning. In the failing light he was experiencing difficulty in maintaining his line on the road and the horses were slowly slackening pace despite his encouragement. They had lit the lanterns either side of the coach but their flickering lights were losing the battle against the dark.

"Another few miles and I must seek guidance. We are not going to make Portsmouth tonight."

He continued to gain some comfort from his two outriders, but a quick glance revealed that they also were stiffening in the saddle with bodies tired and cold. He was summoning up courage to deliver his thoughts to the Sea General when he spied, a half mile ahead, a small collection of lights alongside their future path. It was a welcome sight. It provided a convenient halt, an opportunity to deliver his unwelcome news.

As the lights drew closer Ketch could see that they were approaching a substantial encampment. He could make out wagons and carriages and cooking fires. His cold face managed a smile. He called out.

We have found our own convoy. I think I recognise Captain Treddager and Hedges."

Tull, with great relief, gently pulled the weary horses to a gentle stop. Treddager and Hedges were joined by Beaumont in hurrying to meet them.

"By God we are pleased to see you. Where have you been Ketch? I left you at Westonville three days ago. We thought something was badly wrong with the Sea General."

By now there was a significant group clustered around the coach and there was a sigh of relief when the Sea General opened the door and stepped down.

He was looking over the convoy and was gratified to see Beaumont and Treddager.

"It is a relief you are all here but you should be in Portsmouth. What has happened?"

Ketch had dismounted and pushed his way through to the Sea General's side. He raised his voice.

"We all have tales to tell but I for one am cold and hungry. I need food and above all a hot drink, give us a moment to recover from our day's events and you shall hear all."

Ketch's sentiments were echoed by all who had arrived by the coach and Beaumont swiftly set about doing what he could to meet their needs and make them comfortable.

There was quite a collection of men sitting on boxes, barrels and blankets as Ketch recounted the events of the last three days. Beaumont in particular was desperate to get an understanding of the Sea Generals' experiences. He had not seen his employer since he was taken away at Guildford. There was a deep sympathy for the Sea General when his treatment by Doctor Belpin was explained and a small exclamation of pride in the response of the Men of Hindhead to the Sea General's need of protection. It was the attack of the Spanish agents that aroused most consternation and there was universal approval of their fate. However, there were a few sideways glances at Captain Treddager, when Ketch revealed that it was the Sea General himself who had shot Molly Mosley and that she had been dressed as a man.

By the time Ketch had finished and had answered all questions it was pitch black and most of the people there were ready for their sleep. There was a gradual drift away to settle for the night.

Beaumont considered that the experiences of the convoy should be the subject of a private meeting rather than discussed in public. He arranged this in the Sea General's coach. Present was himself the Sea General Captain Treddager and Ketch. There was a certain resentment in his tone. He turned to Ketch.

"The rest of us felt that we had been abandoned when you rushed off to join the Sea General, we had no idea what was happening. The two seamen in particular were suspicious and resentful. I finally received news of the Sea General's situation from Captain Treddager when we arrived at Westonville. But it was a hard task managing the convoy from that point. We were grinding out hard miles. The rain ruined the overnight stop on Hindhead Common and the men were not only resentful but mutinous the following morning. We had to use our private store of hard liquor to get them started. For the rest it was Treddager and myself who were facing the prospect of arriving in Portsmouth and explaining how we lost the Commander in Chief."

The Sea General could not resist joining Ketch in laughing at the final predicament faced by Beaumont and Treddager. The short silence that followed was broken by Ketch.

"We have all been tested these last few days, but all in all we have succeeded. It is a pity that we have not got the Sea General to Portsmouth in time. But given all the troubles we have faced, arrival early tomorrow morning, I hope, will be acceptable."

The Sea General was gracious enough to remark.

"First thing tomorrow morning will be fine."

Chapter Nineteen   Portsmouth

Beaumont and Ketch stood side by side enjoying the view from the top of the escarpment that looked down to Portsmouth.in the far distance. It was a day of clear blue skies and bright sunshine. It was, however, a sun of little warmth and both men were well wrapped up in their woollen cloaks. Nevertheless, the prospect of journey's end and with the first feeling of spring in the air, both men were in a relaxed mood. They spent some time admiring the great array of masts in the far distance that was the great fleet preparing for sea. It was Beaumont that broke the silence.

"I have misjudged you Captain Ketch. From the first I had some doubts as to how far you were the man for the job of protecting the Sea General. There was a certain lack of certainty in your manner, but events have surely proved me wrong. Your refusal to panic when Captain Treddager virtually kidnapped the Sea General, your immediate understanding of the murder on the stairs, the mobilising of the men of Hindhead and the successful repulse of the Spanish agents, pays tribute to your ability and speaks clearly that you were most definitely the man for the job."

Ketch smiled at Beaumont's remarks. He always remembered a remark made by his master John Thurloe.

"It is always better to exceed expectations than to just meet them."
Ketch was quite happy to praise Beaumont's talents in return.

"You can be pleased with your own efforts this week, Charles. To bring a convoy such as this, intact, through winter weather is no mean feat. Especially as there were the added problems of an attack by Spanish agents and threats of unrest by drivers, carters and grooms. I understand why you have been chosen by the Commander in Chief as his Private Secretary."

There were broad smiles all around as they enjoyed their mutual esteem, but Ketch remembered that his task was not yet completed.

"I think it important Charles, that the entrance of the Sea General into Portsmouth attracts as little attention as possible. There is still a Spanish agent out there and we do not want any crowds in which he can hide to make another attempt. I understand that secrecy is impossible but let us make the effort to minimise the risk. We have yet to get him safely installed in his accommodation."

The convoy by now was beginning its descent from the escarpment and Beaumont was needed to ensure that every means of transport safely reached the bottom.

Much energy was used to secure this transition to level ground and some time was taken whilst the convoy re-organised itself for the final miles into Portsmouth. But in due course it resumed its steady forward motion. Its pace was the same as that which it had employed for the journey to date, but there was a quite different atmosphere around it. It was now the steady joyous tread of horses and men nearing the end of a long journey and anticipating rest and refreshment.

As the town of Portsmouth grew ever closer, Beaumont sought to secure the good offices of Ketch in a particular matter.

"You will know Ketch that we are in fact a little behind our desired schedule and on arriving at our destination I will be extremely occupied in managing the convoy into its final resting place and immediately commencing the transfer of the Sea General's goods and stores to the Naseby. Everything must be completed by this evening. Then there are a range of payments to be made and details of return journeys to be decided."

Ketch listened carefully he did not envy Beaumont's next few hours.

"The Sea General's party which includes you and your two men are all to stay in the Ship Inn at Portsmouth Point. We have taken up all the rooms except, of course, for the large public room. But the remainder are ours. The convoy men, horses, coach, carts and carriages are all to be accommodated in a large warehouse next door. This is where I shall be spending the remaining hours of the day. It will be a scene of furious activity. May I seek your help in seeing that the Sea General is safely into his rooms and that all has been prepared for us."

Beaumont had a worried look but Ketch was pleased to dispel it.

"That is not a problem, Charles. In fact, it is, in a sense, almost the conclusion of our responsibilities. We must both ensure it will end well"

As they approached the inn itself, Ketch moved away from Beaumont and called Tull and Holditch to join him. He needed a quick word with them.

"Now we have arrived at the Sea General's destination there must be no reduction in our vigilance. There is still danger here. The Spanish agent that we know as Michael Gough is still at large. With two murdered colleagues I doubt he has given up on his task. We do not finally relax until Robert Blake is on his quarter deck."

Holditch had something to say.

"This is very difficult, Ketch. If a man is inflamed with revenge and prepared to sacrifice his own life, in a bustling place like Portsmouth he will enjoy many opportunities to achieve his purpose. We cannot put the Sea General in an iron box."

Ketch left Holditch's remarks hanging in the air.

"I want you both to think on this as best you can. Meanwhile I now have the job of settling us into this splendid looking inn. "

The Ship Inn was the pride of Portsmouth Point. It was a large three storied building built of stone up to the second floor and good English oak for the upper story. It was double fronted with large windows either side of the front entrance and multiple windows above promising comfortable well- lit rooms. It extended back over a hundred feet and had communication with its large warehouse next door. Ketch and his two comrades were joined by Captain Treddager together with Hedges and Brown. As a group they strolled purposefully into the entrance hall. Here, there was a long table with a chair on which sat a tall, slim, dark-haired man who was looking decidedly uncomfortable. He was clearly the landlord. Ketch spoke clearly what was required.

"I am here on behalf of Mister Charles Beaumont who has booked all your rooms for this evening. We would welcome a chance to see our rooms."

The landlord looked even more unhappy.

"I am in difficulties sir. Regretfully your rooms have been taken. It is hard to refuse naval gentlemen who threaten violence if their requirements are not met. I am afraid like most naval captains they are used to being obeyed. Six Captains have taken your rooms. Our main set of rooms are now occupied by an Admiral."

Ketch was stiff with outrage.

"This cannot be right, Mister Beaumont has letters confirming these rooms are ours. "

The landlord merely gave a shrug. Ketch could see that he was going to be of little help. He motioned Hedges and Brown to stand beside him

"We may well need their help in this matter."

Ketch looked the landlord full in the face.

"Tell the gentlemen upstairs that they have ten minutes to hand over our rooms. If they refuse, Captain Ketch of the Lord Protector's staff will have them out. He is under direct orders of John Thurloe Secretary to the Council of State. If they resort to violence, they risk their commissions."

A very flustered landlord hurried up the stairs

"Strong stuff," murmured Holditch.

Ketch heard a noise behind him and turned and to look down the entrance lobby to the street outside. There, standing in bright sunlight was the Sea General chatting, quite relaxed, with passers bye.

"For God's sake, "exclaimed Ketch

"He could be killed and stabbed ten times over out there. Tull, bring him in."

Tull retrieved the Sea General and sat him down in the lobby.

"General we are trying to reduce the danger to you by keeping you out of sight. You are not yet on your quarterdeck."

"Are there problems here Ketch?" Inquired the Sea General.

Before Ketch could answer the landlord appeared at the head of the stairs.

"The Captains send their apologies and will return to their ships."

As he was speaking a collection of men, servants and a number of women began to move from the first- floor rooms. In some disorder they stumbled down the stairs carrying bags, bottles and seas chests. There were a series of apologies which grew in number as the sitting Commander in Chief was observed. Following the Captains and their guests, the still unhappy landlord whispered to Ketch.

"There remains the problem of the Admiral, Admiral Godrich, he refuses to move. His exact words were, "I do not know this Captain Ketch and John Thurloe is a jumped-up clerk with no knowledge of naval matters. I snap my fingers at them both."

Ketch looked at the Sea General who gave a nod of approval. Ketch once more faced the landlord.

"Tell Admiral Godrich that his Commander in Chief General at Sea Robert Blake is downstairs and requires that the rooms booked on his behalf are returned to him and any mutinous refusal will occasion naval seamen being sent up to throw him in the street."

The Sea General chuckled.

"A little strong Ketch but it will do."

The landlord once more made his way up the stairs. Ketch wated anxiously for his return, Just, as the landlord on his return reached the bottom, a head appeared at the top. It was Admiral Godrich.

"Dear Lord. My humble apologies, Robert. No idea it was you. The rooms are yours; I shall retreat instantly. There was the sound of cupboards and drawers being opened and shut. Two servants with bags and clothes in their arms followed by Admiral Godrich began the process of clearing a way for the Commander in Chief to secure his rooms. The two naval Commanders Blake and Godrich seemed to think the whole matter an excellent amusement. Godrich made a very low bow to Robert Blake and as he passed and the Sea General threw out a teasing last remark.

"I shall tell John Thurloe your view of him."

As matters began to settle. Hedges turned to Brown.

"It appears Brown that you have just lost the opportunity of a lifetime to throw an Admiral downstairs."

It resulted in an explosion of laughter.

After securing the inn for their own use Beaumont and Treddager took over the management of the Sea General. From his set of rooms, the final preparations for the departure of the fleet could take place without any need for him to leave the inn. With Hedges and Brown at the foot of the stairs there was no immediate need for Ketch and his team to do anything else, other than being available as required. This was the final day of preparation, tomorrow morning the Sea General and the fleet would commence their departure.

Ketch, together with Tull and Holditch, in the public drinking room of the inn, took seats at a table near the window. Holding their mugs of ale, they began to relax. For Tull and Holditch there was a general feeling that they had completed their task; no more than a little escort duty was now required. They could be away to London tomorrow. Ketch was not quite so sure. He stroked his nose and looked carefully at his companions.,

"We have done well so far; we have brought the Sea General in sight of his quarterdeck. There is just the requirement for him to stand upon it. This may be difficult"

"I am not sure Ketch that it is difficult," interrupted Holditch.

"Now he is safely here in the Ship Inn he has the whole English navy around him. I know that Michael Gough is likely to be somewhere, but we do not know if he is in fact here in Portsmouth and there is small opportunity of him getting close to the Sea General."

Ketch turned to Tull for his view, he was the most cautious of agents. However, he was to be disappointed. Tull gave a small smile.

"I agree with Holditch on this Ketch. We have had a few words ourselves on this very problem. The answer to any last concern of getting the Sea General safely aboard his ship is the time it is done. He is expected to leave tomorrow, but in secret tonight, under cover of darkness ,he could be taken aboard, Perhaps two or three o clock in the morning. No one will be in a position to murder him because it is both in the dark and a secret."

Holditch added hurriedly.

"Early morning would probably do just as well. The crucial point is that we control the time of his leaving."

Ketch turned over in his mind the substance of what he had just heard.

"I do believe they have the answer. This looks as if it is going to be easier than I expected. Well done both of you"

He stood up.

"Let me suggest this arrangement with the gentlemen upstairs and, if they approve, we really shall have grounds for thinking London tomorrow. "

Ketch left the barroom and with a nod to Hedges and Brown he strode up the stairs to deliver the proposal. He knocked and entered the nearest room where he found Beaumont and Treddager had set up a working office. They were in deep conversation with a Captain and what Ketch thought was some kind of merchant. Beaumont looked up.

"Will it wait Ketch.

"I think I need an early decision on this "he replied.

Treddager stood up and Beaumont rose to knock on the Sea General' bedroom door and all three entered. They found the Sea General sitting on the side of his bed nursing his leg.
"It doesn't always hold me steady Ketch. I bob up and down, then hobble a bit and then I pick up for a good few yard."

He turned to Beaumont.

"What is it?

"Captain Ketch requires a decision on something."

Ketch could sense that Beaumont had other things on his mind and had a lot of final business to complete so, he quickly outlined the proposed options for the Sea General's Transfer to the Naseby.

Treddager laughed, Beaumont laughed and the Sea General laughed. In good humour they cut their laughter short, they could see that Ketch was puzzled. a After a moment, and controlling his laughter, Beaumont explained.

"The Commander in Chief re-joining the fleet has become a civic occasion. The Sea General will take an open carriage ride to the Old Quay where he will be met by the Mayor. There will be speeches and music, an inspection of the local garrison, as the Mayor formally escorts the Sea General to his Barge. It has become quite an event."

The Sea General rose from his bed.

"I do not intend to skulk on to my ship in the dead of night. The men of the Naseby will expect to welcome, in style, their Commander in Chief and so they shall. Sometimes Ketch, there are moments in life when you not only must take a risk, but you are expected to take a risk. When open bravery is expected of you."

He gave Ketch smile.

"And of course, you are here to see that nothing untoward happens."

Ketch was surprised, but not cross with the news. He was, however, annoyed at his own lack of foresight. He needed to think again. He thanked the company for their news, in a tone of light self-recrimination, and hurried back downstairs. He needed time to think. So, he suggested to his two companions that they enjoy a cold lunch whilst they reviewed this new situation.

"I failed entirely to take account of any civic occasion. We have relaxed too soon, we still have a responsibility for the Sea General's safety."

Despite their best efforts not one of them had any inspiration. Although they did decide to leave the inn and individually survey the town, looking out for Michael Gough and identifying possible areas of danger.

The Ship Inn was to be found half way down East Street. Running East to West it was one of only two main thoroughfares that were enjoyed by the town. At the Eastern end it led into the Old Town Quay the departure point for the

Sea General and the site of the civic occasion. Here were all the shops and houses of quality. At the Western end it ran into Broad Street, a long wide road set at ninety degrees to East Street. One side was totally flanked by the sea, the other was made up of poorer retail outlets, lodging houses, many of them brothels, drinking houses and a number of establishments providing for those whose living came from the sea.

Holditch had chosen to examine Broad Street. He slowly worked his way alongside the various establishments, from time to time breaking off to look closely at back alleys and yards. He was surprised at the sheer numbers of people, mainly men, milling about, some working but others bent on pleasure. He was forced to conclude that finding a particular individual was impossible.

Ketch and Tull decided to examine East Street, especially the route from the Ship Inn to the Old Town Quay. East Street had a pleasant aspect to it. The fine houses and shops being well maintained. The shops were varied and appeared prosperous dealing in, hats, shoes and gloves, books, watches, silver and other luxury items. Both men found themselves viewing the items on display rather than the points of danger.

"Shape up Tull, "demanded Ketch.

"What do you make of East Street. Here the Sea General will pass in an open carriage. It looks uncommonly dangerous to me.

"I agree Ketch. It is quite a narrow thoroughfare. Almost all the properties have upper story windows from which it would be easy to fire down into an open carriage. There are also a variety of flat roofs and balconies that would provide similar vantage points. At the Eastern end, whilst the Southern side continued on its way, on the Northern side there was a turning that led to the Old Town Quay. Here an open square was fronted by the sea. Ketch was slightly happier with the Old Town Quay as offering fewer points of danger for the Sea General. At least here they were manageable, but he despaired for the rest of East Street.

Chapter Twenty   A missed opportunity

Michel, Michael Gough as he was known in England, was in a highly emotional state. The deaths of Raphael and Mary haunted him He had devised their plan of action. They had died whilst he had run away. He groaned.

"Their deaths can only have meaning if I can go on to kill Robert Blake. It must be possible. I can do it!"

For some time, he continued with these self - recriminations. Eventually he realised that such thoughts were not helpful. He needed a plan.

"How can I do this? A great fleet lies in the harbour, the town is full of sailors and the military. If I am discovered as a Spanish agent, I will be torn to pieces."

It was only with great difficulty and a heavy price that he had secured lodgings the night before the arrival of the convoy. He had learnt from Mary that brothels had a variety of uses and for a handful of gold he had secured a room high up in a brothel in Broad Street. As a room, it was small with only a one- foot square window but it enjoyed a large skylight so at times it was flooded with daylight. For his money he had secured privacy and a promise not to be disturbed by anyone. As darkness fell, he sat on the edge of his bed looking down at the pistol cradled in his hands. The bleakness of the room, bed, chair, table and wash stand reflected his mood and his single candle could only throw a weak light. It was not a place that encouraged plans of action but he was able to force himself to think.

"You may be hiding in the dark, Michel, but there is a whole day tomorrow to devise some way of killing Robert Blake. I have learnt that the day after tomorrow he will leave his place of lodging, The Ship Inn, and by open carriage travel to the Old Town Quay where he will leave by barge for his ship. At the quay there will be speeches and music, he will be a perfect target. If only we had known earlier, with three pistols we would surely have killed him. But now it is up to me."

There was a jug of water on the wash stand. He rose to his feet took a long drink and began pacing the room with the jug still in his hand. The movement and the firm grasp became a means for further thought.

"Tomorrow, I will be up early and investigate East street and the Old Town Quay. I shall be seeking vantage points, one of which will provide me with the perfect place to finish our mission."

For a while he dwelt on images in his mind of pointing his pistol, shooting Robert Blake and seeing him fall. With a start he realised he was still standing in the centre of the room still holding the jug of water. He gave his first smile of the day.

"Michel, that is how it will be done.

He slept well that night and was in a lighter mood as he stepped out into the weak sunlight of a March morning. He wrapped his cloak tightly around him as the full force of the wind from the sea buffeted him. He looked at the clouds. Rain would mean a closed carriage. But this morning his courage was up and he dismissed such a negative thought.

His early start did not mean that East Street was empty. There were plenty of people going about their business.

261

Most of them were well wrapped up in cloaks, coats or shawls. There were a few groups of sailors dressed only in trousers and shirts showing how hardy they were, but even they moved about quickly rather than loitering. Michel rather welcomed such a crowd for he more easily blended in. His first consideration of East Street revealed many convenient windows and balconies that at first sight would be very appropriate for his task. But he was most uncertain about the Old Town Quay. He had initially thought that it offered the best of opportunities, but the properties surrounding the quay were large warehouses with few windows and no balconies. He decided to return to his room for further consideration of what he had seen, but in a warmer place. As he mounted the last flight of stairs to his room, he noticed next to the door a metal ladder, that obviously led to the roof.

"Windows and balconies are part of people's property and often part of their daily lives, roofs are rarely bothered with and remain large unused spaces. I think a look at the rooftops may well be worthwhile."

There was a bolt to be drawn but the trap door to the roof opened easily enough. His first sensation on the roof was a nervous reaction to the strength of the wind. But he mastered that quickly and found stretching away before him a series of rooftops that led away along Broad Street but turned to continue the full length of East Street to the warehouse tops of the Old Town Quay. Michel smiled to himself. No one was up there with him. He had a road before him full of vantage points,

"Yes, it is disorderly, jumbled, uneven and in places almost certainly unstable and dangerous, but it is one I can traverse. "

262

He paused to have a quick look down into his own room, noticing how very bleak it looked, but then began to walk and jump and slide his way along the rooftops. It was colder than down in East Street but he enjoyed the usefulness of his discovery and the freedom he felt from being the sole occupant of such a large space.

After a full hour of exploration, he retired back to his room. He felt tired and very cold from his exertions and discarding his outer clothes, he crept into his bed to recover.

He awoke and was surprised to find it was well past noon. He felt very hungry but was full of excitement that he could see a route to achieving success, a rooftop shot into an open carriage. He decided he deserved a substantial late lunch with meat and hot gravy and then a return to East Street to decide from the ground which rooftop to use.

Ketch and his colleagues had reassembled in the public room of the Ship Inn. It had become a scene of busy activity. Members of the convoy had found a convenient drinking place and Mr Beaumont had been quite liberal with payments and bonuses. Beaumont and Clerk Turner were constantly entering on business with various parties

"We cannot think here, let us move on to what looked a pleasant establishment a little further down East Street. "

This suggestion was fully accepted and the three men found their way to The Seagull, a clean drinking establishment that enjoyed the aroma of baked pies that doubled its attraction. Initially no window table was available and they were forced to drink their ale standing next to a large barrel, but it was not too long before one was became free and they quickly settled with their ale together with pies.

"This was a very good idea Ketch," mumbled Holditch through a mouthful of pie.

"It is the most comfortable I have been all week."

Tull, with better manners just nodded his head in agreement.

"Well, I am pleased you two are quite settled but we are here to fix our minds on the danger facing the Sea General. We are at the very end oof our mission and must keep a look out for Michael Gough."

After half an hour they had heard Holditch give a detailed account of Broad Street as a possible hiding place for Michal Gough. They had decided that there was little   likely hood of an attack by the Old Town Quay, there being few vantage points for a marksman Their best reasoning led them to East Street as the source of the attack. It was Tull who came up with the strange idea of packing the Sea General's open carriage with their bodies. Tull explained.

"Admittedly dangerous but if we all dress up like the Sea General surely it would so confuse things that we could disrupt any attempt to shoot him."

Ketch groaned and became positively exasperated when Holditch began advocating a disguise.

"This is nonsense. If you think a civic occasion is going to consider any of this, you are fools. Concentrate on East

Street itself. We may have to divide it up and patrol an area each. That is the best I can do."

An uncomfortable silence fell between them. Ketch let his mind wander out through the windows to the noisy activity outside. His eyes widened and he quickly sat up. He was looking at Michal Gough who was looking back at him. Gough's face and body stiffened and he began walking away at speed. He had initially hoped that Ketch had not seen him but, whatever, he was going to get away as fast as he could. He made straight for Broad Street and his lodgings.

"It's him," cried Ketch.

"Michael Gough! After him."

Tull and Holditch lept to their feet, their chairs tumbled behind them and contrived to get in the way and cause them to stumble. Ketch similarly found it difficult to unwind from his table and chair. A few seconds were also lost when Holditch fell against the door preventing all three leaving cleanly and at speed. Outside the three pursuers broke into a run, dodging as best they could those blocking the way. Ketch could just make out Michael Gough some fifty to sixty yards away. Those in their way were not helpful they resented being disturbed in their efforts to keep warm, and few moved out of the way without a shove.

"Stop that man," cried Ketch.

Unfortunately, in any community there is a proportion of individuals who reject authority, they dislike it, they despise it. Most of them at some time or other have come up against the authorities and, in their own eyes have been treated badly. Many of them are low-level criminals who delight in those opportunities to frustrate authority with no threat to themselves. For such, Ketch and his colleagues were figures to be actively prevented from achieving their object. Their obstruction was not born out of discomfort but positive antagonism. In Portsmouth Point there was a high proportion of such individuals and when Ketch again called out "Stop Him", there was an answering shout of "No! No!" In such circumstances, it was impossible for Ketch and his men to close the gap on Michael Gough.

Michel, grateful for such support had come to the conclusion that it was not wise to run straight back to his lodgings. It was a situation where any place to avoid pursuit was welcome. He turned suddenly and headed through an open doorway. He found himself in a passageway that led past stairs to a garden and to his left was a room and to his right a bare wall. Without hesitation he took the stairs. By the time he had reached the top the pounding in his heart had been joined by a gasping for breath. He pushed aside a maidservant who had just emerged from a side room, he chose another set of stairs. There he opened a door to find a sea of roofs facing him. His familiarity with this part of Portsmouth gave him encouragement but no security of escape. To his dismay he could hear footsteps down below on the stairs behind him. There was a flat roof in front of him which led to another, which he judged, could be reached with a reasonable jump. Beyond, there were chimneys and a pile of broken boxes, roof tiles and water barrels that offered some hope of concealment.

When Ketch, Tull and Holditch reached the passageway they stopped and listened. Uncertain about what he heard, Ketch ordered Holditch to search the garden and Tull the room on their left. He would take the stairs. He started two at a time but towards the top of the first flight he was forced to slow down to one at a time. Here, he found a maidservant sitting on the floor. She gave him a startled look, but only received an urgent inquiring set of eyes to which she responded by pointing a finger to the second flight of stairs. Ketch followed her direction and ran on up to emerge on to a flat roof. There was no immediate sign of Michael. He moved across to the front edge of the roof and looking down saw the garden with Holditch searching amongst the bushes. He turned ran to the right and with a careful leap jumped on to the roof of next door. There he was amongst a jumble of broken boxes and other bits of discarded wood and materials. He carefully looked about him. There were few hiding places here. His judgement was confirmed when a slight movement caught his eye and there was Michael Gough. He stumbled slightly when he reached out to grasp him, but it was sufficient for Michel to turn and run towards a nearby sloping roof. Here it took a great leap for Michel to reach its relative safety. He turned gave Ketch a look of annoyance and ran up and over the roof line. Ketch followed and on reaching the apex of the roof saw Michel once more preparing to leap to a roof with a stone balustrade. He pulled out his pistol, but a great leap from Michel covered the gap and the balustrade to land partly protected. The pistol was too difficult. Ketch replaced it and made to follow the example of

Michael. However, his prepatory, gathering stride was disturbed by poor footing and his leap became mainly a grasping, flailing stumble. As he lurched over the gap, he managed to grasp the top of the balustrade with both hands, where he hung bruised and winded. Having no purchase with his feet, the strength began to drain from his arms. A quick look down showed a forty foot drop to a cobbled alleyway. He began trying to pull himself up to a position where elbows and upper arms could improve his situation. As he struggled to achieve this, a slight raising of the head found Michel's face staring into his own. Slowly Michel took out a pistol. There was a nearby shout from Holditch. Michel looked across, and hit Ketch on the head, turned and hurried away. Ketch managed to hang on with his head reeling. Holditch, had been joined by Tull and they quickly slid down the sloping roof, leapt and hauled Ketch back up over the balustrade. Ketch did not hold back from a series of oaths that helped a bit to quieten his shaking arms.

"Leave him. You will not get him now. I am sorry lads That was a poor performance, although I have never claimed to be a mountain goat."

"I thought he was going to see you on your way down to the ground below, "offered Holditch.

"I think your arrival changed his mind," said Tull. You would have had a good shot."

Ketch had more or less gained his composure.

"Well, whatever his reason. I am afraid he will not get the same clemency from me in the future. I will shoot him if I have the chance."

Ketch's remark brought back the seriousness of their task It was Tull who put their thoughts into words.

"We now know that he is in Portsmouth, he is armed and clearly intent on murdering Robert Blake. He is quick, daring and clever. He is a formidable opponent and circumstances are in his favour tomorrow. We must be very vigilant if we are going to find him and stop him."
They retraced their steps back to the house from which they had come and were met at the roof doorway by a tall man who was distinctly annoyed.

"What the devil are you doing. This is private property. You are trespassers. I'll have you before the magistrate. "

"My apologies sir. We are officers of the state pursuing a wanted man. I am sorry for the alarm we have caused. I do hope your maidservant is unharmed. We have touched nothing and taken nothing."

Ketch felt that was apology enough. He fixed the man with a hard stare. The tall man looked uncertain and did not prevent them leaving the roof top. He satisfied himself with a few strong words.

"I do not want you ruffians here again. Be off with you."

Still upset at his failure, they decided to abandon the Seagull and Ketch led his team back to the Ship Inn. They needed a short rest and then to clarify exactly how they were going to protect the Sea General tomorrow. They had a quiet hour resting in their rooms and then re=-ssembled in the public room below. Ketch was short and to the point.

"At least from our recent experience we have had our attention drawn to the roof tops. The journey from here to the Ship Inn to the Old Town Quay is short and one man can deny a marksman a position on the roof tops. So, Holditch tomorrow you will be up on the rooftops. Tull you and I will walk alongside the carriage watching the windows and balconies. We can ignore those with people looking out and concentrate on those that are blank, especially if we see them opening. Remember, we have only one shot. Only use it if you are absolutely sure."

That was the best that Ketch could do. He was dissatisfied, but he could think of no other. For a few minutes the three of them discussed it seeking improvements but none came. Ketch went upstairs to inform Beaumont and the Sea General what was intended.

The Sea General together with Beaumont and Clerk Turner was dealing with the final immediate naval business in the upstairs rooms. After Ketch had outlined how he saw events the following day they all gave a nod of approval. The Sea General sought to allay the fears of the civilians.

"Do not worry gentlemen. I am certain that Ketch and his men will see us through safely."

He turned to Ketch.

"I have just heard that you were close to capturing the remaining Spanish agent and that he was the new clerk that Beaumont had hired and has been sitting in the carriage with Mr Turner here, all week."

"It was frustrating General. If we had caught him our worries would be over, but as it is, he escaped us."

The Sea General rose to his feet and stretched his arms and leg.

"Well, we must just hope for the best"

Ketch thought the Sea General was surprisingly unworried about his personal safety. But he laughed to himself.

"I imagine that if you have faced volleys of cannonballs, a single pistol shot has few terrors."

As the three men made to leave, Beaumont asked them to stay.

"Oh, by the way Ketch it will be wisest to stay off the streets this evening. Something unexpected will happen, something introduced for the navy two years ago. It is called "empressment." The navy is always short of men and there has always been the tradition that before leaving port a sweep of the town is undertaken to recover from drinking houses and brothels seamen seeking to abscond. This activity has now been extended by Parliament. Tonight, gangs of seaman led by so-called Port Marshals, will take by force any able -bodied man they can find. This does not include gentlemen or citizens of good standing, but anyone else is apt to find themselves taken away on board and enrolled as having signed up. Today they emptied the jails and tonight any man is at risk. Property will be entered and not just drinking dens and brothels. Respectable lodging houses and other public places like shops can be entered and people dragged aboard ship. There is much disagreement and physical resistance which is often resolved by a tap on the head. It is possible, however, as an individual to prove your exemption with a warrant signed by a responsible public figure, a justice or similar. I have no doubt the town will be outraged for few know this is coming."

The knowledge of this was so new to Ketch, Holditch and Tull that for a moment they were quite speechless with indignation. Words tumbled from all three such as tyranny, freedom. Magna carta, English rights.

"Yes! Yes, interrupted Beaumont, but we must deal with the here and now. You will have more chance of being spared if you have these warrants."

He handed ketch three large sheets of paper with a clear statement of exemption and an impressive seal.

"I have told everyone else in our party to remain in the Ship Inn or the warehouse next door. In the Sea General's presence, we will be secure."

Ketch at last began to realise the magnitude of what Parliament had agreed. He found it almost impossible that the law could be abused in such a way. He moved back to his room, on the way handing Tull and Holditch their warrants.

Chapter Twenty-One Problem of the Press

Michel following his escape from Ketch and his men, had made his way to safety, back to his room in the brothel. Hot, flustered and with a heart still pounding he sat on the edge of his bed with his mind boiling with recent events.

"That was terribly close Michel they nearly had you, what a fool I was walking along East Street without a care in the world. I shall keep to the rooftops from now on."

Again, and again, he relived the chase. Each bound and leap passed before his eyes. His limbs were still weak and cold from both fear and exertion. Slowly, however, he began to calm down and the success of escape became the stronger emotion. The defeat of his enemies more prominent in his mind. He finally came to the question of, what next? He decided that two things only would drag him from the sanctuary of his room.

"First I must choose what vantage point I will shoot this Sea General and secondly I must purchase yet a second pistol to increase my chances of success and even aid my escape."

The cold and weakness were still with him, however, and he lay on his bed with both blankets and his cloak covering him. He lay quiet in sleep till late afternoon when, refreshed and more focussed on what was required, he once more climbed up to the rooftops. From there he cautiously made his way to the areas of the Old Town Quay and found a warehouse roof that gave a clear view of the quayside stone steps that would be used by the Sea General on entering his barge. The purchase of the second pistol was a more difficult task. The shop owner of the previous purchase had been made to understand that, with Raphael and Mary he was a traveller to the West Country. He could not risk returning there. Eventually, after a long search he found a second shop that accepted a second story. Both tasks being completed, he retired to the safety of his room just as daylight was fading. Here he would remain, running no risks of discovery. Having nothing else to do he lay down on his bed and fell into a more relaxed dreamless sleep.

His period of rest lasted a good two hours but he woke to the sound of arguments and fighting in the street below. Heated voices full of rage mingled with cries of alarm. He had no means of seeing what was happening so he opened the door to listen from the top of his stairs. The commotion was not only outside. The sounds of raised female voices, doors being slammed and glass and furniture broken, were coming closer to his own room. To his alarm, running feet sounded even closer. Suddenly a rough looking seaman, wide eyed and breathing hard, stared up at him from the bottom of his stairs. The stairs led only to his own room, Michel had nowhere to go and, what was worse, he had no idea what was going on.
The man below began climbing towards him.

"We're looking for volunteers, matey. England's best."

This explanation meant nothing to Michel, but he felt sure there was physical violence ahead. His heart sank when two more ruffians appeared in support of the first. Startled and uncertain, Michel was no match for the intruders, who grasped him firmly, and half dragged him to the landing below.

"Off to sea, you lovely boy"

Michel was not going to submit easily. Shouting and kicking he tried to get his arms free to force release. Then, there was a dull thud and Michel felt something soft but hard hit his head He had been sandbagged. Dazed he was carried away. At the bottom of the stairs, he was dragged out into the street and held up in front of a thin, undernourished seaman carrying a sword and wearing a wig. He gave Michel a cursory glance and said in a rasping voice.

"Shovel him up lads. He'll do. Broadsword will have its quota and we can all go back to the ship."

Michel had recovered enough to understand that he was being taken away for some naval purpose. In a despairing voice he shouted at the man in the wig.

"I am a clerk to your Sea General. Do you hear me a clerk to your chief Captain? You must let me go."

The man in the wig laughed in his face.

"And he is happy with you staying in a brothel? I think not. Take him away."

Desperate Michel again tried to free himself, but to no avail. Instead, he began shouting out at the top of his voice.

"Help! Help Kidnap, Robbery. Murder!"

A searing unbearable pain crossed his back and shoulder. His hair was grabbed, his head pulled back and a rough, unshaven face was rubbed against his. He saw broken teeth and smelt foul breath. A short, thick, knotted rope was pushed up into his cheek.

"Any more of this matey and you will feel pain again. Just like this. "

The cutting, vicious pain forced him to his knees. All spirit gone he became submissive. He had no resistance and no idea what would happen next.

Ketch, Tull and Holditch were sitting around the fire in the public room of the Ship Inn. Each man was nursing in his hand a mug of hot toddy. Apart from themselves there were only two drivers from the convoy quietly sitting in one of the window seats. The inn seemed a warm refuge on a cold dark night. Nearby the sounds of disturbance explained why trade was so slow, as the men of Portsmouth came to terms with the danger of being empressed. There was little conversation each man was lost in his own thoughts. Suddenly the main door to the inn was noisily opened and a head was poked into the public room.

"Evening gentlemen, anyone for the navy?"

A group of large, fearsome seaman filled the room. Everyone there immediately pulled out their warrants and held them out for inspection. The most villainous of the seaman turned to leave.

"Nothing here boys,"

They moved into the entrance hall looking elsewhere for victims. The heavy silence that filled the room was finally broken and conversations of relief broke out. At that moment the head of the landlord popped up from behind the bar. He smiled at Ketch and mouthed across the room.

"Seemed best to be out of sight."

The group of seamen had started to mount the stairs intent on searching the upper rooms, when Charles Beaumont appeared before them carrying a warrant.

"Your Commander in Chief has these rooms above and is trying to get some sleep. What ship is it that wants to see him? I am sure your Captain's name is one he would love to know."

He paused.

"Come now, who is it?"

There appeared in the entrance hall a large seaman more frightening and brutish than those before him. He was clearly enraged, but just managing some self- control. He waved a massive fist at them, scowling.

"Not here fools. Get back outside. "

He looked up at Beaumont

"Very sorry sir. Rough seamen anxious to please. They will be on their way."

He pushed the group of culprits out of the front door.

"Whose idea was that?"

Were the last words that Beaumont and the public room heard.

Beaumont went back into the Sea General's rooms and slowly a mood of good humour returned to the public room. Holditch chuckled.

"Mister Beaumont saw them off. I swear I saw the whole bunch of them turn pale when he asked for the name of their ship's Captain."

Having enjoyed his own remark, he rewarded himself with a long sup from his mug of toddy. As the company settled to enjoy the evening, there was fresh alarm when two more seamen entered the room. Ketch originally startled soon recognised it was Hedges and Brown. Brown stepped towards him.

"Begging your pardon sir, but me and Hedges have seen that Mr Gough, the new clerk, the one that's the Spanish agent and has disappeared."

Ketch rose to his feet.

"You have seen him? Where was this. Quickly?

"Yes, we have sir! not more than ten minutes ago. He had been pressed. We both saw him."

Hedges felt he had to take part in this important news.

"We saw him in a ship's boat sir, being taken. He was in a bunch of sorry looking men, All, desperately unhappy all looking back at the shore for salvation. He is off to sea sir. Six months or more on the Broadsword, a fortytwo-gun ship.

Ketch surveyed both men.

"You are absolutely sure of this?

They both nodded delighted that their news had been received with such interest.

"Well, that is news, very good news. I am grateful that you have told us so quickly. Here, just something in the way of thanks."

He pulled out some silver coins and handed them over to them both.

"Very kind sir. If there is nothing else we will be on our way."

The two of them moved off to enjoy their reward somewhere.

Ketch could not help it, he laughed out loud. He felt a huge weight being lifted from him. He was overjoyed. His whole body relished the moment.

"He will not be killing any Sea Generals now."

Both Tull and Holditch rose to join in their self-congratulations.

. "Well, that is our job done Ketch. We have nothing else to do. We can relax and get on back to London."

"Very true Tull," declared Holditch.

"But you have to enjoy the moment. The man who had hoped to strike a deadly blow at our navy will now be forced to work even hard to run one of its ships named Broadsword. What a wonderful upset to his plans."

The rest of the evening was spent reviewing this change of fortune and offering possible futures for Michael Gough now he was in the Sea General's hands. The arrival of the landlord with fresh candles was taken as a sign that they should be taking their rest and the three men rose to head off for their bedrooms. They were about to leave the public room when the front door to the inn burst open. Three large men dressed in scarfs, hats and heavy overcoats walked swiftly to the stairs and strode up to the Sea General's rooms. Ketch suddenly saw fresh danger and followed by Tull and Holditch he raced up behind to stop them entering the Sea General'sroom. To Ketch's surprise Beaumont at the top of the stairs turned, stood aside, and followed them in. He came to a halt as Ketch and his men arrived at the head of the stairs.

"There is no danger here, Ketch. It is the Mayor and senior council members requiring words with the Sea General.

Back down in the public room they took advantage of the new candles to consider what was the meaning of such a delegation with such furious faces. The sound of heated conversation flowed down to the entrance hall and after half an hour the three men came down looking even more annoyed than when they entered. The entrance hall shook as the front door was slammed shut. After a few minutes, Charles Beaumont came down the stairs and walked over to Ketch.

"Ketch, your life just keeps getting easier as mine becomes more difficult. The Mayor and the whole town are up in arms over empressment. I fear the navy has been too enthusiastic. It was meant to turn idlers and no-goods into fighting sailors. Tonight's activities do not fit well with an Englishman's ideas of liberty. To my knowledge only Plymouth has had this experience and it has come as a terrible shock to Portsmouth. There is talk of kidnap, slavery, retaliation. What has been made very clear to us is that there will be no civic events tomorrow, no celebrations, no grand goodbye, no bunting, no open carriage. The magistrates are furious at the men taken, but of course there is no hope of them being brought

back. The navy has an act of Parliament behind them. "Holditch
had to comment.

"I have much sympathy with them. Overnight you
lose your father, your son or your brother. It is a disgrace."

Beaumont was feeling harassed.

I am not defending it, but if we will have wars this is
what results. My concern is with its consequences. It makes
your position easier; I have a lot of angry people to provide with
explanations. You will sleep easier tonight, I will not."

He put up his hands.

"I am not here to debate this. I have much to do and I
wish you goodnight. You can take it that it will be appropriate
for you to make your goodbyes tomorrow"

With this final remark, Beaumont turned on his heels
and left. Ketch could not help but smile.

Ketch slept very well that night, but was awaken by Beaumont
knocking quietly on his door.

"Ketch, I am sorry to wake you at such an early time,
but I have Mr Turner with me and he has some news that I think
you will want to hear. There is some, fresh bread downstairs
with warm cider. We will wait for you."

It was six o clock. Ketch was used to early starts but
he had hoped for a later rise from his bed that morning.
Nevertheless, he struggled into his clothes, managed a quick
wash and descended to hear Mr Turner's news. Beaumont and
Turner were sitting around a recently revived fire. When Ketch

had collected some food and drink and joined them, Beaumont looked first at Turner and then at Ketch and began.

"Mr Turner spent all of yesterday at the Old Town Quay ensuring that the Sea General's personal possessions and stores were safely transported from the warehouse next door on to the Naseby. For over twelve hours he was loading boats, checking lists so that every item could be accounted for. In this work he is very involved with the movement of boats to and from the fleet."

Beaumont then gestured to Turner that he should now take up the tale.

"Well Captain, I was busy all day except of course for when the Press was in progress, all ship's boats being engaged in that business. When that had concluded we were back into our routine. After half an hour a boat drew up a bit further down the quay with but one man as a passenger. He, without a word climbed out of the boat looked around and then looked directly at me. It was Michael Gough. I was astonished. Seaman Brown had told me that he had been pressed and I did not expect to see him ever again. Nobody ever gets a reprieve once on board the ship."

Turner paused and took a sip from his mug.

"I gave him a wave, the I remembered he was one of the Spanish agents and pulled my hand back. He seemed to laugh at that and took off to East Street. I could not follow, that would mean leaving the Sea General's stores unattended, besides I am not fit for tackling spies. But it was him Captain I am sure of it. Now, there was an empty boat I could commandeer; no one refuses aiding the movement of the Sea General's stores. So, I start the loading and have a word with the bosun in charge and he tells me how Michael worked his release. Apparently pressed men are first lined up before the Captain and, sign their name to be entered into the ship's company.

Everyone whines and complains, but Michael was very curt and aggressive he told the Captain that he was the Commander in Chiefs clerk and started giving details about the stores and men on the Broadsword that quite startled him. He then said if the Captain produced an example of a letter or bill from the Sea General, he would prove it. The Captain was very uncertain of this but found a letter requesting Broadsword to take onboard a particular relative of some acquaintance of the Sea General. Michael then with pen and paper produced an exact copy, letter for letter word for word. The Captain was amazed and very unhappy, especially when Michael said he may well have written the letter himself at the Sea General's dictation. He was put ashore straight away. I fear this is bad news Captain."

Ketch looked grim.

"Thank you Turner, it is bad news, we are back to having a man on the loose with the intent of murder."

He looked at Beaumont.

What are you doing with the Sea General today? When does he join his ship?

"No fuss, no fanfare We shall take him in a closed coach ten o clock this morning. Myself and Treddager will be with him, and Hedges and Brown will be informal escorts."

"Therefore",replied Ketch.

"I must consult with Tull and Holditch, then I will let you know what action we shall take."

They rose to their feet knowing there was no more sleep for them that day.

Chapter Twenty-Two   End Game

Michel was gratified that Turner had merely waved at him and then left him to complete his escape from the navy. He made his way along East Street into Broad Street and back to his lodgings. No one took any notice of him. The "Press" seemed to have knocked the spirit out of the town. There was a sullen silence about and only elderly gentlemen and women and children were on the streets.

His return to the brothel was greeted with great surprise. Despite the urgings of the Madame, Mrs Barley, and her girls, he kept his story short and hurried on up into his room. He was pleased to find his room had been undisturbed. He fell onto his bed, physically and mentally exhausted. He decided to allow himself some rest before taking up the threads of his mission.

He had not bothered to light a candle and he awoke in total darkness. Fumbling around, it took some time to restore his candle light. He felt rotten and his throat and mouth were dry. He found his way to his wash stand, splashed his face with cold water from the jug and drank the rest. He returned to his bed; he had some hard thinking to do about tomorrow.

"Whether or not they know about Broadsword, Turner will have told them I am in Portsmouth. So, there will still be special protection for Robert Blake, and Mrs Barley, in her hate for the navy, mentioned there was to be no civic send off. It seems I must look to the rooftops as providing the best chance of a shot at the Sea General."

He could not prevent memories of Mary and Raphael stealing into his mind.

"They had become friends as well as fellow agents. They had been bold and fearless in their attempts to kill the Sea General."

He felt a deep anguish when he remembered his own weak failings on that occasion.

"I must complete our mission. There must be no weakness this time".

He fell into random nostalgic memories of the Turk's Head, the ghastly woman and her sons, and the excitement of their escape at Guildford. It was strange that those bitter sweet thoughts directed his mind to action A successful attack on the Sea General was now a matter of honour.

"I know the best place on the rooftops for a clean shot. I shall be up early, find a place to hide up there and destroy our enemy and escape. They failed to catch me once on the rooftops and that will happen again."

He retrieved his bag of pistols from outside his window and carefully primed them for the following morning. Holding them in his hand gave him confidence that he would succeed.

Sat at a table with Ketch, Tull and Holditch were not pleased at hearing Ketch's news. Holditch, in particular took it with a world- weary cynicism.

"Events, Ketch, are well and truly against us. We could not catch Michael Gough, the navy had him safely aboard ship and then let him go. There is a certain unevenness in all this. "

Tull, slapped his hand on the table in frustration.

"That puts the Sea General back into danger. Thank goodness he will be away later today. I suppose matters are a little easier. There will be no open carriage and Michael Gough will have only a few moments in which to act probably, at the Old Town Quay."

Ketch continued with his feeling of bone- weary tiredness. He found it difficult to take up the reins of leadership and recover his enthusiasm for the moments ahead. He took a deep breath, shook his head, stroked his nose and made the effort.

"As Tull says we have a good idea of the course of events. I think we can safely leave Beaumont, Treddager and their two seamen to get the coach to the quay without incident. We, therefore, must secure the rooftops. It is annoying to have to make this final effort, but the more we look at it the more straight forward it appears."

I hope you are right," added Holditch.

"Presumably before we take up our positions, we must make our farewells to the Sea General, Beaumont and Treddager."

Ketch ran the pattern of likely events in his mind.

"You are right Holditch, I understand that the coach will leave at ten o clock this morning and it will be no more than a few minutes before they will be at the quay. It is now just seven o clock. If we leave an hour for rest, food and drink, half an hour for checking our pistols, making farewells, donning plenty of warm clothing and getting into position. We will have secured the key rooftops by nine o clock. An hour up there will not be pleasant, but this we will endure."

Each of the six men felt a little awkward at their final farewells. There was a bond between them that was about to end. For a week, day and night they had spent every waking hour to achieve the same purpose, the delivery of the Sea General safely to Portsmouth and the fleet. They had shared much and become close but now it was almost certain that they would never see each other again. It was a fond moment but also bitter sweet. The Sea General and Tull could now share Tull's deception as a sea chaplain with a smile. Captain Treddager was fulsome in praise of all three for their efforts at Westoneville with Doctor Belpin. They exchanged memories of the men of Hindhead and the trip on the Thames with the Osterley brothers. At just the right time the Sea General drew matters to a close.

"Captain Ketch, Tull, Holditch you have served me well. I shall write to Secretary Thurloe and tell him that I am only here because of your protection. I hope I will justify all your efforts by doing well in my duty"

There were a few final exchanges before Beaumont ushered the Sea General and Captain Treddager back to their room. He stopped at the door and turned to Ketch.

"Well, Ketch, for what is worth, I add my thanks to those of the Sea General. I shall make sure that the navy will hear of what you and your colleagues have done."

"Thank you, Charles, "replied Ketch.

"We have one final task which involves us covering your departure for the Naseby from the rooftops. Then we can finally say our commission is over."

They followed Beaumont out into the entrance hall and turned into East Street.

Michel reached the roof tops well before Ketch and his party. He was determined to get as close as possible to the perfect spot for his shot at the Sea General. He dragged broken boxes, rubble and some barrels close but not too close and covered them with an old tarpaulin. Suitably hidden he settled down to wait for his moment.

Ketch and his men made their way on to the rooftops through the house of the thin man. He had not been fully cooperative, but wisely did not challenge three armed men on The Lord Protector's business.

The sea frontage of the Old Town Quay ran from East to West, The Quay itself was a large stone paved square surrounded by warehouses with the entrance from East Street on its Southern side. There were a number of landing steps but the largest was found more to the West than exactly central. This meant the warehouse roofs to the West were the ideal area for Michel and the source of maximum danger for Ketch. It was along these roof tops that Ketch placed himself and his two men. Holditch at the seaward end, some fifty feet to Tull and another fifty to himself. Thus, it was the figure of Holditch that Michel watched carefully.

As Holditch looked down below he saw that the Sea General's barge was already in position and that half a dozen Captains had also arrived and their boats were also lined up along the quay. They stood in a small group in quiet conversation whilst stamping their feet and generally trying to keep warm. There were no other persons on the quay. Today the town wanted nothing to do with the navy

At last, the Sea General's coach rattled into the square and drew up by the main steps. Charles Beaumont stepped out followed by Captain Treddager , Hedges and Brown hastily ran around to the steps to aid the Sea General down to his barge. Finally, the Sea General appeared and gingerly stepped from the coach making his way towards bosun Brown. From his vantage point Ketch waved an arm to signal to Tull and Holditch the arrival of the Sea General. Holditch moved a few yards to make sure that Tull had seen Ketch's warning.

"Why is he pointing like that now?" He shouted to Tull

An unpleasant thought raced into his mind.

""*Ketch is pointing at something.*"

He turned in desperation. All three could see Michael Gough, alias Michel, standing at the sea edge of the roof with his arm out straight, his pistol pointed at the Sea General. Michel fired and the Sea General moving down the first step tumbled into Brown and fell with a groan. Michel had no time for a second shot as Holditch was reaching for his own pistol He turned finely gauged the distance and fired again, this time, at Holditch. The force of the bullet swung him around and then, almost gracefully, he crumpled in a heap. Tull fired as Michel headed for safety, but the shot missed. With rage in his heart for the fall of Holditch and his own failure, he closed on Michel. Ketch, on the run raised his pistol to fire, but Tull was in and out of his line of sight. He made a quick judgement and fired and also missed. But he was thankful that he did not hit Tull, who was now close enough to grapple with Michel.

Michel had prepared himself for this possibility and as Tull approached he threw one pistol at his face and with the other struck Tull a heavy blow to the head. Tull fell to the ground but managed to cause Michel to stumble to one knee This delay allowed Ketch running at speed, and in a blind rage to rush at him, grasp him around the waist and allow momentum to hurl them both backwards.

The Sea General remained part lying on Brown and part on the stone steps. Beaumont and Treddager were all over him searching for the wound. The Captains clustered around them seeking to see the damage.

"Get off me," cried Robert Blake.

"It's my damned leg. What's going on.

Treddager, regardless of the Sea General's words had opened his coat searching for blood.

"You have been shot Robert. You are down. Where does it hurt?"

"You are a damned fool Treddager. Listen, it is my leg. It gave way. I could not manage the bloody steps."

Beaumont took Treddager by the shoulders.

"All is well Ralph, he is unhurt."

291

Amidst the enormous relief a voice spoke up.

"Beg pardon sir! But I am not."

It was bosun Brown, sitting next to the Sea General and clutching his arm. The Sea General demanded to be pulled to his feet,

"Take him into my barge Hedges. Let us get away. We have work for my surgeon. "

To everyone but Ketch, it would have been obvious as to what was to happen. The force of his rush at Michel propelled them to the seaward edge of the roof. Together they toppled over still struggling. First there was a loud, sickening crack and then a dull thud as they hit a stone balustrade and then the rim of an iron balcony. They continued down to splash into an engulfing sea. Tull above, had regained his wits and rushed to the roof edge. There was movement in the sea but no bodies. He began shouting out to the Captains in their boats below. One of the quicker minded Captains had seen the roof top struggle and had directed his boat to the spot where the combatants had fallen. As they neared the spot one figure, with head barely above the water was waving his arms. Every man present knew that the sea in March was a place of numbing cold that could mean shock and then death. A long boat hook thrust into his collar revealed Ketch struggling for air. His heavy clothing had provided some protection from the cold but their weight now proved a serious obstacle to safely pulling him into the boat. It needed three men in concert to finally haul him to safety.

"Well done sir," cried the Captain.

"You got the bastard."

Ketch, between gulps of air had but one question.

"The Sea General is he dead?"

The Captain stood up and surveyed the sea.

"Robert Blake is fine. It was a lame leg that brought him down.'

He spoke to his own coxswain.

"I see nothing of the assailant. I am not going to linger in search of him. We will get you to my ship as quickly as we can. If we are speedy you may recover soon."

Within minutes Ketch was aboard the Jupiter in the captain's cabin. He had been thoroughly dried swathed in blankets and on his second glass of brandy. He had been required to give Captain Jessop a short account of events leading up to the attempted shooting of the Sea General. After brandy came hot stew and fresh clothes from the Captain's wardrobe.

"I shall have yours in return Ketch for the fleet may be away for a year. Without them I will end a scarecrow. "

The ship's surgeon was summoned and agreed that a period of sleep was the best roads to recovery and Ketch was laid out on a handsome couch in Captain Jessop's cabin. Quickly and gratefully, he fell into a deep slumber. It seemed only minutes, however, before he felt the captain's hand on his shoulder pressing him back into consciousness.

"I am sorry Captain Ketch but the fleet is on the move and I must take up my station. I have a boat waiting to take you ashore.

Dusk was falling when Ketch arrived at the Ship Inn. It felt strange in its silence. On entering the public room, he found it darkening and without customers. The fate of Tull and Holditch was uppermost in his mind. He was relieved when the landlord found him so quickly.

"Your men are upstairs Captain, One, is bruised the other more grievously hurt but Sergeant Tull will explain all. I have put them in what was the Sea General's rooms. Here take these extra candles."

Ketch was relieved at the landlord's early good news. Still stiff from his own activities, he slowly climbed the stairs. On entering what had previously been Robert Blake's bedroom, he found Tull, with a bandaged head administering soup to Holditch with a bandaged shoulder. Ketch was pleased to find a positive air in the room.

"I see two invalids before me Tull. perhaps you can bring me up to date?"

"After the soup Captain. Holditch must sleep. The doctor was quite determined about it, despite protests from his patient. The doctor has just left. There was a ball removed from Holditch's shoulder. It was both noisy and a bloody affair. The verdict is that Holditch will live."

Holditch was sitting up in bed but with the soup finished, he leaned back to find more comfort in his pillows.

"Of course, I will live Tull. Yes! I perhaps made a little noise when the ball was being extracted, but that is now all over. A few hours' sleep and I will be fine, almost back to normal. But what about you Ketch? I find you have some new clothing."

"Never mind me Holditch. Tull, finish with the soup and then we must let him sleep. We shall return to the public room to consider what has happened and what we do next."

It was while he watched Tull administering soup to Holditch that Ketch has a moment of deep nostalgic concern for them all.

"We have worked together for some fourteen years as troopers and then as agents for Thurloe. We have survived dangers and hardships through our unity. We have become friends as well as comrades, and yet today each of us has been hurt, Holditch shot, Tull bludgeoned and myself almost drowned. Unity does not protect us from everything, but despite today I think we all will stick with it."

Ketch smiled and, with Tull, left Holditch grumbling but lying down. In a quiet corner of the public room, Tull gave his account after Ketch had tumbled into the sea.

"I found Holditch on his back clutching his shoulder with blood seeping through his layers of clothing. I needed help to get him down to the street and into the inn. Fortunately, the doctor we summoned came quickly. In the upstairs room he took great care in cutting away Holditch's clothing and exposing the wound. It was these layers of clothing that had taken away much of the force of the ball. It had passed through his heavy leather coat, an undercoat, a waistcoat, a shirt and a linen vest. Such was the loss of penetration that the ball broke the skin but lay just below the surface. The doctor declared that it was the easiest of removals. Of course, Holditch made a bit of a fuss and there was a strong gush of blood, but it was all over very quickly. We have seen a lot worse. The final verdict was that if he avoided infection, he would make a strong recovery."

Ketch sat for a moment absorbing Tull's account.

"Your head Tull, not broken?"

"No Ketch but it aches, I shall be glad to sleep myself, but what happened to you?

Ketch gave a quick version of his own experience, essentially the death of the Spanish agent, Michael Gough, and his recovery to the Jupiter. As he was coming to the end, he realised how tired he was. The benefits of brandy and good food taken on the Jupiter were disappearing. Tired, but nevertheless pleased with their day's work they retired upstairs for sleep.

It took four days before Holditch was well enough to travel and another three for them to reach Whitehall Palace. They climbed the stairs to the green door marked enter and Ketch led them into their headquarters. Benson stood before them and a smile lit up his face.

"Welcome back gentlemen you served the navy well"

. Benson rarely smiled and never commented on mission performance. Ketch was surprised at the new Benson, but it was as nothing to that he experienced when all the clerks in the room stood up and clapped all three of them, not wildly but discretely as befitted men of secrets.

Epilogue

May 1657

Ketch was in Whitehall Palace, sitting comfortably with his mentor and senior agent Major Richard Blake. There was no special task facing him at the moment, so the two friends were amiably discussing the issues of the day. Major Blake was particularly concerned about the large number of plots on the life of the Lord Protector.

You would not believe, Ketch, the amount of time myself and Spy Master Thurloe spend tracing and preventing attacks on Oliver Cromwell. There is a group called the Fifth Monarchists forever forging plots, but frankly, the main danger is from rogue individuals who have some, usually quite crazy ideas, that they wish to promote."

Ketch nodded in agreement. Of course, he did know about these threats having been involved in preventing many of them But, he realised that his friend was just venting his frustration he thought he would raise a more delicate topic.

"What about King Oliver, Richard. There is so much pressure from the House of Commons and senior army leaders that this should be so."

Before Richard Blake could answer the door to his office opened and Spy Master Thurloe, himself, entered the room. Such a visit from the Secretary to the Council of State was a rare event. Thurloe had such a range of tasks to perform that increasingly he was relying on Richard Blake to manage the state's intelligence services. Both men rose to their feet and on being offered Richard Blake's chair, he swiftly slipped behind the desk. Thurloe was smiling and clearly in a good humour. Richard Blake retrieved a chair and sat down next to Ketch.

"Well, gentlemen, some good news. I am getting some early reports of a large sea battle in the Bay of Tenerife and that it ended in a great victory for the English fleet. No details yet, but it certainly appears that your efforts last year in getting Sea General Blake, no relation eh Richard, to Portsmouth, was most worthwhile."

Ketch laughed and stroked his nose.

"Sergeant Tull will be pleased, and Sergeant Holditch even more so. You remember that he took a ball in the shoulder in service for the Sea General

Thurloe sat in silence for a while and then spoke quietly and with a strong element of caution.

"What a marvellous man is Sea General Robert Blake. He has a superb reputation as a military commander on both land and sea. He is, as a result, loved as a hero across the land. He is a long- standing Member of Parliament with many influential friends there. He is a staunch republican and deeply religious. He has strong favour with the Council of State. There is no one in the country with his stature."

Thurloe seemed quietly conspiratorial.

"Except of course the Lord Protector but should Oliver Cromwell succumb to illness or pressure of work, or the many plots that surround him. I would certainly see such a man as Robert Blake our next Lord Protector. I am sure the republic would be safe in his hands. I have even dared to have lightly pushed the idea to Cromwell himself. "

This was new ground for both Major.Blake and Ketch. The Major spoke words that Ketch shared.

"You were very brave to take that up with the Lord Protector himself."

Thurloe was quite unabashed.

"You underate our Head of State. He is a great man. I am sure he will reject this nonsense with the crown."

He rose from his chair.

"This is delicate talk, gentlemen. Not to be repeated elsewhere. It is better for us to keep apart from such matters. Believe me, to address them involves dealing with the most dangerous of individuals and it is not to be reccomended."

His serious face dissolved into good humour.

"Well, there we are. We eagerly await more news from Tenerife."

With that remark Thurloe left the room. Ketch and Richard Blake sat in silence for a moment.

"These matters are not for us Ketch. Our world is quite murky enough."

Ketch was ready to move on.

You are right Richard but I have not tasted the good comforts of home life for some time. I am now for Northampton.

Author's Note No 2

On the 20th of April 1657 an English fleet commanded by
General at Sea Robert Blake entered the Bay of Tenerife and
destroyed all sixteen ships of the Spanish treasure fleet. There
were no English ships lost. It was England's greatest naval
victory of the 17th Century. Returning to England Robert Blake,
died aboard ship from illness whilst entering Plymouth
harbour.

.

Printed in Great Britain
by Amazon